Falling Apart
and Other Gifts
from the Universe

A Novel

Also by Catherine Ryan Hyde

Michael Without Apology

Rolling Toward Clear Skies

Life, Loss, and Puffins

A Different Kind of Gone

Just a Regular Boy

So Long, Chester Wheeler

Dreaming of Flight

Boy Underground

Seven Perfect Things

My Name is Anton

Brave Girl, Quiet Girl

Stay

Have You Seen Luis Velez?

Just After Midnight

Heaven Adjacent

The Wake Up

Allie and Bea

Say Goodbye for Now

Leaving Blythe River

Ask Him Why

Worthy

The Language of Hoofbeats

Pay It Forward: Young Readers Edition

Take Me with You

Paw It Forward

365 Days of Gratitude: Photos from a Beautiful World

Where We Belong

Subway Dancer and Other Stories

Walk Me Home

Falling Apart
and Other Gifts
from the Universe

A Novel

Catherine
Ryan Hyde

LAKE UNION
PUBLISHING

Text copyright © 2025 by Catherine Ryan Hyde, Trustee, or Successor Trustee, of the Catherine Ryan Hyde Revocable Trust created under that certain declaration dated September 27, 1999.

Published by Lake Union Publishing, Seattle
www.apub.com

Amazon, the Amazon logo, and Lake Union Publishing are trademarks of Amazon. com, Inc., or its affiliates.

EU product safety contact:
Amazon Media EU S. à r.l.
38, avenue John F. Kennedy, L-1855 Luxembourg
amazonpublishing-gpsr@amazon.com

ISBN-13: 9781662522345 (hardcover)
ISBN-13: 9781662522338 (paperback)
ISBN-13: 9781662522321 (digital)

Cover design by Shasti O'Leary Soudant
Cover image: © Akaradech Pramoonsin / Getty; © New Africa,
© Victoria Moloman, © Zoteva / Shutterstock

Printed in the United States of America

First edition

A Novel

Falling Apart
and Other Gifts
from the Universe

AUTHOR'S NOTE

Before you begin reading, a content warning.

This book contains references to a subject sensitive to many—the attempted sexual assault of two unhoused teens. It's not a subject I enter into lightly when telling a story. My goal was to shed light on the extreme vulnerability of the many young people who have fallen through the cracks of family and protective services. It was not to exploit anyone's suffering. I feel that when something that awful happens in the world, the answer can't be to look the other way and say nothing, even in our fiction.

Not only are there no graphic details, but the attempts fail, and the close calls happen, for the most part, "off the page." Still, I know this can be triggering for some, so I wanted to share these thoughts with you first, so you can make your own choices.

One

Addie

Chapter One

When Your Soul Needs a Good Night's Sleep

Addie Finch fell asleep, her chin leaning on the palm of her hand, well before the meeting ended. The young woman sitting in the next chair jostled her awake with an elbow to her ribs.

"What?" Addie said, sputtering up into consciousness and blinking under the fluorescent lights.

"Addie," the group leader said from the end of the long table. "Do you want to share?"

"Somebody else can go."

"Everybody else has shared already."

"Oh."

She sat up a little straighter. Blinked hard and shook her head slightly to clear away the last of the cobwebs from her half-asleep brain.

"I'm Addie," she said, "and I'm an alcoholic."

"Hi Addie," the group of ten said in nearly one unanimous voice.

"And I'm just . . . tired. I don't know what else to say. I'm just really tired. I know you all know I started a new job a few weeks back, and it's a night-shift thing, and changing your nights and days around is hard. But I have to go a little deeper and tell you it's not just that. It's not only the one kind of tired. Yeah, I'm sleepy, but I'm tired deeper down than that. My brain and my heart are tired. My nervous system is tired. I swear it feels like my soul needs a good night's sleep. I mean, I'm sixty-two years old. I should be getting close to retiring, but there's just no way. I guess it doesn't help that I misspent so many years, but financially I just can't do it.

"I really don't mean to sound like I'm complaining. I just figure if I tell you the truth, even if the truth is not all that pretty, you'll trust me when I say I'm okay. Assuming I ever do. Look, I know there are some newer people here tonight, and I don't want to send out a message like you can stay sober for eight years and still not be very happy. On the other hand I don't want to send a message that people with a little time are liars, or that the new people are the only ones feeling like life is hard. Life *is* hard. But it's better than it was when I got here. By a big margin.

"Anyway . . . I'm sorry. I don't know. I'm just tired and not functioning at a hundred percent. But that's all I've got."

"Thanks, Addie," the group murmured as one.

Then they all rose to their feet and formed a circle around the table, clasped hands, and recited the Serenity Prayer.

———

"Hey," Addie said as the group separated off again. "Hey. Wendy."

Wendy was a tiny woman, barely five feet tall, with a dress size of pretty much zero and hair that always looked like she had just stepped out of a beauty parlor and into a world of no wind.

Wendy stopped on her way to the door.

"What can I do for you, Addie?"

"I wanted to talk to you."

"Talk away."

"I just wondered . . ."

Then she floundered, and felt weak.

Damn, she thought to herself. *A life like I've had, the things I've done, and it feels intimidating to talk to a woman who's probably not tall enough to go on half the rides at the state fair.*

She shoved the feeling down deeper and forced herself to speak.

"I just wondered if you sponsor people."

Wendy just stood a moment, fixing her with a piercing gaze that looked the way Addie could only assume x-ray vision looked from the outside of the thing.

"You have a sponsor, though," Wendy said after a time. A long time from the feel of it.

"Joan was my sponsor."

"Oh. Oh, no. I'm so sorry for your loss, honey. Well, what the hell. Let's go get a cup of coffee, and we'll see if we're compatible enough to pull it off."

———

The waitress was a gruff middle-aged woman with a ton of unnaturally red hair piled up high on her head.

"You eating?" she asked Addie as she filled Wendy's coffee mug.

"Yeah."

"I'll get you a menu. Coffee?"

"Yes to coffee. But if you serve breakfast all day I don't need a menu."

"They serve breakfast all day," Wendy said.

"I'll have two eggs over easy with hash browns and rye toast."

"Coming right up," the waitress said. She flipped over Addie's mug, filled it, and hurried away.

"Why didn't she ask *you* if *you* were eating?" Addie asked.

"Because she knows me."

They sipped their very hot coffee for a minute or two without talking.

"Must've broken your heart when Joan died," Wendy said.

"Definitely not the best thing that ever happened to me."

"Wasn't it almost a year ago?"

"Thirteen months. But who's counting?"

"And you've been without a sponsor all this time?"

Addie shifted around slightly on her seat, as if the padded bench of their booth had suddenly stopped being comfortable.

"I wasn't sure who to ask."

For a moment, Wendy only stared at her with a gaze like an auger. "I'm waiting," she said after an uneasy time.

"For what?"

"For you to dig a little deeper."

"Oh. Okay. Well . . . I guess if I'm being honest, I didn't really *want* to ask anybody else. She knew me so well. And I suppose I wasn't doing a great job of accepting that she was gone. I mean, I know she was ninety-two and all, but she meant a lot to me, and I guess I just had a resistance to starting over with anybody else."

Wendy offered a satisfied nod.

"Now *that* I believe," she said. "Did you have a string of sponsors, or just the one for eight years?"

"Just Joan. For almost seven years. I had just under seven years when she died, and I've turned eight since then."

"Oh," Wendy said. "Right. Well. Okay. We can give it a go. I only have one rule. One gigantic deal-breaker. You have to tell me the truth."

"I always tell the truth," Addie said.

"But I think I mean it on more levels than you do, hon. I don't mean not lying. I do, but not *only* that. I'm talking about no withholding, no minimizing, no lying by omission. For example, I just made reference to the fact that you went a year without a sponsor, and your first answer might not have been a lie, but it wasn't the honest one. I'm talking the truth, the whole truth, and nothing but the truth, like they say in court. And it's not because I'm such a delicate little flower that I'll wilt and die if someone isn't honest with me. It's because if I'm going to be your sponsor, without you telling me the whole truth there's just nothing I can do for you. The whole thing is just a waste of time without that."

"I can do that," Addie said.

"Take a little time and think about it. Make sure you're sure."

"I'm sure," Addie said.

Her food arrived, and she pulled a bottle of Tabasco out from behind the napkin dispenser and doused her eggs with the sauce.

"That's a lot of hot sauce," Wendy said.

"And your point is? I like a lot of hot sauce."

"You always eat breakfast at almost ten at night?"

"Pretty much, yeah. This is my morning. I have to be at work in an hour."

"Oh. Right. Tell me about this new job."

Addie shoveled a huge bite of the spicy eggs into her mouth and sighed. She chewed slightly before answering.

"Security-guard thing," she said. "Night shift. Obviously. I work at that self-storage place over on Hastings. Mostly I just sit in the office all night and stare at a bunch of monitors. There are security cameras everywhere."

"I didn't think those self-storage places bothered to go to the expense. I figured they just told people to put a lock on their unit door and left it at that."

"Usually," Addie said, and shoveled in another huge bite. Chewed. "This place used to do it like that, but there's that old abandoned warehouse right next door. Lots of people live there. And I do mean lots. It's like a whole little underground community over there. Not literally underground, but you know what I mean. Squatters. Teenagers, mostly. They'd come over to sleep in one of the empty units when things got rough over there. Which is most of the time. It's a rough place. So then the owner put locks on the vacant ones. But then somebody got smart and got their hands on a good bolt cutter. And then, well . . . once you've got the bolt cutter it's a pretty short hop to breaking into the rented units and seeing what's worth taking. A few burglaries too many and you either have to get some security or watch your occupancy rate drop down through the floor. That's where I come in, just in time to make my property taxes."

"At least you own your own place. That's a good thing."

"It was my parents' house. I inherited it. But I still have to work to keep it up."

"Aren't you scared out there in the middle of the night all by yourself?"

Addie set down her fork and looked straight into Wendy's face.

"I did two tours with the army in Iraq," she said. "Desert Storm. I did eleven years as a beat cop in Central LA. You think a few homeless teens can scare me?"

"You just did it again," Wendy said.

"What did I do?"

"Gave me defenses instead of honesty."

Addie sighed again. She leaned her head on her hand and wondered if maybe she'd spoken too soon and too easily about her commitment to Wendy's rule. She wasn't opposed to telling her new sponsor the whole truth. The problem was more that before she could report it, she had to know it.

"I don't know," she said. "Maybe. I guess the honest answer is, what difference does it make if I'm scared or not? I need the work, and I just have to buck up and do it."

She picked up her fork again and pitched back into her food, pausing to splash more hot sauce on the potatoes.

"I thought the army and the LAPD had good pension plans," Wendy said.

"They do. If you can hang in long enough to get them. When you flame out with your alcohol problems it doesn't work out so well financially."

"Got it."

Addie ate, and they sipped coffee for a moment in silence. Addie looked out the window and watched the traffic go by. It seemed as though every third vehicle was some kind of emergency responder. Watching them brought a lump of heartburn-like stress into a spot just under her breastbone, and she briefly wondered if that feeling was what other people meant when they talked about fear.

"You at least carry a gun for your own protection?" Wendy asked.

Addie was suddenly acutely aware of the holster under her left arm. The feel of its leather edge. The bulk of it.

"Unofficially," she said.

"I have no idea what that means."

"It means I'm not supposed to, and the job doesn't provide one, but I'm licensed to carry and the owner knows I do. She's made it clear that if I ever have to use it at work, she'll deny she knew anything about it and I'm out of a job."

"Better than being out of a life."

"It all starts to run together in my head," Addie said. "But—yeah. I suppose."

Wendy slugged down the last of her coffee and set a ten on the table. "I should get home to the dogs," she said.

"You don't want change for that bill?"

"Nah. I tip big. When all you ever do is sit and drink coffee, it pays to tip big. Otherwise the waitresses aren't so thrilled to see you coming. Call me every day if you want, but I have no rule about that. Call when you want to call."

She threw on her overcoat and turned as if to walk out.

Then she stopped.

"One more question," she said. "Why me? Why now?"

"That's two questions."

"Ha ha. Very amusing. Answer them."

"Okay. A couple of nights ago I had a dream about Joan. She told me to just go ahead and pick somebody and go for it already. She said hurting myself was no way to pay tribute to her, and that I should just look around and find somebody who had what I wanted."

"And that was me? I'm surprised. We're such different people."

"You have like thirty years sober."

"Thirty-five."

"Okay. Thirty-five. Well. That's what I want."

Wendy paused, as if to think that over, then nodded once and walked out the door.

Addie could briefly see her through the window, standing on the sidewalk, clutching her coat around herself and breathing steam. She seemed to be trying to decide which way she was parked.

Addie glanced down at her plate just long enough to pick up a piece of toast. When she looked out the window again, her new sponsor was gone.

———

Addie sat awake in front of the monitors for a long time. An hour or two at least. But around one in the morning she drifted off to sleep sitting up, without knowing it. She might even have been sleeping with her eyes open, and she might have seen the movement on the monitor for row B. Or maybe the sound of the door being rolled up tipped her, and caused her to open her eyes and see motion.

However it happened, it rocketed her up out of sleep with a colossal start, accompanied by a gasp, the way you might jolt up from a half-asleep state feeling as though you're suddenly falling.

Someone had the door rolled up just a couple of feet on unit B7, an empty unit, and was crawling underneath to get inside. Addie couldn't see the person well, but she thought it might be a teenage girl, because the figure was so small and slight. The person moved slowly and wincingly, as if every movement brought pain.

She saw no bolt cutter. Not in the squatter's hand. Not on the ground nearby. And yet she had checked every lock at the beginning of her shift, just to make sure none had been cut and removed.

She unholstered her pistol, shrugged on her jacket, and grabbed the flashlight on her way out the office door.

As she walked over to row B, she watched her breath flow out as steam and listened to the jangling in her chest and belly. She thought,

Note to self: Admit to Wendy you think you might have been scared tonight. Whatever scared is.

She stopped in front of B7.

Its door had been rolled back down, its lock hanging uselessly open on the hasp. Addie could see a few inches of air underneath.

Holding the flashlight under her arm, she pulled hard on the door with her left hand, pointing the weapon with her right.

The door flew up with a great metallic bang, and a young man of maybe sixteen or seventeen blinked into the light. He threw one arm up to shield his eyes. He was wearing jeans and a pullover sweater. No jacket. No blanket. He had a small backpack that he was using as a pillow. His long hair was dark blond, shaggy and uncombed.

"Oh God, don't shoot me," he whispered. "Please."

"I'm not going to shoot you if I don't need to defend myself against you. But you can't sleep here."

She could hear the young man breathing, but for a long time he said nothing at all. He moved his arm away from his eyes, and Addie saw he'd been crying. A lot, from the look of it.

"Have you ever been just completely at the end of your rope?" he asked her after a time.

"More than once," Addie said, "if I'm being honest."

"I have no place else to go. I just had the worst night I've ever had in my life. Literally. And I've had some bad ones. Please. What am I hurting if I sleep here one night?"

"You're hurting *me*. I need this job, and the gist of the whole gig is making sure you don't sleep here, and I could lose my job for letting you. And I can't let that happen."

"Who would even know?"

"Honey," Addie said, "there are cameras everywhere."

"Oh."

Addie holstered her gun while he struggled to his feet. She watched his movements carefully, and they confirmed her suspicion that he was in pain.

"You get beat up tonight?" she asked him.

"Something like that," he said, his eyes cast down toward the concrete floor.

That was when Addie did something she normally would not have done. She did it with little thought, if any, though she would later look back and wonder what had changed in that moment and why.

"Come with me," she said. "It's nothing bad."

He followed her out into the parking lot.

She led him to her aging SUV and unlocked the back door, holding it wide for him.

"You can lock it from the inside," she said. "One night. But wait. Before you get in . . ."

She took hold of the sleeve of his sweater and pulled him under one of the light posts. Then she took a picture of him with her phone.

"What's that for?" he asked.

"If you steal my car in the night I'll have this to show to the police."

"How can I steal your car without the keys?"

"The fact that you don't know makes me feel more secure."

They walked back to the SUV together, and he threw his backpack in first. Then he gingerly climbed in, easing himself down onto his belly on the back seat.

Addie was helping him bend his legs so she could close the door when he spoke.

"Wait," he said. "Lady."

"What?"

"Do you believe in Karma?"

"I don't know. I don't suppose I do, no. Why? Do you?"

"I'm not sure," he said. "But just now I got bowled over by how much I want it to be true right now. I want the universe to give you some big, wonderful thing as a reward because you were kind tonight to somebody who really, really needed it."

"Just get some sleep," Addie said, and closed the SUV's back door.

But inside her very tired brain she could feel herself clinging to the idea of a big, wonderful thing from the universe.

I really, really need it, she thought.

She checked the lock on B7 to see how it could possibly be open. She found that it was not one of the locks the owner had given her to put on the empty units. Someone had apparently cut and removed that lock and replaced it with a lock that looked similar but worked on a combination rather than a key.

She confiscated the rogue lock and brought it into the office, where she found another official one in a filing-cabinet drawer. She walked back to B7 and properly locked the unit.

Then she watched her car all night on one of the monitors, just to be safe. It never moved, and no one moved inside it. Everything remained still.

Chapter Two

Full of Fear and Searching for Nothing

In the morning Addie made a fresh pot of coffee and poured it into two Styrofoam cups. She left one black, because that was the way she took it. She put two creamers and three packets of sugar in the other. Just on a hunch.

She carried them out into the biting morning and over to the rear door of her SUV. She set one on the tarmac of the parking lot and rapped on the window.

The boy jumped a figurative mile. Or anyway he tried to. But his body seemed to have stiffened overnight, and he was clearly in a lot of pain. It ended up being more of a series of stumbles into a semi-upright position.

He unlocked the door from the inside and swung it open.

"You need your car back," he said. "Don't you?"

"Pretty soon now," she said, leaning over to pick up the second cup. "Here, I brought you coffee. I didn't know how you take it, so I threw in two creamers and three packets of sugar."

"That is *so* perfect," he said. "Thank you. That's just what I would have asked for if you'd asked me how I take it. How did you know?"

"Because it's free calories."

He stepped carefully out into the cold morning and took the coffee from her.

He leaned gingerly on the side of her vehicle and blew into it, sending clouds of steam up into his face.

In the light, he reminded Addie of her son at that age. He didn't really look much like Spencer, but he had a similar build. And there was something else—something indefinable. It might have been a series of physical gestures, or the way he carried himself. Or it might have been something that lived more on the inside of him. It was a hard thing for Addie to chase down.

She didn't tell him so, because if she did, he might think it was the only reason she'd done him a favor. And that wouldn't have been true. She had only just now noticed the resemblance. But that was how empathy so often operated, and Addie wanted no part of the pattern. Hardly a week went by when she didn't catch herself bemoaning the fact that people only seem to extend their caring in that one situation that feels personal.

"You're a nice person," he said, knocking her out of her thoughts.

He took a sip of the hot drink and closed his eyes.

The rear door of her SUV was still open, so Addie sat on the back seat, and they stared off in the direction of the sunrise together.

"I'm not that nice."

"Well, I definitely get that you're trying not to be seen that way," he said.

Addie shook her head in an attempt to rattle away the observation. She decided to move the conversation in a new direction.

"You need some kind of medical attention?"

"No ma'am. I'll live."

"You don't have to call me ma'am."

"I don't know your name."

"Oh. Right. It's Addie."

"Addie," he said. As though thinking it over.

Then they only drank coffee in silence for a while. Addie figured he'd had a chance to tell her his name, and if he'd let it go by, it was likely for a reason. She figured she'd never know. She figured wrong.

"I'm Jonathan," he said after a time.

"Let me ask you a question, Jonathan. Those people who sleep over there in that warehouse. Are they mostly your age?"

"Different ages," he said. "But yeah. A lot of underage teens."

"You think somebody's looking for them? Wanting them back?"

"Oh no," he said, with no hesitation. "Those are not runaways. Those are throwaways. You know the difference?"

"Doesn't seem hard to sort out," Addie said. "Seems pretty self-explanatory."

"That's good," he said, nodding. And nodding. And nodding. "That's a good sign about you. You get it. I used to have this old friend who liked to say 'There are two kinds of people in the world: those who get it and those who don't.' I like to take it a step further and point out that if you say that to somebody and they say 'Get what?' then you know they fall into the second category."

Addie smiled in spite of herself. He looked so fragile and young, but when he opened his mouth to speak he sounded forty.

"What about you, Jonathan? Anybody looking for you?"

"No ma'am. I mean, no, Addie. Nobody wants me back."

He still held the Styrofoam cup clutched in his right hand, and now he had his left arm wrapped around himself, as though he could hug himself warm. He was still staring toward the sunrise, though it could barely be seen through the low-lying layer of smog.

His attention broke suddenly, and he looked over and noticed her noticing.

"Sunny Southern California," he said, "am I right?"

Addie chuckled slightly in her throat but did not answer.

"The main reason I came here from Michigan is because everybody said it was the best place to be homeless. Here or Florida. Never gets that cold."

"I don't know about Florida," she said, "but it gets cold enough here at night in the winter. You don't even own a jacket?"

"I do," he said. "But I had to run out of the warehouse last night without it. I grabbed my backpack and that was all I had time to do. Maybe if I could get in there before it's much lighter nobody will have noticed it, and it won't have gotten stolen yet. But I can't take a chance on running into *him*."

"Him who?"

She knew by context that he was referring to his attacker. She asked because she was hoping he'd offer up more details.

"Him *him*," Jonathan said, and ducked down into a pained but sudden squat to avoid being seen.

Off in the distance in the foreground of the eastern horizon, silhouetted in the sunrise, a hulking figure was walking away from the warehouse. Addie could make out no details of his face or clothes, but the sheer bulk of him was shocking. He looked like one of those NFL linebackers who end up nicknamed after some kind of large home appliance.

"That guy is *huge*," she said.

"Tell me about it."

"He have a name?"

"Skate."

"His name is Skate?"

"Yeah."

"Who names their kid Skate?"

"It's not his real name. It's a street name. Nobody tells anybody their real name out here."

"Did you tell me *your* real name?"

"Yeah," he said, his voice soft. "I did. I figured I owed you that much." He slugged down the last of his coffee and held the cup out in her direction. "Can you please throw this away for me? Thanks for it. Thanks for everything. I have to run over there and get my jacket before it's gone forever."

She took the cup from him and watched him run—figuratively—over there. But he didn't run. He seemed incapable of running. His retreating figure seemed to be engaged in something more like a fast but pained stagger.

She stood, drank the last of her coffee, and walked back into the office. She threw the cups away and locked up for the morning.

She climbed into her SUV and started it up, giving its old engine time to warm before asking much from it.

As she pulled out of the parking lot she saw him again. He was walking awkwardly but fairly briskly down the street, his backpack slung over one shoulder. He was wearing a navy blue down jacket.

He saw her, and gave her a thumbs-up.

She returned the gesture.

Then she drove home and tried to sleep in spite of the fact that the whole neighborhood was just beginning the process of noisily waking up.

———

"When's the last time you did an inventory?" Wendy asked.

They were sitting in the same booth, at the same diner, after the same meeting. Wendy was drinking coffee and Addie was eating corned-beef hash with poached eggs.

"When I was new," she said, her mouth still full.

"You've only done *one inventory?*"

"Yeah. Don't a lot of people just do the fourth step once?"

The step in question, one of AA's twelve, suggested "a searching and fearless moral inventory of ourselves." Addie had found it painful enough the first time around and had never intended to revisit it.

"Well, if they do, they're probably not anybody *I* sponsor. I'm a fan of doing them once a year."

Addie kept her shock to herself. Or tried to, anyway.

"I thought you had just the one rule," she said. "The being-completely-honest thing."

"I do have just the one rule. Think of the yearly inventory as a vehement suggestion."

Addie sighed and rolled her eyes.

"I'm waiting," Wendy said.

"For . . . ?"

"Honest communication."

"Oh. Right. Well. I had a very tough time with the first one."

"Who doesn't?"

"I was really hoping to avoid doing it again."

"Which is how you know you need to."

"Parse that out for me, please."

"If there was nothing important in there, you wouldn't feel the need to push back against it. You'd just kind of say 'I don't know if I have anything to write. I feel pretty caught up.' Resistance is always a red flag. When you resist going somewhere, you know it's a place you need to go. But there's another way I know you're not done. Know how I know?"

"Not really, but I figure you'll tell me."

"Because nobody's done. There's no such thing as done. The day you die, congratulations. You're done."

Addie sighed.

She pulled her phone out of her pocket, thinking she'd block out some time on her calendar to at least get started on the thing.

Instead she accidentally touched the icon for the camera, and it opened. She was surprised to see a photo of Jonathan in a thumbnail at the lower left. She had forgotten she'd taken it.

She touched the image to bring it up to full size.

The boy in the photo was clearly terrified. Cold. Small. Watching life spin out of his control. Utterly demoralized. He reminded Addie of a turtle without a shell, desperately trying to retreat into safety. But there was nowhere to go.

"You know what I really, *really* hate?" she asked Wendy, still staring at the image.

"I give up. What?"

"People who prey on somebody who's smaller and more helpless than they are. Like totally not a fair fight. People who just go ahead and hurt somebody who can't defend themselves because they know they can get away with it. That just chaps my hide."

"Good," Wendy said. "Start there."

"Not following."

"That's the start of your inventory. Go back to the beginning and start figuring out why that's a trigger for you."

"Are you saying it's a problem that I feel for the underdog?"

"Not at all. I'm saying it's a clue."

Chapter Three

When Your Karma Forsakes You

Addie pulled her chair up to the counter and dropped a yellow legal tablet on its surface, in front of the bank of monitors. She found a pen in one of the drawers.

At the top of the page she wrote "Inventory for Wendy."

Then she stopped, and almost scratched it out again. The inventory wasn't *for* Wendy. She was doing it for herself. Wendy was just the person who had suggested it, and the person she would read it to when it was complete.

Suddenly, and without even realizing she'd wondered, she knew exactly what Joan would have said, if Joan could have been there. In fact, she could even hear Joan say it in her head, in that jovial Southern accent Addie missed so much.

Really makes not one whit of a difference what it says at the top of the paper, honey. It's what you write after that. That's all that counts.

Addie sighed and began to write.

"My father was a bully," she began. "He never hit me, but he bullied me in his own way, and it was bad enough. When my mom was pregnant with me he wanted another boy, and he never kept a secret of the fact that I was a disappointment to him. He made me feel small, like I'd never amount to anything. Most of my life I figured I should be halfway grateful because that was the reason I did. (Amount to something, I mean.) It's what drove me to the army, and then the LAPD. But then also I inherited his alcoholism, so no matter how driven I was, no matter how hard I tried, being his daughter always managed to sabotage me in the end. Anyway, I hated the son of a bitch.

"I never saw him hit my mom, but I saw him scream at her and belittle her and generally make her life a living hell.

"But my brother. My only brother, Bill, who's older. My only sibling. He got hit. He got more than hit. He got beaten. Just mercilessly beaten. Enough that we had Child Protective Services sniffing around all the time, because there were too many hospital visits. I mean, honestly, how often does one kid fall off his bike? But they never really stepped in for real, because my father was so charming and so convincing when he needed to be. And I know it enraged him that they came around, because we were his kids and he could do as he pleased with us. I know he felt that way because he said it, on more than one occasion. But not in front of them, he didn't say it. Only after they'd gone. He was always polite in front of them. I think that's when I truly started to hate him, because (even though I was too young to put it into these words) it's bad enough if you just can't control yourself when you're mad. But he could. He proved he could every time the police and a social worker came around, so that's when I knew that he could have controlled himself with Bill. He just didn't want to, so he didn't.

"And it seemed like it wasn't ever over anything big, either. It's like he'd be spoiling for a fight. You could feel it. We could all feel it. It was like this electric charge you could just feel crackling in the air. And then all Bill had to do was just look at him wrong and it was another trip to the emergency room.

"And I probably thought right around then that I couldn't possibly hate the man more, but I was wrong. I hated him even more when he stopped. Sounds weird, I know, because of course we all wanted him to stop. But it was why he stopped that made me hate him so much."

She stopped writing, reread the last sentence, and underlined the word "why" twice.

"Bill got big. And he filled out. And he got strong. And he didn't just take it anymore. Well, he never just took it. He always tried to defend himself, but my father was so much bigger. But then one day he wasn't anymore. Eventually they were a pretty good size match, with Bill getting points for youth, and it wasn't clear anymore who would lose. And my father never raised a hand to him again.

"And that to me is the most despicable excuse for a human being on the planet—somebody who'll beat the crap out of a smaller, weaker person for no particular reason, but only if there's no risk to himself. That's the scum of the earth right there. Somebody who not only wants to pick on somebody, but it's never somebody their own size."

She stopped writing and thought a minute. An inventory couldn't only be about her father. It had to be about how living with her father had affected her. She would have to bring it around to herself.

A movement caught her eye on one of the monitors. And not on any of the internal rows of storage units, either. It was the camera that looked down on the front, street-facing row. The one you had to pass to reach the office door.

By the time she looked up, whatever had been there was already gone, or at least out of camera range.

She got up, moved to the front window, and looked down.

There was someone lying curled on the tarmac of the parking lot just outside her office.

She rapped on the window, and the figure startled and awkwardly scrambled into an upright position. And looked in the window at her. And revealed himself to be Jonathan.

"It's just me, Addie," he said with a shy smile.

Addie sighed and opened the door.

"What're you doing, Jonathan?"

"He's back again tonight."

"Skate?"

"Yeah."

"He there every night?"

"No. He comes and goes."

"And you're going to lie on the cold ground right out in the open all night, and that feels like a good, safe plan to you?"

"I thought if I was close enough for you to hear me, I'd be safe."

Addie sighed again.

"Come into the office," she said. "But if the owner comes around, you're my grandson. Maybe tell her you just got back from camping or something, to explain why you look a little rough."

But she looked him up and down as he came through the door, and he actually looked pretty good. His hair hadn't seen a barbershop in a long time, but it was combed, and his clothes seemed clean enough.

"But there are cameras everywhere."

"Not in the office," she said. "Just in the rows of units that I couldn't see any other way."

"Thanks," he said, and settled in the corner on the floor. "I won't make a sound. I won't bother you at all. I'll just sleep. How often does the owner come in, anyway?"

"Pretty much never, but it doesn't hurt to have a plan. How do you manage to stay so clean? After I said what I said about it, I noticed you really don't look like you've been camping at all."

"Thanks. I wondered about that. When you said that I thought, 'Damn. And here I was priding myself on looking pretty good.' I use the restroom at the gas station three blocks down. Take sponge baths and wash my hair. And I have a change of clothes, so I go to the laundromat anytime I have the quarters. I try to look like I still care about myself."

"Good," Addie said, settling behind the counter again. "I hope you actually do."

"Well, I must. Because I do it. You writing a letter? I don't think I ever saw somebody write a letter on paper before. Everybody emails or texts. Oops. Sorry. I said I wouldn't make a sound, didn't I?"

Addie had just been silently making the same observation. But really she didn't mind. It got awfully quiet in that office at night.

"It's not a letter," she said. "It's an inventory."

Jonathan looked around the office as though there were shelves of goods stored there and he had simply failed to notice them.

"What is there to inventory around here?"

"Not that kind of inventory. Not a business inventory of your products. It's an AA program inventory. A searching and fearless moral inventory of myself."

"How do you inventory yourself? You know . . . morally?"

"It's not easy, let me tell you."

For a time she said no more, and didn't plan to. Then more words came out, even though she hadn't planned them, or even seen them coming.

"You have to put down what you think your character defects are. The things you think you've done wrong. And it helps to go way back to the beginning and see if you can't get some sense of why it all turned out the way it did. At least, that's how I was taught to do it. Some people say you're also supposed to write down what you think is good about you, but I actually find that even harder."

"I can think of good things about you," he said. "And I've only known you for a day."

"You should just go to sleep," she said.

"Yes ma'am. I mean Addie."

They fell silent, and Jonathan curled up on his side in the corner, his down jacket thrown over his upper body like a blanket. From that angle, Addie could see holes worn into the soles of his cheap athletic shoes.

She held pen to paper again, but nothing seemed to flow. She just stared at the words she had written, vaguely comforted by Jonathan's light, breathy snoring.

Addie sat up for the rest of the night, and had no trouble staying awake, but wrote nothing more.

The owner did not come in.

In the morning, about fifteen minutes before the end of her shift, Addie made coffee. She added two creamers and three sugars to Jonathan's, but then realized she dreaded waking him up. He was sleeping like an angel. Like a puppy who had never felt safe before, and was now able to sleep with his head on his new person's arm. He must have needed the uninterrupted sleep.

Before she had to worry much more about it, he shook himself awake.

"I smell coffee," he said before his eyes were even open.

"Maybe because I just made some."

"That has got to be the most amazing luxury in the world. To wake up and smell fresh coffee. I can't believe how lucky I am."

He sat up, wrapping the jacket around his shoulders like a cape, and she handed him the coffee.

He sipped it and sighed deeply, his eyes far away.

"I hope you write this down on your inventory," he said.

"Write what down?"

"This. What you're doing right now. You said you were supposed to write good things about yourself too. Don't you think this is a good thing about you? You think just anybody would do what you've been doing for me? Because I can tell you. They wouldn't."

His words made Addie feel restless and uneasy, so she pushed the conversation in another direction.

"Tell me more about this Skate guy. Why'd he go after you, anyway?"

She immediately regretted asking. The angelic cloud of gratitude around him evaporated quickly, and the air in his corner seemed to darken. Just like that, he felt shut down and stiff.

"What do you mean why?"

"I mean what happened to start it? Or does he just beat people up for no reason?"

Jonathan didn't speak for several beats. When he did, it was with his gaze firmly glued to the faded linoleum floor.

"If you don't mind," he said, "I really don't want to talk about that night. I'm not ready to talk about that. I'll tell you whatever I can about him if you really want to know."

"Sorry," Addie said. "I didn't mean to pry. I'm just trying to figure out if something should be done about him."

"Like what?"

"Well, first tell me if it's happened more than once. To you or to different people."

"It's happened plenty of times," he said, still studying the linoleum tiles in apparent fascination. "To plenty of people."

"And nobody calls the police?"

For a surprising length of time, Jonathan didn't answer. Then she realized her own mistake.

"Right," she said. "Never mind. If you call the police they clear the warehouse like they did when the new owner complained."

"Oh, is that why they cleared it last time? We never knew. Anyway, I'm glad you figured it out. For a minute there I was starting to wonder if I was wrong to think you were one of the people who gets it."

"Gets what?" Addie said. She was wearing a sarcastic half smile, but he didn't see it, because he was still staring at the floor. "That was a joke," she added.

"Oh. Good. Well, look. We'd all like it if he was gone, but nobody wants to be the one that gets everybody thrown out on the street. And if he knows somebody like me is trying to get rid of him, well . . . it better work, and permanently."

"When you take a shot at the king you'd better not miss," Addie said.

She expected him to ask what it meant, but she had underestimated him. He seemed to understand perfectly.

He drained the last of his coffee from the cup, scrambled to his feet, looking excruciatingly painful and stiff, and handed her the cup.

"Thanks for this. Thanks for everything. I'm going to take off now."

"I'm sorry if I was asking after things that're none of my business."

His gaze immediately met the floor again.

"It's okay. I know you're trying to help. It's a hard thing, though."

She wanted to say *Life is a hard thing.* She almost did. But it was such a pessimistic thought, though it felt true enough in that moment. And in any case, he was already out the door.

She walked to the door, opened it, and called after him.

"Jonathan."

He stopped and turned around. Waited.

"How do you eat?"

"Sometimes I don't," he said.

"Sometimes you must, because you're still here."

"Sometimes somebody'll take pity on me and give me a dollar or a sandwich. Other times I walk all the way down to that corner three miles from here where the guys come in a big truck and pick up day laborers. They almost always take me because I'm young."

"Picking crops?"

"Usually, yeah. At the end of the day they pay maybe forty bucks cash. I can make that last a long time."

"You going to eat today?"

"Maybe. I hope so."

"If it doesn't work, come back tonight."

He gave her a smile, followed by a little nod and wave.

Then he walked again.

"You start that inventory?" Wendy asked.

They were sitting on a stone wall surrounding a raised flower bed, outside the seven-thirty sunrise meeting. Addie hadn't even known Wendy attended this one. Addie didn't usually catch it either, opting instead to go home and try to sleep. But that morning she just felt like she needed a meeting.

"Yeah. I started it. Didn't get very far. A couple of pages."

Wendy was vaping, and blew out a truly impressive cloud of steam following a drag on her electronic cigarette.

"Better than not starting," she said.

"Do you believe in Karma, Wendy?"

"That's a weird question."

"Why is it weird?"

"Because that's some of that weird Eastern philosophy stuff. Why? You believe it?"

"I don't know. Probably not. I just wondered."

They sat in silence for a minute or so, the early sun glaring into Addie's eyes. She glanced at her watch to see if it was time for the meeting to start, but they had almost five minutes.

"It's just that somebody put the idea in my head," she said.

"About Karma?"

"Yeah. Pretty much. Like I did something nice, and then somebody said maybe the universe would reward me for it, and I don't know if I believe like that, but it kind of seemed like a nice idea."

"I don't think it works that way," Wendy said.

"How does it work?"

"I think it's supposed to catch up with you in, like, your next life or something."

"I thought you weren't into that weird Eastern philosophy stuff."

"Just telling you what I've heard."

They sat quietly for another minute, Addie wrestling with whether she should just let it drop.

"Thing is," she said, "I kind of . . . need it."

"What? Some big reward from the universe?"

"Even a small one would do. I just feel like I need something good to happen. It just feels like it's been so long since something good happened. It's like one day keeps rolling over into the next, and it's all work, and it all keeps looking the same. And it's all hard, like a grind, and I just feel like I need something."

Wendy snapped the cap back on her electronic cigarette and dropped it into her purse. She leveled a look at Addie that made Addie feel smaller.

"Got a roof over your head?"

"Yeah."

"You eat today?"

"Sure, yeah. I did."

"Know where your next meal is coming from?"

"Pretty much."

"Got any huge problem you don't have the resources to solve?"

"Not really, no."

"Any idea how many people don't get to say that?"

"Okay, yeah, I get it."

A memory flashed through her head. Jonathan, all filled with gratitude because he woke up on a linoleum floor smelling fresh coffee. The way he said, "I can't believe how lucky I am."

"I'm not trying to be unsympathetic, hon. I hear what you're saying, and it's perfectly valid to feel the way you feel about it. I'm trying to show you how to shift your attention a little bit to the good side, just until something better comes along. Now come on. We need to go inside before the meeting starts without us."

———

When Addie got home, she took a look around her place before she even got to the front door. Her across-the-street neighbor was out, watering his neatly trimmed lawn, and it caused her to look at the property through his eyes. Unfortunately.

She really had been letting the place go.

The front yard was seedy and overgrown, and the weeds had taken over everything.

At one time she'd had the energy to keep it all tended herself. After that she'd had a gardener, but since her career on the force had come crashing down, she'd been unable to afford it.

She let herself in, and the place looked dusty and dim inside. Neat enough, but old and not really clean.

She walked through the house and out into the backyard.

It was a huge backyard, nearly half an acre. At one time it had been a garden, with vegetables on one side and flowers on the other and neat concrete paths in between. But it had fallen into a wild state of overgrown, junglelike ruin.

That was when the idea overtook her.

She could bring Jonathan here.

He could clean out the garden shed and turn it into a tiny but decent place to live. And he could be her farmer, and her gardener, and she wouldn't need to pay him much, because she was giving him a place to live.

The idea took on such sudden and overwhelming proportions that she barely slept that day. She mostly just lay awake picturing the place looking tidy and tended and good for the spirit, the way it had used to look.

It was such a lovely mental picture that she began to believe it was that nice thing from the universe. That reward she'd been hoping for.

She couldn't wait to propose it to him when he came around that night.

———

He didn't come around that night.

Or the night after. Or the night after that.

31

Two

Jonathan

Chapter Four

Almost like We're People

Jonathan froze next to the storage-place office, one hand leaning on its stucco wall. From that position he could see the old warehouse. But for the moment he did nothing more than look.

His stomach jangled with an almost electric fear. Not electric as in little tingles. Electric as in a charge that could electrocute a person.

He decided he could not go in. He'd have to find another place to sleep.

He looked over at the wall of the office, as though he could somehow see through it. There were no windows on this side, which was why he'd been coming by this way. He didn't want to seem to be fishing for another invitation from the nice lady. She'd already taken him in far more than any stranger should be expected to do.

He pulled his hand back from the wall and waved to her, mostly with just a little wiggling of his fingers. It was a gesture designed not to be seen.

"Hi, Addie," he said very quietly.

It was nothing new. Every time he went past her office, purposely on the nonwindow side, he waved to her and said hello.

He didn't need her to see it. He just needed to do it.

He turned away and walked six or seven blocks until he found one of those bus-stop benches with a little shelter. He settled in it, curled up painfully on his side on the bench. His body still hurt from that beating, and every part of him felt bruised and stiff. It was cold already, and he pulled his coat more tightly around himself because it didn't zip anymore. The zipper had broken a long time ago, and there was nothing he could do about that.

He knew he wouldn't sleep because he felt so exposed. His shelter was right under a streetlight, and he was on display for anybody who passed by. Just inviting whatever trouble was prowling the city that night.

Not ten minutes later, as if he'd summoned them with his worry, he heard a group of loud and slightly drunk-sounding young men moving in his direction. He skittered out of the shelter and ducked down behind it. It was made of a clear Plexiglas, but there were notices stuck to the back of it, mostly old and half torn away. It wasn't a lot of cover, but it was what he had to work with.

His heart pounded as they grew closer. He could hear their words, teasing each other about women. About whether the stories they told each other about their sexual escapades were even true.

They walked by without noticing him.

He waited a few minutes to be sure they were gone. Then he sprinted back to the self-storage place to sleep on the tarmac of the parking lot in front of the lady's office.

When he got close enough to spot her through the window, he stopped. She wasn't seeing him standing there. She was writing something with her pad and pen, her eyes on her work. And he knew he couldn't do it. It wasn't fair to her.

He'd tried to do it once, quietly and without fanfare, but she'd seen him immediately and invited him to sleep inside. If he did it again, it would be like pressing her for another invitation. It would put her in a bad position. She wasn't supposed to invite homeless teens inside. She'd made that clear. What if she lost her job because of him?

He sighed deeply, letting out air he must have been holding for longer than he'd realized. Then he began the walk across the weedy lot to the warehouse.

At least there were plenty of people in there. Maybe he could plant himself inside a tight-knit group of people and not be such an inviting target.

He could feel his heart hammer, and hear and feel the pounding of blood roaring through his ears.

When two dark figures stepped outside through the doorway, it made him jump the storied mile. He even let out a little squeak of alarm, though he hoped they hadn't heard.

"Hey," he said to them, a little louder than a whisper. "Is Skate in there?"

It was that couple he'd seen many times before, a man and woman in their early twenties. The man was missing his two front teeth, and they both had tattoos on their necks. It was fair to say that he knew them, to the extent that anybody knew anybody here.

"No, it's safe, son," the woman said. "We heard he's over at that construction site on Church Street. That's pretty far."

"Nothing's far enough," Jonathan said.

"We got a new arrangement, though," the man said. "You know how nobody's ever all asleep at the same time?"

Jonathan knew, all right. Because there were always people talking and laughing and yelling while he was trying to sleep. Always.

"Well," the man continued, "we made a deal that somebody'll always be watching the door, and if he comes in they'll yell it out real loud. That way people can scram out the door, or unsheathe their knife, or whatever they feel like they got to do."

"Thanks," Jonathan said.

And, doing his best to ignore the pain and the self-electrocution, he walked inside.

The moon was about halfway illuminated and shining strongly through the broken warehouse windows, and Jonathan kept opening his eyes to make sure somebody was sitting up watching, and awake.

He was still deeply bruised and sore from the experience, and he had only just barely gotten away last time, and this time he figured he would probably lose. If he was unlucky enough that there would be another time.

And then, much to his retroactive surprise, he was jolted awake by a shouted word.

"Skate!"

He had been sleeping sitting up, and possibly even with his eyes open, and he briefly considered the possibility that no one had shouted. That maybe he had only heard that word in a dream.

But then he scanned the moonlit room, and saw the big guy skulking around.

The moon was so bright that Jonathan could see the empty liquor bottles scattered around the floor and the long, dusty ropes of cobwebs arcing down from the high ceiling.

The plan had been to run if Skate showed up. But now there was a problem, something Jonathan had not correctly anticipated. Skate was between him and the door. Or close to blocking him, anyway.

He thought he'd chosen a spot sufficiently near the door for a quick getaway. What he hadn't realized was that if Skate hung close enough to that exit, Jonathan would risk being seen if he tried to run. If he bolted for the door, he would immediately become the center of his tormentor's attention. So he only sat frozen and watched his attacker skulk.

He wasn't focused on Jonathan, or moving his way. He had plenty of people to harass, and he seemed to be choosing and considering.

There was something disturbingly restless about his pacing.

There was another door at the back of the place, but it would be a long and very exposed sprint across the warehouse floor, and Jonathan was still slow and stiff from his injuries.

He decided his best bet would be to hold very still.

Everyone seemed to be holding still. No one spoke or moved, though they clearly could not have slept through the barked warning unless they were literally passed out. The whole room full of people seemed to be holding its breath, collectively, like one complicated entity.

And still Skate prowled.

It was something like watching a man-eating lion survey the room. You could feel the sheer weight of the menace. Every movement struck fear, and made Jonathan afraid to move and afraid not to move at the same time.

A good three or four minutes later Skate had gradually moved his prowling closer to the back of the warehouse.

Jonathan quietly gathered his feet under him, moving into a ready crouch, and bolted for the door.

He burst out into the safe-feeling night, but as soon as he did he heard the struggle of a victim. A young-sounding girl was loudly objecting to being attacked. It wasn't a scream, exactly. More a series of breathy words, probably meant to be shouted but stifled by a lack of air.

The only individual words he could make out were all the word "stop."

He almost ran on.

But before he got far, his eyes fell on the storage-place office. And, without really thinking it through, his imagination connected him to the night he'd been the victim. Nobody had helped him at the time. He'd had to fight off Skate on his own.

But then the lady had let him sleep in her SUV. She'd even brought him coffee in the morning.

There was that whole situation with Karma.

He turned and looked back into the warehouse, still hearing the sounds of a scuffle. Despite every nerve, every cell of his body jangling with alarm bordering on panic, he ran back inside.

On his trip across the floor, zigging and zagging to avoid filthy sleeping bags and bodies, he picked up an empty vodka bottle.

When he reached Skate, who had the struggling girl mostly pinned, he raised it high over his head and brought it down as hard as he could on the back of Skate's skull.

What happened after that was different from anything he expected.

He thought Skate would keel over. Be knocked unconscious, the way it would have gone in a movie. Instead the huge guy just stopped moving. He reached one hand back to touch that spot on his head, and grunted a word that seemed unique and yet somehow related to the word "ow."

But it was enough.

It gave the girl her opening, and she broke away from her not-quite-pinned position, and together they bolted for the door. Jonathan looked back over his shoulder to see if Skate was giving chase, but he hadn't moved. He was looking at his hand in the moonlight, as though trying to see if he was bleeding.

They ran to the street together, Jonathan reaching out to take the girl's hand. It didn't quite work at a sprint, and he ended up pulling her along by the wrist.

They didn't stop until they reached the alley on the other side of the dry cleaner's, where they ducked down behind a dumpster to wait it out.

"Thanks," she said in a whisper.

"Sure," he said breathlessly in return.

"Nobody ever does that for anybody else."

"I do. And also, don't I know it."

"He came after you too?"

"Yeah. A few nights ago."

"You get away?"

"Barely."

"What's your name?"

"Jonathan."

"Thanks, Jonathan. And thanks for telling me your real name. I hate it when people only have those street names, and it's always the

name of a thing and not a person. I just hate that. Like we don't have
enough reasons not to feel like real human people. Like people don't
treat us that way all the time. I don't see why we need to turn around
and do the same thing to ourselves."

"You didn't tell me your name," he said.

"Jeannie," she said. "Jeannie the real human person."

———

They sat in that cramped position on the hard and dirty concrete, afraid
to move from their hiding place, until the light came again.

"I could really use some breakfast," she said.

"Like what?"

"Anything hot. Even if it's just coffee."

"Food would be better," he said.

He felt as though his stomach were trying to tie itself in knots, like
a twirled rubber band on a child's balsa-wood airplane.

"You got any money?"

"Not a dime," he said.

"I'll get some. If people are up and walking around, I'll get enough for
breakfast. But you stay here. If I don't come back for a long time it's just
because people weren't waiting for their buses yet. But I should definitely
do this just by myself. When you're asking strangers for money, it always
works best when a girl my age asks grown-up men. It won't help to have
an older boy along."

He hadn't asked her age, and wouldn't. He didn't figure it was any
of his business. Or, rather, he had learned that certain things were not
your business on the street. But he made her to be around fifteen, with
hair dyed an electric blue, quite a few piercings, and a hoodie covering
everything but her face.

It couldn't cover the bruises, swelling, and discoloration on her face,
though. It could not hide the fact that she had been assaulted.

She must have seen him looking, because she said, "That'll help, actually. People give you more money when they feel sorry for you. When you look like you're in trouble. Don't go away. I'll be back. The least I can do is get you breakfast."

———

They walked down the boulevard side by side, eating microwaved gas-station burritos.

"There's that homeless shelter on Fifth," he said.

"That's almost all the way downtown."

"Yeah. We'd have to take a couple of buses and walk some. But we can't go back to the warehouse."

"No. We can't go back to the warehouse."

A woman in a neat skirt suit and heels and a long, open coat approached them on the sidewalk, looking down at her phone. Just as she was a few steps from plowing into them she looked up at them and frowned in an overblown reaction of disapproval.

Jeannie gave her the finger, but the woman had already passed and didn't see.

It filled Jonathan with a deep wash of resentment, the way she had looked at them. Like it wasn't bad enough to be reduced to living this way. It wasn't enough that he was constantly hungry and deprived of sleep and in danger. No. She had to make it clear that his condition troubled *her*.

He tried to shake the feeling away again. He had a burrito, and a friend, and that made it otherwise a decent morning. He didn't want to let one rude woman ruin it.

"You have to be there by five and get in line," he told Jeannie. "That's when they let people in. But really you have to get there two or three hours earlier, because there's a cutoff. There's never enough room for everybody who's waiting, so you have to be near the front of the line. Otherwise you came all that way and waited all that time for nothing."

"You been there?"

"Once. Yeah."

"How is it?"

"It's okay. It's safe. And there's soup. But that's pretty much it. There's not much more to be said for it than that."

———

They sat cross-legged on the hard concrete of the sidewalk near the shelter's front door. They had been sitting that way for hours, so the discomfort was getting harder for him to ignore.

But they were near the front of the line, so that was good.

Jeannie was playing cards with two guys. Gin rummy. Jonathan was not playing, because he'd never played and didn't know the game.

Now and then his eyes kept going back to a sign on the door.

It said: "You are responsible for your belongings and may not buy, trade, and/or sell your belongings with others. Weapons are not allowed in the shelter and nothing may be used as a weapon. Possession, use, or distribution of alcohol or illegal drugs is not allowed within the shelter."

He'd practically memorized it by that time.

"We should play poker," one of the guys said.

"Except I don't know how to play poker," Jeannie said in return.

"We could teach you," the other guy said.

"Yeah, right. Sure," she said. "That's a surefire way to win at a game. Let the people you're playing against teach you."

The guys both had very long hair and seemed reasonably clean. They looked almost like they could have been brothers, but maybe that was only a coincidence. Jonathan couldn't shake the sense that she was flirting with them in some very subtle way. It was something you could feel, but never really substantiate. And it bothered him. Not because he thought she should flirt with *him*. He didn't feel that way at all. More because he worried about her leading herself—and possibly him as well—into trouble.

"I have to go to the bathroom," she said suddenly.

"Where?" Jonathan asked.

"No idea," she said. "I guess I'll just find an alley or something."

"They'll let you in for that," a big woman in her fifties said from two places behind them. "If you tell them you have to go, they'll let you in just long enough for that."

Jeannie stood, dusting off the seat of her very well-worn jeans.

"Here," she said to Jonathan, and handed him her cards. "Don't let these guys see my hand."

Then she moved to the front of the line and rapped on the door. A few seconds later it opened slightly, and she disappeared inside.

"Your girlfriend is pretty," the older woman said.

"Oh, she's not my girlfriend," he said, craning his neck to address the lady. "I only met her last night."

"Future girlfriend?"

"No," he said. "I don't see it going that way."

He looked back toward the door and saw the two card players staring directly at him. It made him uneasy.

"Why?" one of them asked. "She's pretty."

"I just think of her more like a kid sister."

"You gay?" the other one asked.

They were still staring directly into his face, and he still felt like a bug pinned onto a card and examined with a magnifying glass.

"My life is none of your business," he said.

He heard a little "oooh" sound from someone in line. Because, honestly, it had been a brave thing to say. They were physically bigger than he was. Most people were. And there were two of them.

And then, amazingly, Jeannie was back. Either she had used the bathroom unusually fast or time had experienced some sort of bend or warp.

He remembered something he'd read in a textbook in school, back when he'd been able to go to school. Albert Einstein saying something along the lines of *Time isn't what you think it is.* But he still had no idea what that meant it was.

"We should play for money," the first guy said as Jeannie settled onto the sidewalk again.

"Except we don't have any," Jeannie said.

"Damn."

Yeah, Jonathan thought. *Damn.*

He actually believed she did have a little. He had no idea how much she'd gathered from panhandling earlier that morning. He hadn't figured it was his business to ask. But he'd seen her take money from her pocket when they got on the bus, and she'd had something left over to stash away after that.

But it couldn't have been much, and if she was smart enough to save it for something more important than losing at cards, he was grateful for that.

———

They lay side by side in cots arranged with just inches between them. Just barely room enough for people to squeeze through.

Neither of them seemed to be sleeping. Then again, why would he expect otherwise? The snoring was outrageous, and every time someone moved through to use the bathroom they ended up banging their shins on one of the rows of cots.

But Jeannie wasn't even trying. She had her head up and was looking around the mostly darkened room.

"I'll be right back," she said.

"You have to use the bathroom?" he asked in a loud whisper.

But she was already gone.

He lay alone for what felt like a very long time. Longer than it takes for a person to use the restroom.

While he waited, he felt a little cheated, and very, very alone.

———

It was the second night in the shelter when things went south.

Jeannie was up and down again, as she'd been the night before. When she got back she seemed restless. Unable to hold her limbs still.

That went on for what Jonathan guessed was two or three minutes before one of the big men who worked at the shelter came and tapped Jeannie on the shoulder.

"You need to come with me," he said. "And bring your stuff."

"Wait," Jonathan said. "Where are you taking her?"

Then two people in nearby cots yelled at him to shut up so they could sleep.

He grabbed his jacket and his backpack and followed her to the door.

When he got there, the man was taking a picture of her with an old-fashioned Polaroid camera. Not that it wasn't new-looking. Just that Jonathan had been under the impression that they no longer existed.

When the picture popped out with an odd zipping sound, the man waved it around and blew on it, then tacked it up on a bulletin board behind the front desk.

"What are you doing?" Jonathan asked him.

"Throwing her out."

"Why did you take her picture?"

"It's how we know not to let her in next time. She's banned."

"What did she do?"

Jeannie tugged at his sleeve and shook her head at him.

"Never mind," she said. "Just leave it alone. Go back to bed. You're not thrown out. Just me."

But he knew if she walked out without him they might never meet up again. It was a big city. And she needed him. And maybe, a nagging thought in the back of his head told him, the reverse was true as well.

It had been nice having a friend for a couple of days. Not being completely alone in the world.

"No," he said. "If you're out, I'm out."

"Suit yourself," the big man said. "But *you're* not banned. You can come back if you want."

They stepped out into the cold night together and began walking, for lack of a better plan. He watched her as best he could when they passed under streetlights. She was sniffing a lot, and swiping her nose with the back of one hand, and her movements seemed jerky and strange.

"Sorry," she said after a few blocks.

"You're high," he said. "Right?"

"Pretty much."

"Where did you get drugs?"

"From some guys. Sorry I got us kicked out. Damn. It's so cold out here."

He pulled his down jacket more tightly around himself when she said it, though it was not the first time he'd noticed the cold. And she didn't have a good jacket. Just a hooded sweatshirt.

"I'd kill for a cup of coffee," she said.

"Do you still have enough money for one?"

"Yeah, but nothing's open."

"We could take the bus back to where we started. There are all-night gas stations there."

"But once we take the bus we won't have money for coffee."

"Let's go back there anyway," he said, aching for the feeling of something familiar. Anything familiar. "If we can get back there, I might know how to get us some coffee."

It was only the smallest of favors to ask. Not like asking her to let them in to sleep. Not even like asking her to let *him* in to sleep. Just coffee. She probably didn't even have to pay for it herself, and he could not imagine her losing her job over giving away a couple of cups. And she could always say no.

And, anyway, it would be nice to see the lady again.

Three

Addie

Chapter Five

I Am Not the Jury

"I'm not sure it was such a great idea anyway," Wendy said.

"Why wasn't it?"

"Well. You can make that little shed look as pretty as you want, but it's not really intended for human habitation."

"Neither is that old abandoned warehouse."

They were sitting in their usual coffee shop, after their usual meeting. Wendy was drinking coffee and Addie was having French toast and sausage for her evening breakfast.

"Does it have a bathroom?" Wendy asked.

"Of course not. But—"

"I know, I know. Neither does the warehouse. But now he's on your property, hypothetically speaking at the moment, and it's kind of your problem where he goes to solve that inevitable situation."

"It could have a porta-potty," Addie said.

"And then this homeless stranger would have to come into the house to empty it."

"Not really. He could dump it straight into the sewer pipe and clean it with the garden hose."

"And then how does he eat?"

"I guess I'd have to bring him something."

"And what do you get out of all this?" Wendy asked, staring at the foot traffic going by the big front window.

"A gardener. My place back looking like something I can be proud of. Again. For a change."

"Don't you have a son?"

"I do, yeah," Addie said.

And she cut her eyes away so Wendy could not see in.

"You talk to him?"

"No. I mean, I would. I'd be happy to. But he won't talk to me."

"Are you sure you're not just lonely?"

"What if I was? I still need a gardener. One thing doesn't cancel out the other, you know."

Wendy sighed and set down her mug.

"Well, it doesn't really matter anyway, hon, now does it? What with his being gone and all."

"Just when I was starting to care whether he's okay," Addie said.

She was looking down at her food when she said it. Cutting a sausage link with the edge of her fork. When she looked up, Wendy was drilling that serious gaze right through to the back of Addie's brain. Maybe through to the back of her soul.

"Has he got a higher power, this boy?" Wendy asked.

"He does."

"Is it you?"

"It isn't."

"Turn it over, honey," Wendy said. "Turn it over."

———

It was a little after five in the morning—less than two hours from the end of her shift—when she looked up to see him smiling nervously at her through the glass of the office door. When it was clear that she saw him, he gave a little wave with just his fingers.

She was halfway to the door when she realized there was somebody with him.

The new person seemed to be a girl. She was standing a few steps behind him, mostly outside the circle of light that spilled from the fixture over the door. She looked to be his age, or maybe a year or two younger, and she was wearing a dark hoodie with the hood up. She was small and slight, like Jonathan, or maybe even a little more so.

Addie opened the door.

"Who've you got with you there?" she asked, feeling a strong resistance to this new development.

"I know I shouldn't be asking you for favors," he said. "You should just offer if you feel like you want to. It's not like you haven't done a lot already."

Her first thought was that he was about to ask her for money, and she wasn't sure what her reaction would be, or even what it should be. She had a nagging feeling that she would have been more receptive if he'd come alone, rather than foisting someone unfamiliar on her, despite the fact that she could never have defended that position in words. Or even in the silence of her own brain.

Before she could open her mouth to speak, he clarified the favor.

"I was wondering if we could hit you up for coffee."

"Oh," Addie said, a little stunned. "Is that all? That's not much of a favor."

"I was hoping you'd see it that way. We don't have to come in. I'm not asking for you to let us in there to drink it. I know you've let me in before, and I appreciate it, but I'm not using that as an opening to push my luck. And that was when it was just me. Now there are two of us. It's just that it's cold out here and we've been walking and riding the bus for hours and coffee would just be really nice."

"I wish I could let you in," she said. "If it was just you I might chance it. But I'm not sure about having two of you in here. I'm not really supposed to."

"It's okay," he said. Then: "It's okay," again. "We can drink it outside. No problem."

But he sounded a little disappointed.

Addie stuck her head out into the cold, dark morning and looked around the parking lot. As if the owner could be standing anywhere, seeing everything.

"It's okay, I guess," she said. "I guess you can both come in. Just, if the owner shows up for some reason, you're my grandchildren. And you came here to ask for my help because you just got mugged."

She said that last sentence because as she spoke, the girl came closer. Stepped into the light. And she looked as though she had just been mugged. She had one black eye, and her face was swollen and discolored on one side.

Addie also saw that her hair was bright blue where it stuck out from under her hood, and that she had a nose ring and two eyebrow rings. And none of that punk stuff did anything to endear her to Addie.

Still, Addie stepped back from the door and let them both come in. The girl made a point of not meeting her eyes.

"Addie, this is Jeannie," Jonathan said.

"Jeannie," Addie said, quietly, by way of a greeting.

Jeannie did not speak. She might have grunted slightly, but if the sound had existed at all, it was so quiet that Addie would never be sure if she'd heard it or not.

Jeannie walked straight to a corner on the customer's side of the office and sat cross-legged, her back against the wall. She pulled off her hood, and Addie saw that her short, spiky blue hair was growing out from its dye job, leaving a couple of inches of brown at the roots.

"Where've you been?" Addie asked Jonathan as she started a pot of coffee. "I was worried about you."

"You were?" He sounded breathy and childlike. Almost unable to believe what he had heard. "That's so nice."

For a minute he said no more. Just stood with his hands in his jacket pockets, watching her make coffee. Just as she was beginning to think he would never volunteer where he had been, he spoke again.

"Jeannie had a problem with the same guy I did," he said. "So we went to a shelter."

"I didn't know you had that option."

"Well, sometimes. Sometimes you can get in, but it's a long way away, and you have to get there early. If they fill up, then they just do. And then they turn you away, and you're just out of luck."

"Don't say I had a problem with him," Jeannie said from the corner. Her voice was small and meek and yet somehow hard at the same time. "Call it what it really was."

"Oh," Jonathan said, and looked down at the linoleum floor in what appeared to be shame. "She got attacked."

Addie hit the "brew" button on the coffee machine and walked back behind her counter. She could feel the situation with Skate begin to rankle her again—a growing, angry, unlivable knot in her belly—and she had no idea what to do with all that negative emotion.

"What is it with this guy? He just starts beating on people whenever he happens to feel like it?"

"Not exactly," Jonathan said, still staring at the floor.

"Tell her," Jeannie said.

But Jonathan didn't tell her. Jeannie did the job herself.

"He doesn't come after you to beat you up. He comes after you for something else. But if you won't let him do the something else, he gets mad and starts in on you. And the more you try to get away the worse it gets."

"Wait," Addie said. She plunked down into her chair, her brain reeling. "Wait. Are you telling me this was a sexual assault?"

"He meant for it to be," Jeannie said. "But Jonathan helped me get away."

"Wait. Just you, Jeannie? Is that just what he tried to do with you? Or was that what happened with Jonathan, too?"

The room fell quiet. Eerily quiet.

Jonathan just kept staring at the floor.

When it was clear Addie did not intend to withdraw the question, he said, "If it's okay with you, I'd really rather not talk about that night."

"Holy crap," Addie said. "I'm going to kill that guy."

In her peripheral vision, Addie could see Jeannie perk up in the corner.

"That would actually be great," she said, her voice sounding bigger.

"Well, I'm not actually, literally going to kill him."

"Why not? Jonathan says you've got a gun."

"I'm not going to kill him because attempted rape is not a death-penalty crime, and because, anyway, even if it was, I'm not the judge, jury, and executioner."

"You can't call the police," Jeannie said.

"But maybe I could chase him out of here."

"Yeah, okay," Jeannie said. But it was clear that she was sorely disappointed, and that she had liked the idea of his death much better. "But . . . just so you know . . . not everybody gets away."

———

"Why did you leave the shelter?" Addie asked him.

They were sipping their coffees on opposite sides of the counter. He had his elbows on its hard surface and was leaning in, as though wanting to be just a little bit closer to her.

Jeannie was fast asleep and snoring lightly in the corner, her mouth wide open, her head on Jonathan's backpack.

"We got kicked out," he said.

"For what?"

He stared out the big front window for a minute without answering. Then he leaned in a little closer and spoke in a low voice.

"They threw us out because Jeannie was using."

Addie sat up straight, pulling her head back away from him.

"She can't be on drugs here either," she said.

"I know. I know. She's not. She's not anymore."

"You sure? You sure she's not passed out over there in the corner?"

"I'm sure. No, she's not passed out. She's just asleep. We haven't slept at all tonight. We've just been walking. She's not high anymore, and she doesn't have anything on her. I know you're a sober person, or clean, or whatever, or both. I mean . . . I know you don't do any of that stuff. And I would never bring anybody here who had any drugs on them, or in them. I would never do that."

"Good. I'm glad we're clear." She leaned forward on the counter again, wishing this Jeannie had never come into the picture. "I was all ready to offer you a job," she added, trying but failing to keep the regret out of her voice.

His eyes went wide, and yet also somehow soft at the same time.

"You were? What kind of a job?"

"Gardening, mostly. And grounds maintenance. My house is on a really big lot, and I just can't keep it up anymore. It's a mess. I don't know how my neighbors stand it. I figure they must be sticking pins in a voodoo doll that looks suspiciously like me. I don't have much money to pay you, but there's a little shed that could be fixed up nice. You know. More of a room-and-board kind of deal."

"Ooh, I would love that," he said. "It sounds so safe and happy and so much better than this. But I can't leave Jeannie."

"She's your girlfriend?"

"Oh, no. No. Nothing like that. It's not like that with us at all. I just can't leave her because she needs somebody. She needs not to be left."

Addie nursed her disappointment for a moment before answering.

"I guess it's nice that you're that kind of friend," Addie said. "But the place is barely big enough for one."

"If it's big enough for two people to lie down side by side, then it's big enough. And you'd get two workers for the price of one."

"I don't know, Jonathan. There's the drug thing."

"She's not a bad person."

"Jonathan. Honey. I know addiction as well as anybody. Better than most. If having addiction issues made you a bad person, then I'd be bad and so would just about everybody I know. It's just a tricky thing, though, addiction. You can walk away, but it wants you back, and it'll try everything. People have to hit some kind of real bottom with it before they manage to break the cycle. My old sponsor used to say it's like dancing with an eight-hundred-pound gorilla. You're not done dancing until the gorilla says you are."

He tried to smile, but it was a sad-looking little thing.

"Will you at least think about it?"

"Yeah, I guess. I guess it can't hurt me to think about it."

But based on the feeling in her midsection, it already did hurt.

———

"Bring her to a meeting," Wendy said.

They were on the phone later that morning while Addie microwaved a TV dinner.

"That's not what I thought you'd say."

"What did you think I'd say?"

"I thought you'd tell me not to have anything to do with her."

"We don't shun the people who're out there struggling in their disease, hon. We reach out to them. Just don't get the idea that you can fix her. If she's ready, she'll stick, but you can't make her ready."

The microwave beeped, and Addie pulled on hot mitts and took her dinner/breakfast out and set it on a woven mat on the table, the phone clutched between her cheek and shoulder.

"I don't think she's the AA type," she said into the phone. "I think it's mostly drugs with her."

"So? There's a Narcotics Anonymous meeting at the same time, right down the hall. Every day."

"At the sunrise meeting or the evening one?"

"Yes. Both. Reach out and see if you can help her, but don't forget the part about how you probably can't. I mean, the odds are not that great that she's ready. But at least she'll know where to go if she ever gets ready later on. But a word to the wise, hon. Think long and hard before you offer to let her stay on your property. If you take on those two, you take all of them. All their baggage. All their problems. And you're not doing her any favors to keep her safe and warm while she's still using. You're just helping her postpone hitting her bottom and making any real changes. Remember, we carry the message, not the alcoholic."

Still, it was a lot more encouraging than anything Addie had expected her to say.

Chapter Six

What You're Asking When You Ask a Thing Like That

"Where's Jeannie?" Addie asked as she walked back into the office.

It was the following morning, and Addie had just come in from checking all the locks at the end of her shift. She didn't know where those two had been all night, but they'd been in her office when she'd stepped outside a few minutes earlier.

"She's in your bathroom, getting cleaned up for that meeting," Jonathan said.

Addie had been walking toward the area behind the counter, but her feet stopped cold, and she just stood a moment, nursing her surprise.

"She's actually going?"

"If she can ride with you, yeah."

"What did you have to say to get her to go?"

"Nothing, really. I just told her you suggested it, and that they don't take your name or lock you in or anything. And that there's coffee and cookies."

Addie began to walk again.

"Let me ask you a question," she said as she settled behind the counter. She purposely lowered her voice so she wouldn't be heard from the bathroom.

"Okay," Jonathan said.

He moved closer to the counter and leaned in.

"She has no money, right?"

"Hardly ever."

"Then where's she getting drugs?"

"Well. Somebody'll always have drugs."

"And that somebody wants to give them away . . . why?"

"I don't really know."

"I'm afraid I *do* know. But clarify for me."

"I guess if they want somebody to hang out with . . ."

"In other words she's prostituting herself for drugs," Addie said.

"I have no idea, but I hope not."

"Were the people she got the drugs from male or female?"

"I don't know. I wasn't there. But I think the only people she knew at that shelter were two guys. But still—"

"Look," she said, cutting him off. "I'm not trying to judge her here. I just wanted to know how much trouble she's in, since we're hoping to help her get out of it."

"I know she's not as user-friendly as I am," Jonathan said, pulling things in a new direction. "I mean . . . 'user' is a weird word. I'm not suggesting anybody is trying to use her. It's just an expression."

"I know what it means, and I know exactly what you meant by it."

She watched a little satisfied smile play at one corner of his mouth.

"See?" he said. "You always get it. Anyway, what I'm trying to say is . . . even if it's not as easy to be around her, she still needs help."

Addie was going to say that was why they were on their way to a meeting, but the sound of the bathroom door opening stopped the conversation where it stood.

Jeannie stepped into view.

"Jonathan says you're taking me to some kind of meeting," she said. "I'm ready to go when you are."

"Are you going to be there?" Jeannie asked in the car.

The question, and her voice as she asked it, made her sound several years younger than her already young age. Addie had never been so painfully aware that Jeannie was a child.

"No, I go to AA, right down the hall. You can come to that one if you want, but it's supposed to only be about alcohol. I figured the NA one would feel more right to you, being about drugs and all."

"Drinking just makes me throw up."

"Yeah, it pretty much had that effect on all of us, but some of us didn't let that stand in our way."

They drove in silence for a few blocks.

A split second before Jeannie opened her mouth to speak again, Addie realized the girl was scared, and seeking some kind of reassurance. It was something Addie could just feel circulating in the air.

"Do I have to talk?"

"No. You don't have to. Somebody might call on you to speak, but you can just say your first name and identify, and then say you only want to listen."

"Isn't saying my name identifying?"

"Identifying . . . sorry, that was not self-explanatory, was it? In the program it means to identify yourself as someone who qualifies for the program. In AA I'd say 'I'm Addie and I'm an alcoholic.' You'd say 'I'm Jeannie and I'm an addict.'"

She glanced over at Jeannie, who was staring out the window as if something fascinating were happening out there. A rocket launch, maybe, or some kind of flashy parade.

"But what if I think I'm not?"

"When you're new, it's okay to say you're just kind of . . . looking into whether you think you belong there or not."

"Can I say my name and that *you* think I'm an addict?" Her voice had turned cold quite suddenly. It was a surprisingly abrupt change of mood. "This was all *your* idea."

"I'm not forcing you to go."

"I guess. Right. I don't know, though. The whole thing just seems a little weird."

"The people there will be welcoming. You'll see. They've all been in your shoes."

"Oh, I doubt that."

"Prepare to be pleasantly surprised," Addie said.

Then they ran out of things to say and fell silent for a long time.

As they pulled into the parking lot of the community center, Jeannie said, "Jonathan really, really wants that situation you were thinking about giving him."

"Being my live-in gardener, you mean?"

"Right. That. But I know he probably won't get it, and I know it's because of me. But he wants that so bad, and he deserves it. You know?"

Addie pulled into a space and shifted the SUV into park.

"Tell you what," she said. "You get clean and stay clean, and I'll extend the invitation to cover both of you."

Jeannie offered no response to that statement, so Addie had no idea where that left them. Then again, she did know that getting clean and staying clean was not as simple as all that. It was not one of those cut-and-dried situations where you just agree to do something and then do it.

"He thinks you can't make it without him," she told the silent girl.

"He's right. I'm just really, really close to the edge right now. I just don't have a whole lot of rope left, if you know what I mean."

"I know exactly what you mean," Addie said.

———

Wendy had been chosen to lead the meeting that morning, and right from the beginning, Addie had a strong sense that Wendy would call on her first. She just felt it coming, and had been attempting to avoid eye contact and make herself as small as humanly possible.

It was all to no avail.

"I'm going to call on Addie," Wendy said at the end of her share.

"I'm Addie and I'm an alcoholic," Addie said with a deep sigh.

"Hi Addie," the group said in return.

"Still tired," she said. "Maybe more tired. And still feeling a little prone to complain. But I've just been thinking about people a lot lately. Sounds weird, I know. But . . . on the subject of other people . . . for a long time I didn't have much in the way of other people in my life, or if I did, I kept them pretty much at bay. It was completely true when I was drinking, and it's been a little bit true since. And since my old sponsor died it's been so true it's scary. But now I have more people in my life, and I've honestly got to tell you . . . people are a royal pain in the ass. Life is so much simpler without other people."

She stopped and waited for the ripple of laughter to move through the room. She had not intended it as a joke, and the other members likely knew that. But it was common for laughter in the rooms to reflect identification with what had been said, along with a spirit of not taking oneself too seriously.

"But I helped a new person get to her first meeting today, and I guess that's something. And I know it wasn't much, what I just shared, but it's all I've got to say. I don't want to call on anyone. I'd rather just leave it open for someone who *wants* to share. Or who needs to."

A young man named Tom raised his hand.

"I'm Tom, and I'm an alcoholic."

And the group said, "Hi Tom."

"Thanks, Addie. For your share, and for leaving the sharing open. Because I did need to. Anyway, I have news. And not the good kind. I drank again. Threw away seventeen months. And then I purposely came in late so I wouldn't have to raise my hand as a newcomer. But that's stupid, isn't it? I can't avoid it forever. So I'm admitting it. And if some of the guys want to give me their phone numbers, I promise I'll actually use them this time."

It had the effect of making Addie grateful for her own problems. Which was probably one of many reasons to keep coming to meetings.

"How was it?" she asked Jeannie on the drive home. Although dropping her back in the general area of an old abandoned warehouse was a strange use of the word "home."

"It was different than I thought."

"Different good, or different bad?"

"Mostly good, I guess. I shared. I didn't think I would, but then I did. A bunch of people came up to me after the meeting and gave me their phone numbers, not that that helps much when you don't have a phone. But it was nice, I guess. And they told me to keep coming back. And one of them said something I really didn't think anybody would ever say to me. She said, 'Even if you get loaded, come back.' Which I totally didn't expect. I sort of figured I was welcome there so long as I was doing what they're doing, but not if I messed up. I don't think anybody's ever told me they wanted me back someplace if I messed up, or if I didn't want to be like them. So that was interesting."

Addie felt her hands tighten on the steering wheel, because she wanted to ask the girl if she'd go back to another meeting. Instead she loosened her hands and said nothing. And let the moment go by.

Honestly, sometimes it was better just to let that first meeting experience percolate. Often, Addie knew, one could get further by letting the program speak for itself. By choosing not to push.

They drove without talking for at least a mile.

Then Jeannie said, "Everybody really would be better off if you just took him out, you know."

"Skate, you mean?"

"Who else?"

It was another one of those moments when the girl suddenly and unexpectedly changed the temperature of the room. Or of the inside of the car, in this case. Addie had been enjoying talking to the new, more open Jeannie. And then, just like that, Dark Jeannie was in charge again.

It felt almost as though there were two of them in there.

"*He* wouldn't be better off," Addie said. "Not that he's my prime concern. But I'm not sure I would be either. Actually, I do know for sure. I wouldn't be."

"I just think the world wouldn't be any worse off without him. At all. Who would miss him?"

"Maybe his mom?"

"Here's the thing, though," Jeannie said, as if she hadn't heard. "You'd have to not miss. With that gun, I mean. That kind of missing, not the kind we were talking about a minute ago. You'd have to do it right, because if you don't get it right the first time, he'll mess you up."

"I don't miss," Addie said.

"That's a pretty confident statement."

"I did two combat tours in Iraq. I spent eleven years on the streets with the LAPD. I'm considered a sharpshooter. My scores on the range were generally in the top five percent. There are people fighting on the front lines of wars right now who aren't nearly as good a shot as I am. Most of them, in fact."

"Then you've killed people before."

Addie drove past the parking lot of her work and pulled up halfway to the old warehouse.

A day person would be on shift now in the office, and Addie didn't want anyone to see her with one of the homeless teens in her car. Whether anyone else knew them by sight, Addie had no idea. But she was not inclined to take chances.

"I have," she said. "Which is how I know it's not nearly as clean or as easy as you make it out to be. But you're missing the point, Jeannie. Easy or hard is not the point. Justified or unjustified is not the point. The point is that when the army and the police force gave me a gun, it came with rules of engagement. I was authorized to use deadly force if the situation called for it, so long as I stayed within those rules. Nobody's giving me any authority to walk over to that warehouse and shoot that boy. That's just called murdering someone. A murder is a murder regardless of how much you think the victim deserved what he got. And I'm not a murderer. And I don't think you know what you're asking when you tell me you think I should be. But I might just go over there and pay the boy a visit."

"He won't take you seriously. Even if you're pointing a gun at him. He'll just figure you're an old lady. I mean . . . sorry. An old-*er* lady is what I meant to say. He'll just take one look at you and figure you wouldn't really do it. He doesn't scare easy, and he won't believe you."

"There are ways to make people believe you," Addie said.

Chapter Seven

Monsoon Season

"How's that inventory coming along?" Wendy asked her.

They were sitting in their regular coffee shop, Addie eating oatmeal with raisins and walnuts, Wendy eating a soft-boiled egg with white toast.

"You never eat when we're here," Addie said, though she certainly could have brought it up sooner.

"And you figure I won't notice that's evading the question, hon? Let me try it again. Hey, Addie. How's that inventory coming along?"

"Good," Addie said.

Then she stopped eating and rested her closed eyes in the palms of her hands. When she looked up again, Wendy appeared expectant. To phrase it mildly.

"I just broke your drop-dead rule," Addie said.

"So I noticed."

"I haven't gotten any more work done on it since you last asked. I've been sort of preoccupied."

"Which is certainly an excellent excuse."

"I'm going to guess you're being sarcastic."

"Good guess," Wendy said.

They ate in silence for a minute or so.

Then Wendy said, "Is this about those two kids?"

"Yes and no," Addie said with her mouth half full. "It's more about this guy who hangs out in the warehouse with them. Comes and goes. He's got a bad habit of trying to sexually assault anybody he thinks he can take. Which is pretty much everybody, because he's a huge guy. It's starting to get under my skin. And it's even worse than it normally would be in my brain—like it's not already bad enough in there—because I'm writing about my father, who never sexually assaulted anybody as far as I know but who used my brother for a punching bag until he got to be a near size match. And the two situations are coming together in my head, because he's tried it on both those kids, the boy and girl both, and it's bugging me a lot. I just can't seem to keep my mind focused. I think I'm going to have to do something about it."

She was afraid Wendy would ask her what she planned to do, but fortunately it never came to pass. Probably Wendy would just think Addie was talking about a call to the police. That was what most people would think. Especially if they didn't know Addie all that well.

"What do your two new friends think about that?" Wendy asked.

"Not sure," she said, which was not entirely true, because she knew Jeannie thought she should kill him. "They haven't been around for a couple of days."

"Well, I hope they're somewhere indoors. I wouldn't wish it on my worst enemy to be sleeping outdoors during this."

Addie stopped eating and gazed out the window for a moment. As if there were something to see out there. A firestorm or a tornado she had somehow missed. But it was just a night like any other.

"During what?"

Wendy raised an already high and arched eyebrow.

"You don't watch the news?"

"Sometimes. Not lately."

"Or look at weather reports?"

"Not usually. I figure I'll see what the weather is when it gets here."

"Every now and then there's weather you might want to see coming."

"Rainstorm?"

"More than just that, hon. More like a monsoon. Two gigantic atmospheric rivers, back to back. The old Pineapple Express, as they call it, from Hawaii. Pretty much time to start building an ark. We're looking at maybe twelve inches in less than a week. Last time we got that much rain, cars floated away in those underpasses under the freeways and idiots tried to drive through the floodwater and got stuck. Because they always do. Some fool or another'll probably have to get airlifted out of the concrete river, like last time. They're calling for mudslides in the hills, and the winds might gust up over sixty. Trees down. Should be bad enough for people who live in a house. I hate to even think about the rest."

Addie chewed without speaking for a time, her brow furrowed in concern. She couldn't decide if the solution to this stress was to insist Jonathan always tell her his whereabouts, because she cared, or to let it go and try not to care. Then again, when did it ever work to try to feel something other than what she felt?

"I guess they know where to find me if they're really in trouble," she said.

———

Addie brought up a browser on the office computer and typed "atmospheric river" into the search window.

What came up first was a bank of news stories. National news stories about the weather event that was about to hit California.

Her goal was to try to find out when to expect it, but she had to read pretty deeply into the stories before she found a general prediction that the first storm would land late the following day. And by that time she'd digested a lot of pretty alarming details of what was about to hit them.

She thought all that gloom and doom would make it easy to stay awake that night.

She was wrong.

She woke a little after six a.m. with her head resting on her arms, which were crossed on the counter. Her back muscles screamed as she straightened up.

She squinted at her watch, then squinted at it again. She found it hard to believe it was morning because it still seemed so dark.

She walked to the glass door and looked out.

Jonathan was leaning against her old SUV.

He had his feet well out, away from the vehicle, and was leaning the small of his back against the front fender, his head dropped back, looking at the sky.

Addie stepped out without her jacket.

An eerie wind was picking up, feeling almost warm, and uncomfortably humid, and somehow electric.

He dropped his head level and looked at Addie when he heard her approaching, but didn't seem startled. Then he gazed up at the sky again.

"Lose something up there?" she asked him.

"Looks like it's going to rain," he said.

"That would be putting it mildly." She leaned her back up against the SUV's driver-side window, her shoulder a foot or so away from his. She looked up too, because it was hard not to copy that. The sky was socked in with clouds that looked nearly black. "Supposed to be biblical," she added.

"Biblical?"

"Like Noah and the flood. And the ark."

"Oh, right. That kind of biblical."

"You're here by yourself this morning."

Jonathan sighed. Then, after a weirdly long time of not answering, he said, "Jeannie threw me out."

"Of what?"

"We were sleeping in one of those little bus-stop shelters."

"And she threw you out."

"She feels like she can't get clean. And so she said she wanted me to come back here and take that gardener job you offered me. She doesn't want to hold me back."

"Got it. That's why you two have been gone for a few days. Because she can't get clean."

Addie didn't phrase it as a question. And Jonathan didn't answer it. Then again, he didn't need to.

"Well, let me go make us some coffee," Addie said. "And then at seven o'clock we'll go home."

It was dawning on her at a raw-feeling level that Jeannie was out of the picture and she was getting her wish of having Jonathan in her shed and her place looking picture-perfect.

Then she felt guilty for feeling that way, because she wished the girl no harm.

"Home," he said, still gazing at the blackening clouds. "That's such a nice word. I haven't been able to use that word in as long as I can remember. And it doesn't even matter that I haven't seen the place yet. Just calling it home makes it feel like it is. That and the fact that I've been needing someplace to be home."

———

They drove together down an avenue lined with palm trees, the wind howling. The tarmac in front of Addie's wheels was littered with downed fronds. They made a thumping sound—and feeling—as she drove over them.

A new one came down, clattering against her windshield and making them both jump. Then it skittered away past her driver-side window.

"Wind's really picking up," he said.

"I'll say."

"Bad time to be living outdoors."

"You're worried about Jeannie."

"I'm worried about everybody I know who lives on the street. But yeah."

"Well, I only know two people who live on the street. You and Jeannie. And I'm worried about her too."

"Really?"

His voice sounded vulnerable and laced with wonder, both at the same time. She glanced over to try to match that tone to a facial expression. He looked as though he didn't dare believe her.

"Yeah. Really. I took that girl to her first meeting. She's suffering, like I was for so many years. So, yeah. I'm going to wonder how she's doing after that."

"That's really nice," Jonathan said, his voice softer. "I really like that about you. I'm not saying it's good that you suffered. But you understand. Nobody else understands Jeannie."

I almost wish I didn't, Addie thought. But she didn't say so out loud.

"She knows where to find me if she wants to make a change," she said.

———

They stood together nearly shoulder to shoulder—the wind blowing their hair around and making them squint—and stared into the shed. It was about fifteen feet long and ten feet wide, built to look like a barn. In fact it was painted in a classic barn red—now slightly faded—with white trim and gray roof shingles. It had a window on each side and a concrete floor. At the moment it was stuffed with tools and equipment. Big items such as a power mower, leaf bagger, and push tiller, along with rakes, shovels, hedge trimmers, and dozens of other assorted gardening tools leaning against the walls in a line.

"Wow," Jonathan said.

He spoke up a bit to be heard over the wind.

"I know. It's going to be a lot of work."

"It wasn't that kind of 'wow.'"

For the few seconds before he continued, Addie was curious about what kind of "wow" it had been. But she didn't have time to ask.

"I was thinking how nice this is going to be," he said.

"Really?"

"Absolutely. It has windows. I didn't think it would have windows. I can look out onto the garden. And up at the stars at night, when the storm passes and we can see the stars again. And it looks like it's built nice and tight. Like it'll be warm and dry."

"It has a light," she said, reaching in and pulling its string. "And there's an outlet in the corner. I put that in a few years ago to recharge the leaf blower and such, now that all that stuff is battery-powered instead of gasoline. You need to get all this out of here and into the garage. And I need to go get you a rug and a space heater. And I have an air mattress. We'll blow it up and I'll bring out sheets and blankets. I have a chair for the corner, and a little chest of drawers so you can put your clothes somewhere. I don't see that you'll have room for much more. Oh, and I have thoughts on the bathroom situation, which I'll share when we're done here."

"Wow," he said again. "This is going to be so nice."

He was looking up for some reason. Maybe at the bare electric bulb. Maybe at the ceiling, which was some kind of knotty wood. He had a look on his face that Addie initially couldn't find a word to describe. Then she settled on "wonder." And it reminded her of something. A moment, a stray memory, that started as an unidentified tickle and then roared into sharp focus. It was Spencer, at seven or eight years old, at the circus. Looking up at the trapeze artists and the high-wire act with that same look in his eyes.

Addie had never in her wildest dreams expected anyone to look at her gardening shed with the wide-eyed wonder of a kid at the circus. It was just one of those things she could never have imagined until the moment it arrived.

———

She gave him about three hours before checking in to see how he was doing, and to bring him one of the straight-backed dining room chairs. Still the rain threatened, but had not let go.

She was more than surprised to see his progress.

He had moved everything she'd once stored in the shed to the garage and scrubbed the floor and the insides of the walls. He had washed the windows inside and out, set up and inflated the air mattress and made it up into a nice bed with the sheets and blankets she had given him.

"Wow," she said. "You got a lot done. Here, I brought you a chair."

"Thanks," he said. He was sitting on the low bed, his knees drawn up to his chest, staring out one of the high windows. "When's it supposed to rain like we were Noah in the Bible?"

"Later this afternoon," she said.

She set the chair in the corner and sat down on it.

On the concrete floor next to his bed was a photo of a woman. It was surrounded by what looked like a sterling-silver frame. The woman was about forty, with long brown hair and a slightly nervous-looking smile.

She said nothing about it for the time being.

"I guess you'll be dry in here at least," she said. "I know it's not much."

"Are you kidding? It's everything."

"Oh, it's not everything."

"It's safe," he said. "And that's everything."

She looked back at the photo again. It was hard not to stare. He looked over and noticed her looking.

"Your mother?" she asked.

"Yeah."

"Pretty woman. That frame looks like sterling silver."

"It is."

"Nice that you managed to hang on to it all this time."

It struck her as she said it that she really had no idea how long or short a time he had been out on the street. And she didn't ask, because it felt less important than the other questions that lay in front of her.

"Why do you think I grabbed my backpack and left my jacket?" he asked. "You know. That first night. When I met you."

"You obviously love her very much."

"And she loves me," he said, staring out the window again. His face was blank of emotion, but maybe purposely so. Anyway, that was how it seemed to Addie.

"Then what happened? It's none of my business, so you can just not answer. But I couldn't not ask."

"She kind of . . ." He faded away. Sighed. Paused for a strange length of time, looking almost dreamy, but in a dark, shadowed sort of way. "She has this thing about relationships. Men. When she falls in love with one, it's almost like an addiction. She'll do anything to keep him. Anything."

"I've known people like that," Addie said.

"My father left her. And she met this new guy. And he didn't want me around."

"So she put you out on the street?"

Her voice came out squeaky, like a badly played violin. She had tried to keep her judgment out of the question, but she knew she'd failed miserably.

"No," he said. "She sent me to live with my dad. But he's a mean drunk."

"Got it," she said.

They sat without talking for a time.

Then she said, "I swear I don't know how you do it."

"Do what?"

"You always seem so . . . hopeful. So grateful for the tiniest little things. I would think you'd be traumatized."

"Who says I'm not?"

"You do a good job of hiding it."

"It's not hiding it exactly. That's not really what it's about. It's like you have two things going on at the same time in life. Always. The really good stuff and the really bad stuff. And you can't do anything about the really bad stuff. The only thing you can do is just decide what you're going to pay attention to. What you're going to spend the most time looking at. Thinking about. You know?"

Addie let that run around in her brain for a full minute or two.

Then she said, "I know adults three times your age who can't do what you just said."

"Sometimes it's like that," he said, still staring out the window at nothing. There was nothing to see from that angle but dark and threatening clouds. Maybe the branches of a few trees swaying wildly in the gale. "Sometimes you learn a lot early in life, because you have to."

Addie felt herself overwhelmed with a wave of empathy for him. She didn't like the feeling, so she shunted it aside.

"I need to go to bed soon," she said. "Come with me for a second so I can show you a couple of things about the back of the house."

He rose and followed her through the swirling overgrown jungle of garden to the back door.

"This is the mudroom," she said, opening the door.

"That's a weird name for a room. Why do you call it that?"

"It wasn't my idea. That's just what you call a room off the back of the house like this."

She stepped inside and he followed.

"Why do they call it that?" he asked, looking up and all around.

He had a tendency to look up, Addie had noticed. But she wasn't sure why.

"I'm not sure. I guess I always figured it was because you came in through the back in bad weather and left your wet raincoat and your muddy boots in here and went into the house clean."

"Oh. Okay. That should come in handy in the next few days."

"There's a washer and dryer in here. As you can see. And it's fine for you to use them."

"Really?"

"You sound surprised."

"Just seems like quite a luxury. Clean clothes on demand."

"We're going to try to raise your standards regarding what qualifies as a luxury," she said. "Laundry soap and dryer sheets and such are on that high shelf." She pointed with her chin. "Help yourself. And there's a bathroom right off the mudroom there that nobody ever uses. Right through that door."

Jonathan walked to the bathroom door, opened it, and looked around inside. Yes, including up.

"There's a shower *and* a tub."

"There is."

"And I can use all that?"

"Anytime you want. This door into the kitchen locks with a dead bolt. I thought I'd leave that locked and leave the back door open so you can do laundry or use the bathroom anytime. I don't mean I'm locking my house *against you*. I'm not afraid of you. I just mean I can't leave my house unlocked all the time. You know. But there's nothing to steal in the mudroom. Now I'm going to make us each a sandwich. And then I need to get a good day's sleep."

Four

Jonathan

Chapter Eight

Weeding in the Rain

After Addie left, Jonathan stretched out on the air mattress, not intending to sleep. In fact, he was sure he wouldn't. His brain was buzzing with excitement, and the purpose of lying down at all had been only to take a moment to feel grateful and good because of the unimaginable luxury of resting on something soft.

He laced his fingers behind his head and stared at the knotty wood grain of the ceiling and tried to remember when he had last been physically comfortable. Since leaving his father's house, all he could remember was the back seat of Addie's SUV.

Next thing he knew he burst awake, sitting bolt upright, unable to breathe for a second or two. He had apparently been deeply asleep, though he had no idea for how long, and he blasted into consciousness thinking he was still at the warehouse. Thinking Skate could be there without his knowing it.

Thinking, *How could you fall asleep? What a rookie mistake, to fall asleep.*

Thinking, *What if it's already too late?*

Then he looked around, and the dream state faded, and he was not at the warehouse. But for another couple of seconds he was unclear on where he was.

When it came back to him that these were his new accommodations at Addie's house, he breathed deeply for a long time. It struck him that he must have been a lot more tired than he'd realized.

As he looked around the room, the picture of his mother caught his eye.

His reaction was to wonder why he had even taken it out of his backpack and displayed it there. Had he wanted Addie to know that someone had cared about him sometime? He hadn't questioned the move much at the time, so he knew only that it bothered him to look at it now.

He leaned over and turned it face down in its sterling-silver frame.

Then he rose, and stretched, and stepped outside.

The sky was just as black as it had been before he'd gone inside, but the rain still had not let go.

The nature of the coming storm—its biblical proportions—gave an excess heft and gravity to the act of waiting for it. It was such a significant threat, and seemed almost to be flexing its muscles and purposely holding back, just to scare the people on the ground below.

Just because it was bigger and stronger, and it was in control. And it knew it.

Just because it could.

He looked around at the overgrown weeds, the tangled climbing vines, the hedges tall enough to argue with the smaller fruit trees. He wished he could start on it right now. Well, he could start now. If he wanted to. But he would never finish any significant part of the job before the storm let go.

A movement caught his eye, and he looked through the kitchen window to see Addie puttering around in there. He had figured she would be asleep by now. But maybe his little accidental nap had been only a few minutes long.

For a moment he was seized with an idea. He would call his mother and tell her he was okay. Partly for her sake, but there was a selfish aspect to it as well. He wanted her to know that there was someone in the world who wanted him around, and she hadn't even given birth to him.

Of course he'd need Addie's permission to make a long-distance call on her phone. He'd need some kind of plan to pay her back for it, though he had no idea what kind of plan that might be.

He walked through the back door into the mudroom, then rapped lightly on the locked kitchen door.

As soon as he did, he changed his mind about calling his mother. And not because of the money. Or at least not entirely because of it.

It felt too much like letting her off the hook. And he was angry, and not ready to do that for her. It would be like saying, *You can stop worrying now. I have it all worked out.* He had no idea how long he'd be invited to stay with Addie, and besides, the least his mother could do was worry. It was a very small price to ask her to pay for what she had done.

The door opened, and Addie stood in the doorway looking reasonably happy to see him. It felt like the best thing that had happened to him in as long as he could remember.

"You need something?" she asked him.

"I just wanted to tell you something. But if now's not a good time, that's okay."

He was hoping she would invite him in. Instead she just leaned her shoulder against the doorjamb.

"Now's okay, if it's not hours long."

"I said something to you that wasn't entirely true."

"Oh?" she said.

It seemed to pull her back into herself a step or two, and ruined his best moment, and he wished he had never started with this. But he *had* started it, and now he couldn't just leave it where it lay. She would imagine it to be worse than it was.

"Before, when you were in the shed with me, we were talking about my mother. And I said I loved her very much."

"Well, not exactly you didn't," Addie said. "I said you obviously loved her very much, and you didn't say otherwise."

"Oh," he said. "Right."

"What's the truth, then?"

"I do love her. But I also hate her."

"I think a lot of people feel that way about one or both of their parents," she said.

"Really?"

Jonathan thought that was a good answer, because it didn't make him feel like a freak or a bad person.

"Oh yeah," she said.

"Do you love and hate your parents?"

Then, the minute he asked the question, he wanted to lasso it and pull it back inside again. Who was he to ask her anything personal? What right did he have to intrude?

But she answered as if his misstep was nothing at all to her.

"They're both dead now," she said. "I loved and hated my mother, because she didn't do anything to save us from him. She didn't leave him, or stand up for my brother. Or for herself. I didn't love and hate my father. I just hated him. I guess a psychiatrist would take exception to that statement. They say hate is something like the flip side of love, and that one doesn't exist without the other. But I'm not a psychiatrist, and I'll just say if there's part of me that ever loved him, I've never met it and I don't know where it lives. And I'm fine leaving it that way."

They stood awkwardly in silence for a moment or two.

Then she added, "I feel like there's more you wanted to tell me about your mom."

"Oh," he said. "Yeah. I guess so. I kind of made it sound like when she sent me to live with my father she couldn't possibly have known I would end up on the street. But she did know. Not then, I mean, but later. She knew where I was headed. And I'm not sure why I lied about that. It's like I was covering up for her, but I don't know why I would do that."

"Human nature," Addie said.

Another good answer.

He wanted to tell her it was a good thing to say, but he wanted to rush forward more. To get the truth out on the table at long last. The truth of this thing he'd been hiding.

"She knew what my dad was like because she lived with him. But there was more to it than that. When I left my dad's house I had a phone. So I called her. Five times I called her, but she never picked up. Maybe she wasn't there. I go back and forth on that, but one way or another it's bad, because I left five messages and she never called me back. The first time I said I'd be sleeping on the street if she wouldn't let me come home again. That I'd be literally homeless. And then the second time I said I'd slept outside for the first time in my life. And then I told her I was out of money and didn't know how I'd eat next, and it just kept getting worse from there. Then I just waited for a few weeks, thinking she'd get to feeling guilty and call me back. But she never did. By then it had been a long time since anybody had paid my cellular bill, and I sure didn't have enough money to pay it, and the phone lost service. And finally I just took it to a pawnshop because I was hungry. How can you not hate somebody for doing that to you?"

"I can't imagine," Addie said.

"I'm not even sure why I put that picture of her out where I can see it, because it just kind of makes me feel sick inside to look at it. But anyway. I'm probably keeping you up. I shouldn't be bending your ear like this."

"Actually, it's good. You're making me feel like a better mother. Granted, my son hasn't spoken to me in years, but I never did anything *that* bad to him. I'm really sorry you had to go through that."

Jonathan shifted from foot to foot, wanting to move the conversation in a different direction, away from his own mother.

"Why doesn't he talk to you?"

"Honestly? I have no idea."

"Was it the drinking?"

"You'd think so. But he knows I've been sober for eight years, so if that was it, I would think he'd have given me another chance. Seems like there's something else, but he won't tell me what it is."

"I'm really sorry *you* have to go through *that*," he said.

She smiled sadly, and then he felt doubly bad, because not only was he talking to her when she needed to sleep, but he was making her unhappy.

"I was wrong to ask you about that," he said.

"It doesn't really matter."

"People don't like to talk about personal things like that."

"I'm program people. It's what we do."

"I should let you sleep."

"I don't mind your talking to me," she said.

"I probably shouldn't have said all that, though."

He turned and hurried through the mudroom, feeling deeply ashamed because he had bared so much of his feelings. And, accidentally, so much of hers.

Before he made it to the back door he heard her say, "You hungry?"

"No, I'm good," he said, and rushed outside.

He let himself back into his little shed, and opened the back of the silver picture frame, and took the picture of his mother out. He took it out of its frame because he intended to tear it into tiny confetti-like shreds. But he sat on the edge of his air mattress for what must have been a good ten or fifteen minutes, and he just could not bring himself to do it.

She was his mother.

He slid the picture into the bottom drawer of the nightstand Addie had given him, and stashed the frame into his backpack in the corner.

Meanwhile he was thinking, *See, this is the problem with your mother. She never stops being your mother, no matter what she does to you. It's just a thread that doesn't break, even if you really, really want it to.*

He stepped outside again, preparing to lose himself in gardening.

Not thirty seconds after he did, the rain let go.

There wasn't even so much as a drop of warning. It let go like the bottom breaking out of a bucket the size of the world. He didn't try to go back inside to stay dry, because he was already soaked before he could even process the thought.

Instead he chose to simply accept being soaked.

After all, when he got tired of being wet and cold, he could take a hot bath or a shower and get into dry clothes. It was a thought so welcome that it almost made him cry. Or, anyway, something did. But the hot bath was definitely a big part of the feeling, because his bottomless gratitude over that small comfort underscored what a comfortless life he had been living for so long.

Sometimes it's best not to let something really get to you until it's safely over.

For several hours—maybe even as many as six or seven, though he didn't own a watch—he pulled weeds out of his future vegetable garden in the driving rain.

At times the rain lashed so hard into his eyes that he had to squeeze them closed and work by feel. But the work got easier and easier, because the ground grew so saturated. In time it felt like pulling weeds out of water, rather than out of muddy dirt.

As he worked, he fantasized about offering Addie vegetables.

He would grow lettuce, and pick it right before dinner, and wash it in the kitchen sink, and whatever Addie was having he would make a salad to serve on the side of it. And it would be more special than any other salad had ever been, because it was all full of the vitamins found in food that had been living and growing fifteen minutes before you ate it.

And because Jonathan had literally created the food himself. Made it appear out of nothing.

And there would be tomato plants, and cucumbers, and rows of carrots. Maybe jicama. And he would ask her if he should dig up a few little red potatoes to roast in the oven and have on the side.

They would eat like royalty, and never, ever eat anything that was sold in a gas-station convenience store. They would eat only the things you get hungry for after all that time on the street with no money. Fresh things, that nature wanted you to eat.

And she would never, ever be sorry she had invited him into her life. He would see to that.

Five

Addie

Chapter Nine

Be Careful What You Celebrate

Addie woke at about six in the afternoon to an absolute thunder of rain. Not actual thunder. More like a thunderous downpour. It seemed to be hitting the roof in sheets. There was a downspout just outside Addie's window, and rainwater was clearly flowing much faster than the spout could possibly accommodate. She could hear the splatter of the excess water tumbling off the rain gutters and splashing onto the concrete below.

She rose and walked to the second-floor window, which looked out over the back garden.

Jonathan was weeding in the downpour.

He was on his knees on the concrete next to her former vegetable garden, pulling up weeds from the wet soil by their roots. Stacking them high by his side. He wore no hat or jacket. He was utterly soaked, and seeming not to mind it. Or, actually, even to notice.

She pulled on her old corduroy robe and walked downstairs and to the back door. She opened it and watched him for a few seconds.

"Jonathan," she called. But the rain was so loud it drowned out her voice. "Jonathan," she called again, louder this time.

He turned and saw her standing there in the open doorway, and his face lit up in a smile. He jumped to his feet and ran to where she stood, stepping under the protection of the awning over the back stoop, his hair and clothing dripping.

"You sleep okay?" he asked her.

"What there was of it, yeah. Why are you out in the pouring rain?"

"I'm weeding the future vegetable garden."

"Why are you weeding the vegetable garden in the pouring rain?"

"Because I can."

She offered him a twisted and somewhat skeptical expression, so he said more.

"And because I wanted to get it planted while there's still some rainy season."

"I have running water, you know."

"But it's not free. Rain is free. And because I know when I'm done I can take a long, hot bath and get into clean clothes fresh out of the dryer. And I haven't been able to do that in just so long. I can't even remember how long."

"Okay, I guess. I have a green waste bin for all those weeds, you know."

"Yeah. I saw that. But I figured I'd put them in later. I didn't think it would be good to have the lid sitting open on a big bin in this kind of rain."

"Ah. Good thinking. I'm going to have something to eat and then go to my meeting. You want something to eat?"

"No thanks. I still have half that sandwich you brought me before. I'm not used to eating so much all at one time. Just think. When I get the vegetables planted, I can start offering *you* something to eat. I can say 'Hey Addie, want some tomatoes? Just picked them.'"

"If you're willing to grow vegetables, they should be for you."

"Oh, no," he said. "I would want to share them."

"Okay. Tell you what. You share your vegetables with me and I'll share my eggs and bread and tuna fish and such with you. And we'll both eat well."

He didn't answer. Just grinned and stuck out his right hand. It took her a minute to realize he was inviting her to shake it.

She did.

It was soaking wet, but clean from having been rinsed in the rain. It felt slight and cold but generally reassuring.

"Now go to your meeting," he said. "I'll be fine."

———

Addie worked on her inventory for the first two or three hours of her shift. She produced six or seven pages, but hadn't managed to move on from her father, and her father's treatment of her brother. She also hadn't managed to bring it clearly back to herself and her own character defects.

Addie was feeling increasingly sleepy. The sound of sheets of rain had become a kind of white noise, like meditation music, and it wasn't helping at all.

I don't really even like that term, though, she thought. *Character defects. Because little kids only barely past toddler age can't rightly be accused of being defective. They are what they are. A kind of blank slate. And if what they see and experience warps them into a bad state, is that any defect on their part? Or are they just a product of what they survived?*

She remembered, quite suddenly, something Joan had said. So suddenly that it felt as if Joan had appeared and said it again, straight into her ear. Addie had been newly sober when she'd heard it. She hadn't thought about these words for a long time.

"Sometimes I like to call them character *defenses,*" Joan said in the silence of Addie's brain.

And then, with that same suddenness, Addie realized the part of her brother Bill's situation that was about her. The failing she needed to admit in her fifth step with Wendy, when she was done with the inventory and ready to read it out.

"I didn't do anything." She spoke those four words out loud as she wrote them down on the page. "I didn't help Bill. It played out right in front of me, and I watched, and when it got really bad I hid my head or covered my eyes, but I could still hear the blows landing, and the grunts of pain coming from my brother, who was trying so hard not to admit he was in pain. I was there but I didn't try to stop it."

She looked up, toward the door, and sucked in her breath in a little gasp of surprise. A wet figure was standing just outside, staring at her through the glass insets of the office door.

It took a couple of seconds to realize it was probably Jeannie.

The fact that the girl was soaking wet was causing her hood to droop down and cover her blue hair, and a lot of her face. Addie moved closer to be sure.

It was Jeannie. And her eyes looked haunting and deep.

Addie opened the door.

For a minute they just stood there, considering each other. Blasts of wind shot rain through the door, where it whipped into Addie's face. She winced, but she didn't move. She waited for the girl to make a move.

"I don't want to keep living like this," Jeannie said.

"Glad to hear it."

"It's not right. People shouldn't have to be outside like this with no place to go. It's not the right way for a human person to live."

"I thought you were living in a bus shelter."

"The rain blew right in. I came back here to sleep in the warehouse, but Skate is there. I can't take this anymore. It was never supposed to be like this. I never thought I could sink down this low."

"Maybe you're ready for a change," Addie said, still taking gusts of rain in the face.

"I'm not using and I don't have anything on me. I swear."

"Then you can come in."

She stepped into the office, and Addie closed the door behind her. Addie wiped her face on her sleeve and watched a pool of rainwater form and grow around the girl's feet.

"Thank you," Jeannie said. "I want to go live where Jonathan is. That . . . I don't know . . . shack or whatever it is in your yard. Please don't say no. Please. I'll go to meetings and I'll never, ever bring anything onto your property. Not in my pockets and not in my blood. I promise you. If I think I can't stay clean, I'll just leave. I'll disappear, and that's how you'll know. But I'll never be anything but clean at your house."

"It's up to Jonathan, you know. It's his place."

"He'll let me stay there."

"I suppose he will," Addie said, walking behind the counter again. "By the by, if the goal is to get clean, then I'm not sure it's such a good idea to have a contingency plan for when you fail."

"Yeah, I guess," Jeannie said, and settled in a puddle of her own wetness in the corner. "You didn't talk to him."

"Who, Skate?"

"Who else?"

"No, I didn't. I didn't think I knew anybody who had to try to live over there."

"Lots of people have to try to live over there. Just because you haven't met them doesn't mean they deserve Skate."

"That's true, I suppose. But there are a lot of wrong things happening all over, and sometimes you have to decide which ones have something to do with you and which ones don't. Like when you take somebody to court. Sue them for something. The judge has to decide if you even have standing to bring the case."

"He tried it on *Jonathan*," Jeannie said.

It made Addie feel seen. Uncomfortably so. Jeannie knew exactly where to place the knife to hurt her. Jeannie knew that Addie cared for Jonathan, and that it angered her to think of someone hurting him. And Jeannie knew not to use herself as the example. Skate had "tried it" on her too. But she knew that would not draw quite the same momma-bear reaction from Addie.

"Maybe I'll go over when I'm off shift in the morning."

"You're scared of him," Jeannie said.

She was egging Addie on to act. Addie could feel it, and it made her mad.

"A couple of things about that," Addie said, her voice formal and hard. Like a door she had just closed to make sure the girl knew to stay out. "First of all, what idiot wouldn't be nervous confronting a huge, violent person? You'd have to be insane not to feel some sort of trepidation about that." Addie noticed she was dancing around words like "fear" and "scared," but she didn't correct it. "But that's not why I would wait till morning. I'm on my shift. I'm at work. I can't just walk over there and confront somebody with a gun like it's part of my professional duties. I need to work my shift, and then in the morning we'll see what's what."

———

In the morning the girl was snoring lightly in the corner, her wet head on her balled-up wet jacket. Addie was staring at the big old-fashioned clock over the door, its second hand moving one audible click at a time.

When it finally, finally clicked onto seven o'clock, Addie pulled on her hooded rain jacket and stepped out into the miserable weather. It was vaguely warm, and the wind had died completely. And still the rain came down in sheets, as if a few acre-feet of rainwater were being dropped onto the scene all at once. It hit Addie's eyes and made her wince.

As she crossed the dirt lot to the old abandoned warehouse, she asked herself if she was scared. After all, just a few hours earlier she had made it clear that any fool would be scared in that situation. But the honest answer seemed to be that she didn't know. It felt as though the whole middle of her body, where her organs lived and functioned, was filled with something blank and heavy and inert, like concrete.

It was barely light, but she could see. It should have been much lighter at seven, but it didn't help when the rays of sun couldn't find their way through the black, rain-heavy clouds.

She saw a small figure duck out of the warehouse and into the downpour, which was her first signal as to how to get inside.

She walked to that open doorway and unholstered her gun, holding it tightly in her right hand, which she slid into the slash pocket of her raincoat. Then she stepped inside.

She stood a minute, allowing her eyes to adjust to the light. Or lack of light.

There were maybe forty people on the ground floor of that three-story building. Some were sleeping. Some sat up, staring at her. The walls were bare and dirty, the floor littered with leftover shelving and discarded pieces of equipment. Most of the filthy windows were broken. A forklift sat in the corner, having long ago fallen into disrepair, apparently already too old and useless to be taken when the place was cleared out all those years ago. Cobwebs hung limply from the ceiling.

"I'm looking for Skate," she said in a booming voice. It was the voice she had learned on the force.

"Nobody's ever looking for Skate," a young man's voice said.

Addie could not see who had said it.

"You a cop?" an older, deeper voice called out.

"No," Addie said.

"You have to tell us if you are."

"I'm not," Addie said, shouting to be heard across the entire floor. And maybe even the floors above. "I just want to talk to this Skate."

Then he was there, on the stairs, moving downward. Addie knew it was him, even though she had never seen him at close range, because he was the one coming closer. And because very few people were that big.

He stopped at the bottom of the steps and looked at her, and she at him.

In her peripheral vision, Addie was weirdly aware of the devastation all around her. The shabbiness and filth of the place, but also the human devastation. The smell of urine and unwashed bodies.

The weird part of that sudden awareness was the sense that her attention should have been completely focused on the enormous boy in front of her. But the mind can play tricks at a moment like that.

He had a round, undefined face. Soft, almost. His curly hair fell over his eyes. He was wearing a denim jacket at least two sizes too small for his giant frame. He stared at her the way a bird of prey watches a mouse after it pauses in the open as it crosses a field.

He did not look like evil incarnate. Then again, Addie hadn't expected him to. She had encountered many people in her life who did terrible, evil things on a regular basis, and not a one of them had had horns and a tail. They all just looked like people. Because they all were.

"You want to talk to me *why*?" he said.

His voice was oddly childlike. A bit too high and soft for his imposing frame.

"I want you to leave and never come back to this place," she said.

"I can go wherever I want."

Addie pulled her right hand, and the pistol it held, out of her pocket. Almost without thinking she assumed a shooting stance, the gun gripped in both hands.

She heard a small handful of people suck in their breath.

"True," she said. "But I can also shoot you if you come back here. Everybody has a similar case of free will like that."

They both held still for a few seconds. Everyone did. Even the dank air in the place seemed to hold still.

"You're not going to shoot me," Skate said, and began moving in her direction. "You're just a harmless old lady, and you can hold a gun and point it, but you don't have the nerve. And even if you did pull the trigger you'd probably miss."

He was still moving slowly in her direction. He stepped under a long-defunct light bulb, still screwed into its useless fixture in the ceiling. Addie raised the pistol and shot the bulb, which shattered, raining glass onto Skate's head.

He touched his scalp, and his fingers came away bloody.

"That's just a *thing*, though," he said, his voice eerily calm. "It takes guts to shoot a person. I'm a person."

And he began to approach her again.

"*Are* you now?" she asked, to buy time.

But she knew the answer. He was. It would be a relief to Addie to think people who committed terrible crimes and abuses were inhuman. But they were not, and she knew it. And that was the bad news, in her opinion.

"No more steps," she said.

He took another step.

She lowered her hands and the gun, and put a bullet through the top of his bare right foot.

It was just that fast. A thing that happened almost before Addie knew it was about to. And it would never unhappen. She had been around the block enough times to know, immediately, that it never would.

He let out some variety of animal grunt and raised his right leg suddenly. The wild, unplanned movement caused him to fall over. He sat up and just froze a moment, looking quite shocked and bleeding onto the concrete floor. He raised the leg again, as if to reach for the injured foot. As if to touch it and comfort it. But he did not dare touch it.

He looked up at Addie and said, "You shot me."

"And I'll do it again if you ever come back here. At least now you've got one good foot. If I hear you're back I'll put a bullet through the other one, and then getting around will be a real challenge. But even with one bad foot, I figure this way your victims have a pretty good chance of outrunning you."

Addie turned and walked to the open warehouse door.

As she did, she heard the sound of applause. At first she thought it was some kind of auditory illusion. A hallucination. She *was* in a mild shock, making everything feel dreamlike. But in her peripheral vision, she could see people clapping. Sitting up, banging their hands together.

Don't do that, she thought. *Don't ever celebrate a thing like that. When you do, you're just letting him pull you down to his level.*

But she never said it out loud. Or anything else, for that matter.

She stepped out into the rain, which had turned to a light drizzle.

She walked back to the office, where she let herself in. Jeannie was still sleeping in the corner.

She walked to the girl, put a hand on her shoulder, and shook her awake.

"Come on," she said. "Shift's over. Let's go home."

"No coffee?"

"I'll make coffee when we get home. It's after seven. Let's just go."

But as she was waiting for Jeannie to shake herself awake, she glanced at the clock. It was only four minutes after seven. That whole chapter of drama in her morning had only taken four minutes.

How could so much change in four minutes? Addie could not make sense of that.

They walked to the door together and out into the humid morning. The rain had paused entirely.

"It finally stopped raining," Jeannie said, blinking into what light existed in the overcast dawn.

"For now," Addie said.

She unlocked her SUV and they climbed in. Addie started up the engine and sat a minute, giving it time to warm up. While she waited she stared at the old warehouse, but nothing moved there. No one came out.

The feelings she had successfully cast in concrete were waking up now. Shaking loose. It felt like a buzzing electrical connection in her chest and gut. Her brain felt fuzzy and disconnected. And none of it felt good.

She shifted into reverse and backed out of the parking space.

"So you're not going to talk to Skate," Jeannie said. Her voice was full of a disappointment that she clearly wanted Addie to hear.

"Actually, I already did," she said, pulling out into the partially flooded street.

She could see a bank of mud on the right that marked how high the water had been before receding slightly.

"Really?"

"I wouldn't make a thing like that up."

"You think he'll really leave?"

"I expect he might," Addie said.

Chapter Ten

Turn It Out, Turn It In

She stood in front of Jonathan's little shed, a pizza box in one hand, and knocked.

He came to the door quickly, rubbing sleep out of his eyes.

"Hey, it stopped raining," he said.

He was looking up as he said it, as he tended to do. He was wearing an oversize sweater over boxer shorts as pajamas, and his long hair was messy from its contact with the pillow.

"For now."

He looked down at her again. Right into her face.

"What's wrong?" he asked. "What happened?"

"Who says something happened?"

"You just look . . ." But he never finished the sentence. He never told her how she looked to him. "Hey. You brought pizza."

"Yeah. That. But that's just one surprise, and I brought you two."

She looked over her shoulder to make sure Jeannie was still back there. Then she stepped aside and let the girl step up.

"Jeannie!" he said. Practically shouted.

He stepped in to give her a hug, but she held up a hand to stop him.

"I'm still soaking wet," she said.

"Are you . . . ?"

"Yeah, I'm clean. For now, anyway. I want to be here with *you*. Can I be here with *you*?"

"It's up to Addie," he said. "It's her place."

"I told her it was up to you," Addie said. "If you want to share this little shed or not. And of course depending on her staying clean."

"Of course," Jonathan said. "Of course I'll share. Addie has an actual clothes dryer."

"I can give you something to wear," Addie said. "While your clothes are tumbling."

———

"You sure you're okay?" Jonathan asked.

Addie looked up to see if he was talking to her. He was.

They were outside in the yard, sitting in Addie's big Adirondack chairs, which they had covered with blankets because their wooden slats were wet and cold. Jeannie was wearing a big sweatshirt of Addie's that came down past her knees, her lower legs looking skinny and white and childlike in the damp morning. They had been eating their pizza in silence before Jonathan spoke up.

"Nothing a good day's sleep won't fix," Addie said.

It was a lie and she knew it.

"Jeannie told me you talked to Skate," he said. Cautiously, as if stepping out onto a high plank that might or might not hold his weight. "But she said you didn't really tell her anything about how it went. We thought maybe something happened. You know. Skate being Skate and all."

Addie said nothing.

"Did he hurt you?" Jonathan added.

Addie snorted.

"Other way around," she said.

"I'm not sure what that means."

Addie set her pizza down on its paper plate and looked him dead in the face. Caught his eyes and held them.

"Okay, fine. You really want to know? I'll tell you. I shot him in the foot."

Then she looked at the sky for a few seconds, watching heavy black clouds scud. She purposely did not watch his reaction to that news.

"Is that . . . ," he ventured after a time, "is that like an expression? Like when you say 'I shot myself in the foot' but you don't mean it literally?"

She looked down into his face again. It registered no judgment. It was just open and curious, and a little bit confused.

"No. It's not. I mean I literally put a bullet through that boy's foot."

"Which foot?" Jeannie asked, her mouth full of pizza.

"*Which foot?* You mean left one or right one?"

"Yeah."

"That's a weird thing to wonder. It was his right foot."

"Good," Jeannie said.

"Good that it was his right and not his left?"

"No, just in general. Good that you shot him."

"I'm not able to see it that way," Addie said. "But maybe that's because it was my finger squeezing the trigger and not yours. It's no small thing to shoot a person."

"He deserved it," Jeannie said.

"Maybe. Or maybe even probably. But I'm not in the habit of meting out justice all on my own. And I'm curious as to whether you know that people who abuse others were generally abused themselves. If he's running around molesting people, he was probably molested. If we'd seen him back then, this innocent little boy having these terrible things happen to him, we'd feel for him. But then he grows up all twisted and we just hate his guts and we don't feel for him in the slightest."

She glanced up at Jonathan as she wrapped up those thoughts. He was not eating. He was not speaking. He just sat there and took it all in.

It was Jeannie who spoke.

"Does everybody who gets abused grow up and abuse?"

"No, not everybody. Unless you count self-abuse. Seems like hurt people go one of two directions. They either turn the pain inside and take it out on themselves or they turn it outside and go after others."

"Well then, he deserves it for being one of the ones who goes after others."

"Except I don't know why different people have those two different reactions," Addie said. "And I don't know if it's anything they can control. Maybe it's something wired into them, or maybe the ones who can't keep it inside got hurt worse than we know."

"Well, I don't feel for him," Jeannie said. "I don't feel for anybody who hurts people, no matter why."

"Which in my opinion is one reason we're going so wrong in this world. It's like we all have empathy to one degree or another, but it only goes just as far as it goes and no further."

They fell into silence for a time.

Addie picked up her slice of pizza, which was thoroughly cold by then, and took another bite. But she was acting mostly out of habit. She had lost her appetite.

At least three or four minutes later Jonathan finally broke the silence.

"Did you . . . just . . . I'm trying to picture what happened. I can't imagine you just walking in there and shooting him."

"No, it wasn't like that. I said a few things, and he said a few things, and he said I wouldn't really shoot. And he started to move on me. Not fast, but like a challenge. You know? And then I fired a warning shot at a light bulb over his head, but he kept coming. So I said, 'Not another step.' But he took another step."

"It was self-defense, then," Jonathan said.

"You could look at it that way."

"What other way could you look at it?"

"You could say I shot my way out of a situation I could have just not walked into in the first place." Another long silence fell. Or maybe it wasn't that long. Maybe it just seemed long because it felt awkward and strange. "I had to think fast, and I thought a foot wound would be the best, because even after it heals, it'll slow him down. Pretty much everybody will be able to outrun him now."

"Not as good as killing him," Jeannie said, her arms wrapped around her drawn-up knees. "But good."

"I think it's brilliant," Jonathan said. "I think it was a really good solution."

Addie opened her mouth to say it, but he beat her to it. He said it for her.

"Then again, it wasn't my finger squeezing the trigger. Right? It was yours." He ate in silence for a moment. Then he said, "You did that for us? To protect us?"

"You and everybody else," she said. Then she pictured Wendy looking over her shoulder and clucking her tongue, because that wasn't the truth, the whole truth, and nothing but the truth. "Well. Yeah. You. Pretty much you."

———

Addie was just stepping away from the table at the end of the meeting when she turned toward the door to see Wendy standing right behind her. So close behind her, in fact, that Addie startled slightly and let out a quick breath that both she and Wendy could hear.

"Sneak up on people much?"

She moved toward the door and Wendy followed.

"What's going on with you?" Wendy asked, pulling level with Addie and giving her a squinty-eyed look.

"Why does something have to be going on with me?"

"You were called on to share and you didn't share."

"I *sort of* shared. I said my name and identified and said I just wanted to listen tonight."

"Exactly," Wendy said.

"People do that all the time."

"People do. You usually don't."

"Is that all you've got to go on?"

They stepped out into the dark night. The rain had not begun again, but it felt as though it planned to let go any second. Addie could hear distant thunder.

They stopped and stood facing each other, and Wendy looked into Addie's face as much as was possible in all that darkness. A wash of cigarette smoke near the door of the meeting room hung around them, feeling dense and uncomfortable. Addie had liked the smell of it for a few years after quitting, but she didn't like it now.

"Call it sponsor's intuition," Wendy said.

Addie sighed deeply.

"Okay," she said. "Here's the thing. I said I'd tell you the truth, the whole truth, and nothing but the truth. But we never discussed the time frame on that. Does it always have to be immediately, every time? Or might there be other times when I get to take a beat and let things settle first?"

"Take all the time you need," Wendy said. Her voice sounded a bit tight with suspicion. Or maybe Addie was reading that in. "You have my number."

Then she walked away without looking back.

———

Addie had the night off, her first of two, and it would have been a luxury to sleep in the dark, with the neighbors inside their homes and things fairly quiet. But she could not sleep. She had successfully turned her days and nights around, but that was not the only problem—not even the biggest one—and Addie knew it.

After half an hour of trying she sat up and turned on the light.

It was only ten thirty.

She pulled her phone off the bedside table and called Wendy, who picked up on the fourth ring.

"Too late to call?" Addie asked in place of hello.

"Pretty much. Are you at work?"

"No, I'm home."

"Why aren't you at work?"

"I don't work seven days a week, you know. Also my shift starts at eleven."

"Oh. Right."

"If it's too late I'll talk to you tomorrow."

"Unless it's really important," Wendy said, which felt surprising. It was a more open, nonbristly sense of reaching out to help than Addie was used to.

"Define 'really important.'"

"Let's assume you didn't kill anybody."

"No," Addie said. "I didn't kill anybody. But I did shoot him."

A long silence on the line.

"If that's a joke," Wendy said, "tell me now."

"I wish it was a joke, but I got into a bit of an altercation with that bully who tried to sexually assault both those young kids I've been looking after. And it ended up with him taking a bullet through the foot. Though I suppose that's not the best phrasing for a person planning on taking responsibility, is it? Makes it sound like it was all his doing. I ended up shooting him in the foot, I should have said. And it's not sitting well with me."

Another long silence, followed by Wendy clearing her throat.

"Here's a tip, hon," she said. "If you ever call me and say you put a bullet through any part of anybody and it *is* sitting well with you, I'm going to tell you to find a new sponsor. I know we always said it was just the one rule, but come on. I can't anticipate everything that might come up. I guess I sort of figured 'Don't shoot anybody' could go unsaid."

"Understood."

"You'd best get over here," Wendy said. "Drive carefully. We have another storm about to hit us over the head, and it's supposed to be a doozy."

———

"You need to do the right thing," Wendy said.

"Yeah. Duh. I could have gotten that far on my own, Wendy. The problem is . . . I'm not sure which of the things I can imagine doing might be right."

They were sitting on an overstuffed and faded fabric sofa in Wendy's living room. Wendy was vaping with one hand and petting a tiny, scruffy blond dog with the other. He looked like a cross between a teacup poodle and some kind of wirehaired terrier. He alternated between half closing his eyes in bliss and staring defensively at Addie.

Wendy's house was cluttered and as overstuffed as the sofa. She was into framed pictures covering every inch of every wall, and ceramic knickknacks, and too much furniture for any given space.

A second dog, a massive beast who appeared to be at least half Saint Bernard, sat in front of Addie with his chin on her knee, staring up into her face. She was doing her best to ignore him, but her best was not good.

Meanwhile the rain hammered relentlessly on the roof and the windows.

"You used to be in law enforcement," Wendy said. "That should help."

"It's not helping so far."

"Know anybody who still is?"

"I suppose I could go back to my old precinct. Some will have transferred out or retired, but somebody I know will still be there."

"Do *that*," Wendy said.

She vaped in silence for a minute or two while Addie watched the huge dog stare at her.

"What does he want from me, this dog?" Addie asked after an awkward pause.

"He just wants you to give him a pat on the head."

Addie reached out cautiously and gave the huge beast a couple of perfunctory pats. He wagged his tail obsessively and wiggled his body even closer to her.

"*Now* what does he want?"

"Now that he knows you're willing to pat him on the head he wants you to do it some more. Not much of an animal person, are you?"

"I like cats. To a point. But getting back to the heart of my situation. You want me to go into my old precinct and tell them everything I just told you. And then what?"

"Then they tell you what price you need to pay for a thing like that, and you pay it. I can't imagine you serving jail time for it. Maybe probation or some sort of community service. Or maybe nothing. From what you just described, there was a good bit of self-defense involved."

"Except if I'd just stayed in my office until it was time to drive home, then no self-defense would have been needed."

"Darlin'," Wendy said on a long vapor exhale, "nobody wishes you'd stayed in your office more than me."

"One person might," Addie said. "Actually . . . make that two."

"You know what you need to do," Wendy said. "You just came over here on the very off chance I might say you didn't need to bother with it. But you knew you didn't have a snowball's chance in hell of me letting you off the hook, right?"

"It was worth a try," Addie said.

For a moment she only watched the rain stream down Wendy's big picture windows, its miniature rivers illuminated by the streetlight on the corner. It made her worry for the drive home.

Wendy spoke up suddenly.

"The guy is big, right? The one you shot?"

"How'd you know that?"

"And those kids you wanted to protect are not."

"Where are you getting all this?"

"You told me the first night we ever talked. In a roundabout way. You said the one thing you really, really hate is people who prey on somebody who's smaller and can't defend themselves because they know they can get away with it. You said that just chaps your hide. It's all coming together for me now."

———

As she walked Addie to the door, Wendy said, "You never had pets growing up?"

"Not as I recall."

"Wouldn't that be a thing you'd recall?"

"You would think so. Why are you even asking?"

"I don't know. You don't strike me as someone who wouldn't like animals."

"Seems like a strange thing to say when you just saw it with your own eyes. What makes you think otherwise?"

"People like you usually do."

Wendy opened the door, and the sound of the rain dominated everything. They stepped out onto the covered porch together so the dogs would not get out.

"Define 'People like me,'" Addie said.

"You know."

"I *don't* know. Or I wouldn't bother asking."

"You know. People who are sensitive like you are."

Addie only stood listening to the rain and blinking for a moment or two.

"You think I'm sensitive?"

"Yeah. Don't you?"

"I think I'm just about the least sensitive person I know."

"Then maybe you don't know yourself as well as you think you do."

Addie shook her head. Not so much as a message of "no" but more as though she could make the whole conversation fly out and leave her alone.

They stood awkwardly for a moment, as if they'd forgotten something absolutely necessary to ending the meeting. But Addie had no idea what that might be. It just felt like something missing.

Then Wendy said, "You're not a hugger, are you?"

"That's putting it mildly," Addie said.

"I watch you in meetings, and people come up to you afterward to talk. And you always take a step back from them at the end. You always make it clear you don't want them coming any closer."

"That's because I don't want them coming any closer."

"You have to have people in your life, though."

"I do have people in my life. Too many, if you ask me. But I don't have a choice about that. I do have a choice about not letting them grab me."

"I hope you rethink that decision at some point," Wendy said.

"I need to go home and get some sleep," Addie said.

And she did.

At least, she did the first of those two things.

Chapter Eleven

But What Could You Have Done?

"You look like hell," Wendy said.

They were standing outside the meeting the following night. Wendy vaped while Addie squinted and stared at the cloudy sky.

"Thanks a bunch."

"I'm just saying you look like you didn't sleep."

"Well, I didn't."

"That would explain it," Wendy said.

"I had too much on my mind, and I just tossed and turned, and then I got up and started looking for this picture. I remembered I had a picture somewhere of me with a dog. This little sheltie, and I was just hugging that dog for dear life, but I don't remember if it was our dog or maybe somebody else's who was just visiting."

"Odd thing not to remember," Wendy said on a billowing vapor exhale.

"I was really little. Three or four maybe. I knew I had this picture in one of my photo albums somewhere, but I didn't know where the album was. Took me a couple of hours, but I finally found it in the attic."

She pulled the small, dog-eared print out of her pocket and held it out for Wendy, who peered at it in the light spilling through the meeting-room door. Addie was wearing a dress in the photo, which she had always hated for as long as she could remember but which had been forced upon her regularly. She was on her knees on the carpet, the hem of her yellow dress touching the rug, her arms around the small dog's neck. Her face was not visible, being buried in the thick ruff of fur around the dog's collar, but Addie knew it was her.

"Any living relatives you could ask?"

"Yeah. I could ask Bill. My brother. We talk on the phone a couple times a month or so."

"Should be interesting," Wendy said.

"Not sure why you're so fascinated by the topic."

"Because," Wendy said, "in my experience you can divide non-animal people into two groups. Those who just naturally don't like them, and those who got hurt bad enough by losing one that they vowed never to like them again."

"I don't remember making a vow like that."

"I'm sure you don't. But that's the thing about writing an inventory, hon. It brings things up. Out of the woodwork, you know? That's the beauty of it. That's the inventory doing exactly what it's supposed to do. So, look. How long are we gonna dance around whether you made any progress on that legal situation?"

"I called," Addie said.

"And?"

"My old lieutenant is still there. Nice lady. Kind. Well, maybe 'kind' is the wrong word. She *is* kind, but kind of tough, too. But I guess I mean she's someone you feel like you can depend on. Anyway, she's on leave for a time. Her mom is on hospice, and she might not be back for at least a couple of weeks. Hard to know how long in a situation like that."

"Suit yourself," Wendy said.

It was a huge relief to Addie, something she could feel like a figurative sigh flowing out of her chest. She had worried that Wendy would think she had to do it immediately, with whomever was available.

"I'm going for coffee," Wendy said. "You coming?"

"Nah. I think I'm going to go home and call my brother and then work on that inventory some more."

"You'll get no argument from me," Wendy said.

———

When she got home, she texted Bill with the message "You around?"

It took a few minutes, but then she got a "Yup" in reply.

"Got time for a quick video call?"

Addie had never asked Bill to use any type of video-call app, so in the stillness that followed she pictured him literally scratching his head, frozen in confusion.

But then her phone rang—a different, more musical kind of ring than the one for voice calls—and it made her jump.

She touched an on-screen button to accept the call, and there was Bill.

Before anything was said, they just looked at each other for what felt like a long time. It had been almost four years since they had visited in person. He lived in Texas, and neither had any love for flying. And Bill was suddenly old.

He had only gotten four years older, of course. She knew that with her rational brain. Addie thought the shock of his appearance had to do with a long, thick white beard he'd grown. And his bushy, wild hair had gone snow-white in only four years—or so she thought for just a moment. Then she realized that made no sense, and he likely had been coloring it and then stopped. It made her feel as though she wanted to look more closely, really peer into the screen to find Bill in this unfamiliar older man.

But the part of the moment that really made an impression on Addie was the realization that it wasn't only Bill who had grown old. If he was older, so was she, and he was likely thinking the exact same thing about her.

"Is everything okay?" he asked.

As soon as he did, the sense of unfamiliarity evaporated. In the animation of speaking, he was Bill again.

"Yeah," she said. "Fine. Why?"

"You never ask to do a video call."

"I just wanted to show you something."

"Oh. Okay."

A little girl's face popped up between Bill and his phone, smiling. A girl of maybe six or seven.

"Who *is* that?" the girl asked in a screechy voice.

"That's your aunt Addie. Go play with MomMom, okay? Aunt Addie and I are going to have a talk."

The face disappeared, and Addie could hear the drumming of footsteps running away.

"Got the grandkids," she said.

"For the whole weekend, yeah. Might kill us."

"Don't tell me that was Kaitlin."

"It was, though."

"She's supposed to still be a baby!"

"Tell *her*, don't tell me."

Addie smiled a bit sadly and pulled the picture out of her pocket. But she didn't show it to him yet. She had one thing to take care of first.

"Look, Bill. I swear I'm not prying, and I'm not after any details or any confidences. But I just have to ask. You talk to Spencer lately?"

A pause fell that seemed cautious on his part, though she could not have explained how.

Then he said, "He calls now and then."

"Just wondering if he's okay. Nothing beyond that."

"He's okay. Relationship problems. But who doesn't have relationship problems?"

"*I* don't. I've found the magic cure: Don't *have* any."

He smiled, which was nice. It struck her that they didn't do a lot of smiling, either one of them.

She held the photo up in front of her phone, peeking around it to be sure he could see the whole thing.

"You know this dog?" she asked.

"Sure I know that dog. That's Sheena."

Addie lowered the picture to see that Bill's face had changed. He looked troubled now. He looked as though the outside of him had turned into the inside of her—always waiting for another shoe to drop. It made her feel sad to see that she had wiped his smile away.

"Whose dog was she?"

"Yours," he said.

That big word just sat a moment, sounding like something that would almost be best left unaddressed. But it was too late for that now.

"Odd that I wouldn't remember, if she was mine. Really mine? Not everybody's? Not the family dog but my dog?"

"Well, I guess in some ways the family dog. But the thing is they got her as a puppy right around the time you were born. You know. So you could grow up together. So more yours. I think maybe the reason you don't remember is because you were so young. We only had her till you were five."

"So much for growing up together. What happened to her when I was five?"

"Dad sold her."

"That sounds like Dad all right."

"It might have been traumatic for you, and that might be why you don't remember. You loved that dog. But she was terrified of Dad. I didn't see a special reason with my own eyes, but she might have had her reasons. Who wasn't terrified of Dad? But he really spooked her. Well, not permanently. Happy to say. The people who bought her just lived about two miles from us. I used to walk over there and visit her, and she bounced back really well at their house. But between the time she got so scared of him and the time he sold her, she was kind of a mess. Hiding under the sofa and peeing if he came near her. And then he announced he was disgusted by her because she was so timid and scared. That's why he sold her."

"Wait," Addie said. "I need a minute to take all this in."

What she really needed was a beat or two to process the absolute loathing that rose up through her chest and seemed to be trying to escape via her throat.

"I think we should dig that man up and kill him again," she said a minute later.

Bill barked out a rueful laugh but didn't answer.

"Then why didn't you take *me* over there? I would've liked to visit her. I mean, I know that sounds strange, since I don't even remember her. But it sounds like something a kid in that position would want."

While she spoke, Bill's expression deteriorated. His face appeared more pained, if such a thing were possible. He looked to Addie like an old abandoned building being brought down by a dynamite charge. Imploding on itself.

"I'm really sorry, Addie," he said, and for some reason his emotion cut like a knife in her gut. "Mom said it would only make things worse for you. I don't know if she was right or not, but I didn't want to hurt you. They told you Sheena went to live on a farm. And finding out they lied, and that she just didn't get to be your dog anymore . . . I don't know, Addie. Did I do the wrong thing? I'm sorry if I did the wrong thing."

Addie pulled in and released a few breaths before answering. She felt as though her chest were filled with something, blocking the way. Blocking air. Blocking words. She had to push harder on everything to get it free.

"I don't know, hon," she said when she could. "You tried. The whole thing sucked, but not because of you. But look. While we're on the subject of apologies, I've got one for you too."

"Oh?"

He seemed curious and surprised. As if he had never imagined that such a situation existed, or even could.

"I'm doing stuff out of order," she said. "Steps-wise."

"Steps?"

"Program steps. The Twelve Steps, you know? I'm writing an inventory about all this, and the amends are supposed to come a few steps down the line."

"I thought you already wrote an inventory."

"I did."

"I thought you only had to do that once."

"You and me both, brother. I mean, I knew that some people do them regularly, but I didn't see myself being one of them. But I got this new sponsor, and she's really got me hopping."

"I can't imagine why you'd need to apologize to *me*."

"Because I didn't do anything about it."

"About what?"

"You know."

Addie could hear the pitter-patter of grandchildren's feet on his end of the call, which was why she chose not to spell it out clearly.

She heard and saw him take a huge breath and then blow it out slowly.

"What do you suppose you could have done?"

"I don't know. Something. Anything."

"But there *wasn't* anything."

"At least if I'd screamed at him to stop you'd have known I was on your side."

"I knew you were on my side."

And with that, Addie found herself desperate to get off the phone. As desperate as she might be if submerged in water, waiting to gasp a breath.

"I think there's somebody at my door," she said.

There wasn't, at the exact moment she said it. But not two seconds later she heard a knock. The coincidence was almost too much to take in.

"Go take care of that," he said. As though he needed to inhale as well. "We'll talk another time."

The window that had shown his face disappeared from the screen.

She walked to the front door and looked out the small window, but there was no one there. Then she heard the knock again, but this time she could tell it was coming from the back door.

She moved through the house, and when she reached the door to the mudroom she paused and called out, "Jonathan?"

"Yeah, it's me, Addie."

She opened the door.

His face was open and soft, as if nothing were wrong anywhere in the world. As though nothing ever had been, or ever could be. And she still had no idea how he did that.

"I brought in your mail," he said, handing her a thick stack of bills and circulars. "I hope that's okay. I saw you were home but also I saw the yellow flag was still up. I thought maybe you forgot, and maybe it wasn't okay to leave it in there overnight. You know. In case there's a check or something."

"Ha!" Addie said. "I should be so lucky."

"This is none of my business, so just tell me to get lost if you want to. I just wondered who Adam Finch is. But you don't have to say. I just figured we could start to get to know stuff like that about each other and that would be a good thing. Just the everyday stuff. Up to you, though. I thought maybe he was your husband once, or maybe your father. I thought I remembered you saying he died and left you the house . . ."

Addie looked past him into the yard to see if it was raining. It wasn't, but neither was there a star in sight.

She always hated getting into the name thing. On the other hand, she hated where her head had been when he had first knocked, and it felt like an easy distraction.

"*I'm* Adam Finch," she said.

"Your name is Adam?"

"Fraid so."

"Addie is short for Adam? But it says on this bill 'Mr. Adam Finch.'"

"Yeah, they pretty much all do. When your father gives you a boy's name, people make assumptions."

"Why did he name you Adam? Oh, I'm sorry. Was that rude? It's just so . . . unusual."

"The word you're searching for is 'weird.' And I get this all the time, so I'm pretty used to it. Nothing to be gained by acting like it's not weird. It just is what it is. My father wanted another boy, and he wouldn't let it go, and he wouldn't let it go, and he wouldn't let it go. Along with everything else in his life. You two okay out there?"

"Oh yeah. We're doing great. We got more done on the garden. It's going to look so good."

"Where's Jeannie?"

"She's doing an NA meeting on Zoom. Nice of you to let her use your iPad."

"Yeah, well, I realize you guys are a little bit isolated from things out here. But if she wants to go to more in-person meetings, she can always come to my work with me at night. We'll hit one in the evening and another in the morning before we come home, and she can sleep in the SUV overnight."

"Thanks. I'll tell her. Well, I'll let you get some sleep."

But Addie didn't get much. She wasted a second night off doing very little sleeping. Instead she sat up in her easy chair and stared at the picture of Sheena.

Then she wrote more on her inventory.

A lot more.

Chapter Twelve

Already Angry

It was about six days after the call to her brother, and Addie was out in the backyard talking to the kids. Jonathan was showing her the little stakes with their signboards, marking where he had planted the green beans, as opposed to the carrots or tomatoes.

Then he stopped and craned his head around to the other side of the garden.

"Do you think we pruned the bushes back too far?"

"Maybe a little," she said. "I might have done a little less. But they grow, so it really doesn't matter."

"Whew. Okay, good. Think it's going to rain again?"

"It is."

"Doesn't look like it," Jeannie said.

She was sweeping dirt off the stone walkways and back into the planting beds. Except Addie could see no dirt on the stone in the first place. Still, better the kids take the job too seriously than not seriously enough.

"How it looks is subject to change," Addie said.

Then she took hold of the elbow of Jonathan's sweater and pulled him a little closer to the house.

"Can I talk to you in private?" she asked him.

But unfortunately Jeannie overheard.

"You're going to talk about me," she said.

"We're not going to talk about you," Addie called in return.

"Then why private?"

"I just want Jonathan's opinion about something. And the something is not you."

He followed her into the kitchen. It was the first time he'd been on the house side of the mudroom door.

"You should let me make dinner," he said.

"Not much to make it with."

"Can I look?"

"Knock yourself out."

She sat at the kitchen table and watched him rummage around in the pantry.

"You've got all kinds of stuff in here," he said. "I could make pasta."

"If you really don't mind."

"Good. This'll be fun." He came to the table and sat across from her. "What did you want to talk to me about?"

"I was just thinking . . . wondering . . . about something. Let's say a young person is living in that warehouse where you were . . . What options would they have if they needed some kind of medical care?"

He only blinked for a moment or two.

Then he said, "But we're here now. And we're fine."

"I know. I just wondered."

"Well. There's a free clinic. But it's all the way downtown. You'd have to take a couple of different buses to get there. And I hear it's hard to get into. Like, people line up at the door and all the way down the block and then somebody goes down the line and tells most of them they won't get in that day. And I guess you can go to one of those general hospital emergency rooms. I don't think it's actually free. I think they bill you. But I think they do have to treat you if it's a life-threatening thing. Even if they can see you've got nothing. Why?"

"No reason."

"Doesn't seem like a question you'd ask for no reason." He tilted his head like a puppy, almost as though it might help him think. "Wait. Are you thinking about Skate?"

"Maybe."

"And that's why you didn't want to talk about it around Jeannie. Because she would just say she hoped he got gangrene and died."

"Pretty much, yeah. You can tell her what we talked about. I don't care. I just didn't want her weighing in. You know. In real time."

They sat in silence for what felt like a few minutes.

Then Jonathan said, "I like that about you, that you don't really wish death and devastation on anybody. But . . . still. It's Skate. Are you really worried about whether Skate is okay?"

"Yes and no," she said. She was twisting the fingers of one hand roughly with the other, which was unlike her. "If somebody else had shot him in the foot and he got gangrene and died, I wouldn't celebrate, but I wouldn't take it too hard, either. I'd say 'Well, that's Karma for you.' Or I'd note that the world was no poorer for the loss of him. But it wasn't somebody else who shot him. That was me. And I believe we're responsible for the consequences of what we do to other people."

He opened his mouth to speak, but Addie never did find out what he was going to say. At that moment her phone rang in her pocket, ending the conversation.

She pulled it out and looked at it, and her stomach—her entire midsection—turned to tingling ice. It was her old lieutenant, returning her call. She knew because it came through as "Work," which was a designation she'd given to the precinct number ages before. Nearly nine years and two new phones later, she still hadn't changed it.

"I need to take this," she said. Her voice sounded far away to her, as though her ears were plugged.

"Okay. Come let me know when you're done. I'll start cooking."

She gave him a chance to take two steps toward the door. Then she clicked onto the call.

"Tish?" she said.

"Yeah, it's me, Addie. I heard you called while I was out. How've you been doing?"

"Pretty good, actually. Doing the work of pulling my life together, at least." She watched the kids working in the yard as she spoke. It provided a sorely needed sense of comfort. "I just celebrated eight years sober."

"Well, good for you!" Tish said, and her voice was bold and strong, and she seemed to really mean it. Then her tone changed dramatically. "I have to say, though. I don't think it makes you eligible for rehire. If it were only up to me . . ."

"Oh, this is not about that," Addie said. "No. I just wanted some advice."

"From *me*?"

"Not personal advice. I have other people I'd go to for that. More like police-related advice."

"Ah. I see. But you *were* police. For more than a decade. What do you think I know that you wouldn't know?"

"The right thing for *me* to do. I think that's always an easy call to make for someone else but not a smart thing to try to apply to ourselves. Too easy to mix up what we think is the answer with what we want the answer to be."

"And I'd say that's very wise. Okay, fine. What say we get together in the next few days and I'll buy you a drink."

That seemed to land with a thud, and for a moment it was followed by only silence.

Then Tish said, "Holy crap, that might just be the dumbest thing I've ever said, and it has some competition. I am so, so sorry, Addie. I didn't mean to be insensitive. I just wasn't really thinking."

"It's okay. It's not your job to frame everything in terms of alcoholism. That's just what *I* have to do."

"I'll buy you a fancy coffee drink."

"I'll take it."

"How about tomorrow at five, at that place on the corner near the precinct?"

"Perfect," Addie said. "See you then." She was almost off the call when it hit her. "Oh. Tish. Before you go . . ."

"Yes?"

"I was so sorry to hear about your mother."

"Oh. Thank you. It was hard."

"I think it always is."

"We were close. We had a really good relationship. Is that how it was with your mom?"

"No. We had a terrible relationship. And it was still hard. There's just no way a thing like that can go that isn't bad. Anyway. See you tomorrow."

They clicked off the call.

Now all I have to worry about is sleeping in between now and then, she thought.

She called Jonathan in to make pasta for dinner, because it was something she could do that wasn't worrying.

———

Addie was driving down an endless multilane avenue in heavy traffic, because it was far too close to rush hour to get anywhere near the freeway.

She was talking to Wendy on her cell phone—hands-free, of course—because she was more than a little bit terrified by being on her way to meet with Tish. The odd part was that she knew how scared she was, though she had not decided whether that kind of knowing was the good news or the bad news.

"You're doing the right thing," Wendy said.

"I know," Addie said. Her eyes flickered back and forth between the road and the rearview mirror, because some idiot was tailgating her. "I hate the right thing."

"Don't we all?" Wendy said. "In the program we call that an AFGO. Another F-ing Growth Opportunity. But it's better than not growing."

"I—"

But Addie couldn't finish the sentence, because the idiot behind her had pulled up even closer on her tail, as if threatening her to make her go faster. But she couldn't have gone faster if she wanted to, because she was backed up in traffic like everybody else.

She spotted an empty loading zone and pulled over to let him pass. And that would have been fine, and a reasonable way to handle things, if she had only left it at that. But she could not resist flipping him the bird out the window, which she had quickly powered down for just that reason.

He stopped level with her car and powered his passenger window down. The cars behind him honked, but he paid them no mind.

He was an angry-faced thirtysomething man with greasy-looking hair and a baseball cap on backward.

"What is your problem?" he shouted.

"My problem is tailgaters," she shouted back. "Don't take it out on me because you want to go faster. We all want to go faster. But I can't go any faster than the car in front of me. And . . . here's a news flash. Neither can you!"

He gave her the finger in return and hit the gas.

"You could've saved us a lot of time by just doing that in the first place!" she shouted, her head out the window. But she didn't figure he heard.

He was good and gone.

"Damn," she said more quietly, putting on her left-turn signal. "Now it'll take forever to get back into the traffic lane."

She said it more or less to Wendy, who she could see was still on the line.

At first there was no reply.

Then Wendy said, "Is this because you're scared?"

"Is what because I'm scared?"

"All the yelling at other drivers."

"No. It's because I hate tailgaters."

"So you always drive like that."

"Pretty much. I can't help it that people drive like idiots."

Meanwhile she watched for a break in traffic, but there was none on the horizon. And no one seemed inclined to let her in.

"Ah yes. The alcoholic's disease. 'If only all the other people in the world would behave the way I think they should. Then my life would be perfect.'"

"Are you saying tailgaters are not a problem?"

"Addie."

"What?"

"How long have you known that people drive like idiots?" Wendy asked.

"All my life."

"Then explain to me why you haven't accepted it yet."

The request threw Addie so far off her game that she forgot she was looking for a break in traffic.

"How do you get used to a thing like that?"

"You practice acceptance. You say to yourself 'Hey, the world is full of bad drivers, and I've known that all along, so I shouldn't be too surprised that I just ran into one.' It's okay to think to yourself 'Somebody ought to teach that guy to drive.' Just stay clear on the fact that you're not the universal instructor. Got it?"

Addie looked up to see the break she'd been waiting for. She pulled into the traffic lane and headed for her meeting with Tish again.

"You still there?" Wendy's voice said from her console.

"Yeah, I'm here."

"Answer me this. When you hurt yourself, do you fly into a rage?"

"Hurt myself how?"

"Like bang your thumb with a hammer."

"Oh hell yeah. I'll jump around and use some pretty colorful language. What else would a person do at a time like that?"

"Maybe put some ice on it and feel empathy with yourself for a few minutes?"

"I'm not sure where you're going with this," Addie said.

Several blocks down, she could see the familiar sign for the coffee place, and it made her stomach ice over again.

"I'm going here with it. Are you clear on what it means when you flare up into anger regularly, and with very little notice or provocation?"

"It means life is really maddening sometimes?"

"It means you were already angry."

That sat in silence for a moment, because Addie had no idea what to say.

"Think about it," Wendy said. "And write some more inventory when you get home."

"If I'm not in custody."

"We'll talk more later," Wendy said.

Addie pulled up in front of the coffee place, in a space that was—against all odds—just open and waiting for her. There was even time on the meter.

She shut off the engine and sat with her eyes closed for a couple of minutes.

Then she said, out loud, to no one in particular, "Remember that Karma thing? How Jonathan thought maybe some nice thing was about to happen to me because I gave him a break on his very bad night? I could really use something like that. If there really is something up your sleeve, I need a break here."

If asked, she might have said she was talking to Karma. But that would have been papering over the fact that she still didn't believe such a thing existed. No matter how badly she wanted it to exist.

Chapter Thirteen

You Don't Say That Like It's a Good Thing

The coffee shop's outdoor patio had a high brick wall blocking the view of neighboring buildings. The brickwork looked old and distressed, seeming to have been mortared or plastered over at some point, but with that outer coating now flaking and fading away. Or maybe it had been made that way on purpose, to look historic. A massive vine grew and spread along it, clinging as it reached for the sky. From the width of the base of it, Addie guessed it was older than she was.

And still she waited for Tish to respond to her story. And she did not wait patiently, either.

Tish hardly looked a year older, which seemed unfair. Her dark hair was cropped shorter than it had been when Addie last saw her, as though she had decided to push all forms of fussing and nonsense out of her life.

Women do that as they get older, Addie thought.

She was wearing a neat gray pants suit and looked every bit the professional, as always.

And still Tish was offering no response to what she'd just been told. And Addie was feeling as though she might be about to spontaneously detonate.

"Your thoughts?" she asked, to avert the explosion.

"Reporting the incident to the department would have been good. That might be the only thing I'm sticking on just a little bit."

"Well, I called you. To get your advice about reporting it. But you were on leave."

"Right, right. How long after the incident did you call?"

"Pretty sure it was the next day."

"That's not bad, then. That's not bad at all. Tell me you're legally licensed to carry that handgun."

"Of course. I wouldn't be carrying without a license."

Tish fell silent for quite a bit longer. She seemed to be staring at the vine-covered brick, but Addie doubted she was taking in any of the visuals. Her dark brown eyes looked far away. Addie felt she could almost see her mental effort.

"You realize I'm only talking to you as an old friend," Tish said after a time.

"Of course."

"This is not official legal advice."

"Got it."

"And whatever I say stays between you and me."

"Absolutely."

"I think you should go home and put it behind you."

Addie was suddenly and surprisingly aware of huge quantities of air moving in and out of her lungs. It was like a great lifting. But the relief had a catch hiding underneath it—a scratchy thing, like a sharp little thorn. Because she instinctively knew she wouldn't be able to put it behind her.

Part of her had actually been hoping for some mild form of punishment. Community service or probation. She could have easily completed either one of those sentences, allowing her to feel as though her debt had been paid.

Instead Tish was assuming she was a person who could let things go. She was not.

"That's it?" Addie asked after a time.

"I just don't think the DA's office would go near this. What judge or jury is going to want to punish an Iraq war vet and a former LAPD officer for a thing like this? A known violent individual, coming at you. You gave a verbal warning. And then you fired a warning shot. And then you purposely fired a nonlethal round. Just enough to stop him. Why didn't he stop, I wonder?"

"He thought I was just a harmless old lady and wouldn't really do it."

"Ha!" Tish barked out. It came out so loudly that people at neighboring tables turned their heads. She lowered her voice again. "Well, obviously he doesn't know you like we do. And then you self-reported what had happened. I'm sure I don't have to tell you that the DA is extremely busy trying to prosecute people who did harm because they meant harm. People who shouldn't be out on the streets because they're a danger to the citizenry. I just can't see them wanting to pursue this."

Addie opened her mouth to speak, but Tish was still going.

"And it's more than just the self-defense aspect, though that's big. We have no complainant. We don't even know where this young man is. We don't know his name. All we know is that he hasn't walked into a police station anywhere wanting justice. We really just have your word for the fact that a shooting took place. I'm not saying I don't believe you. I'm just saying there's nobody on the prosecution side. I mean, of course it can be tried as the people versus you, but it still helps to have a person with a bullet wound who can tell his side of the story, you know? Otherwise what have you got to take into court?"

"You *sure* he hasn't walked into a police station anywhere?"

"I'd be very surprised. If you were him, would you want the police investigating why somebody might want to take a shot at you? But when I get back to the precinct and my computer, I'll check."

"I thought about all those things," Addie said, "but I thought maybe I was letting myself off the hook too easily. I just keep thinking, 'If only I hadn't gone over there.'"

"But you went over there to chase him off, so innocent parties didn't get raped and beaten. Not exactly evil intent."

"And now different innocent people will just get raped and beaten elsewhere."

"At least he doesn't move so fast these days. At least his victims have a chance to outrun him."

"That's exactly what I said!" Addie's voice came out louder than intended, almost an accidental shout. This time nobody turned. Maybe they were used to the sudden blasts of vocal energy by then.

"You can't solve all the problems of the world, Addie. Eleven years on the force must have taught you that. Look. I'm glad you take this as seriously as you do. It's always a big deal to discharge a round into another human being. I'm glad your conscience is asking a crap-ton of questions. But the justice system has a lot to do in this town, to put it mildly. It really doesn't want or need to mess with you. Anyway, that's my unofficial two cents' worth. I think you should just go home and let it go. The only thing I can see changing would be if he popped up somewhere and filed a complaint. Then we'd have to revisit this in a more official sense. But the chances of that happening are not very high. I really think you can let go of this one. And I really think you should. And that's my honest opinion."

———

On the drive home, Addie called her sponsor from the car, stuck in traffic on the crowded boulevard. That was safer than it might have sounded, as it was a little before six p.m. and she was literally standing still. In fact, she had shifted into park to take pressure off her braking foot.

She put the phone on speaker just as Wendy's voice came on the line.

"Did you do it?" Wendy asked immediately.

"Oh yeah," Addie said. "I did it."

In the brief silence that followed, she stared out over the sea of white headlights and red taillights. Dusk had fallen, causing them to glare into Addie's eyes.

"And?" Wendy asked after a time.

"She told me to go home and let it go."

"Then why do you sound disappointed?"

"Turns out letting things go is not a specialty of mine."

"Well, there's a surprise. Who could have seen that coming?"

"Are you being sarcastic?"

"Extremely."

"So . . . do you agree with her? It's just over?"

"You can add it to your inventory. Write out your feelings about it. And also how you think your actions might have contributed to a bad situation."

The traffic eased forward slightly. Addie shifted the SUV into drive and allowed it to crawl forward a few yards. Then she shifted into park again.

"And then I'm supposed to be done with it?"

"I'm not sure what to tell you, kiddo. The idea was to let a law enforcement professional advise you. We agreed you'd take her advice, even if it meant jail time. I think you have to take her advice even if it means no punishment. I mean . . . done with it? . . . as opposed to what? It *is* over. The guy's gone. You'll probably never see him again. It's only going on in your head at this point. You have to decide how long you want to keep it alive up there. But then of course to cap off 'being done with it' there's always the living amends, where you do your best to live out the rest of your life without shooting anybody. And then the whole thing just kind of tails off on its own because the past is the past."

"There's just this one thing, though," Addie said, shifting into drive again and creeping forward a dozen feet or so.

"Okay. Tell me the one thing."

"She's checking right now to be absolutely sure the guy didn't report it to the police. We don't figure he did. But even if he didn't . . . yet . . . she said if he does happen to walk into a police station and file a complaint, we'll have to revisit the thing in a more formal sense. So I have that hanging over my head. What do I do with that?"

"Turn it over?"

"I might've seen that answer coming," Addie said with a sigh.

"Yeah. You might have. I'll see you at the meeting tonight."

"Maybe. If I feel up to it."

"When you don't feel up to a meeting is exactly when you need a meeting."

"That one I saw coming," Addie said.

———

Halfway through the hour drive, Tish texted her. Traffic was moving slowly, and Addie had to pull over to read it.

It said, "No complaints matching your description."

She texted back, "Thanks."

Then she drove home to eat dinner with the teens and not go to a meeting.

———

Addie walked straight through the house, out the back door, and through the meticulously tended yard, where she knocked on the door of the shed.

Jonathan answered it in a matter of seconds. Then again, how long would it take someone to walk across the shed to that door?

It was dark now, and Addie couldn't see the sky, but the air felt warm, humid, and strangely static. And the moon had disappeared completely.

"I thought you two might want to come in and have some dinner," she said.

She watched his face change. It darkened, like the sky, blotting out his bright moon.

"In your *house?*"

"That's what I was thinking. Yeah."

"With *you?*"

"Not sure what part of this you're not getting."

From deeper inside the shed, Addie heard Jeannie's voice.

It said, "Uh-oh."

Addie didn't know what had warranted the comment, and she was too tired and preoccupied to worry about it, so she talked right past the situation.

"I thought you might be hungry," she said.

"Both of us?" Jonathan asked tentatively.

"No, I thought you got hungry and Jeannie lived on rainwater and air. Of course both of you."

"Did you want to talk to us?"

"I wanted to offer you something to eat."

"In your house?"

"Wow," Addie said, feeling frustration build up around her ears. "We just went around in a big circle, didn't we?"

"Sorry," he said. Then over his shoulder he added, "Come on, Jeannie. We're going in the house."

They followed Addie through the mudroom and into the kitchen.

No sooner had she closed the door than the rain let go all at once. They all three winced at the sheer volume of it on the roof and windows. It sounded as though an entire ocean had been lifted up and poured on them.

"How much rain have we been getting?" Jeannie asked, settling nervously at the kitchen table.

"Seventeen inches in the last two weeks," Addie said.

"Is everything flooded?"

"Not really. Not too bad. Some, in a few places. But somehow it keeps stopping just long enough for the excess to run off."

Jonathan was pacing slightly by the windows, but Addie wasn't sure why.

"Did you want to talk to us?" he asked.

"I didn't say I wanted to talk to you."

"Right. Right. But I just thought you might."

"Why would you think that?"

He exchanged a look with Jeannie. It was a dark exchange.

"You don't usually have us in the house, so I figured you were going to break it to us that it isn't working out and you want us to go."

She looked into his face, and he looked back, and the precariousness and vulnerability of his position broke her heart. Almost literally, from the feel of it.

"Nothing like that," she said. "It's working out fine. Sooner or later I was going to ask you in. When I felt like I knew you a little better."

Jonathan appeared to sigh out something approximately the size of the world. He sat next to Jeannie at the table, his shoulders slumped slightly. As if without his fear, there was nothing holding him upright.

Addie sat down herself, across from them, rubbing her face briskly with both hands. Still the rain pounded the roof and streamed down the windows.

"If I'm being honest," she said, "I really didn't feel like being alone tonight."

"Oh," Jonathan said. He sounded surprised. "I thought you liked being alone."

"Normally I do."

He leaped up from the table, this time animated in a positive way, and headed for her pantry.

"I could make us something," he said. "Unless that would take too long. You probably want to get to your meeting."

"I don't think I'm going."

"I thought you always went to your meeting."

"Normally I do."

He stared into the pantry for a minute or so.

"You have navy beans," he said. "I used to make a really nice navy bean soup. Fills you up, you know?"

"When did you learn to cook like this?"

"Early," he said. "When I was pretty little. In our house, if you wanted something to eat you had to make it. You'd like my navy bean soup. Everybody does. But I'd need onion and carrot and celery and garlic."

"I've got those," Addie said, face in hands. "But they might be a little old."

He left the pantry and rummaged in the refrigerator for another couple of minutes.

"These are fine," he said.

He pulled carrots and celery out of the crisper drawer, but they looked a bit sad. A crisper can only keep things crisp for just so long.

"Kind of saggy, don't you think?" she asked.

"Which is just the kind you use in soup, so they don't go to waste. Once they simmer in the broth for a while, you'll never know the difference. I see spices there on the wall, but I need a big pot."

"In that cupboard next to the stove."

In the silence that followed, punctuated by the occasional banging of pots, Addie glanced at Jeannie, who glanced back. The girl offered a little smile, but it looked sad to Addie. She said nothing.

It was Jonathan who spoke up from the area near the stove.

"Are you going to tell us what's wrong?"

"Who said anything was wrong?"

"You don't always have to say things for me to know them. Some things are just there for anybody to see."

Addie didn't answer for a long time. She only watched him take down a hanging colander and rinse the beans, then begin to chop vegetables on the cutting board.

"I had to go in and talk to someone from my old precinct," she said after a time. "You know. About that situation with Skate."

"I didn't know there was anything to talk about," he said.

"I discharged my weapon into a human being."

"That's no human being," Jeannie interjected.

"Well, I have bad news for you, young lady. He is. I know it's easier to think actual people can't be that awful, but they can be, and somebody or another is out there proving it every day. If not many somebodies."

"Are you going to get in trouble?" Jonathan asked over his shoulder.

"Probably not. The only bad scenario would be if he hopped into a police station and filed a complaint against me."

"How would he even know who you are?" Jeannie asked.

"He might know I work next door. He might've seen me coming and going. But even if he didn't . . . if he files a complaint, it'll get matched up with what I said happened when I was talking to my old lieutenant today."

"Then why did you even *go*?" Jeannie nearly shouted. She sounded quite exasperated. "Why didn't you just keep quiet about the whole thing?"

"Because that's the difference between an innocent person and a guilty one, my young friend. The innocent person explains what happened and expects people to understand. When you try to cover your tracks, that's clear cognizance of guilt, and it'll end up being used against you in court."

They sat in silence for a long time. Several minutes. Except Jonathan continued to stand and dice vegetables in silence.

He was the first to speak up.

"I'm sorry we got you into this," he said.

"You didn't. I got myself into it."

"Well, I'm not sure about that. But we both really appreciate that you did that for us. We talk about it all the time. We think it makes you kind of a hero."

Addie snorted but offered no words of reply.

"He won't go to the police," Jeannie said. "Nobody in that whole place would. They're not there to protect *us*, the police. They're there to protect other people *from* us. And most of us never even did anything wrong except sleep someplace nobody wants us. Skate did plenty wrong. He's not going to ask them for help."

"That's what I'm banking on," Addie said.

Jonathan found a plastic basket with onions and garlic in the pantry, and they filled the kitchen with their piercing aroma as he chopped them and dropped them into the sizzling oil in the pot.

Still the rain hammered.

Addie had planned to leave the conversation at that. End it on a hopeful note. But without advance planning she found herself saying more.

"Right now he just has a hole in his foot," she said. "Which is bad enough. But if he doesn't manage to hook up with any medical attention, things will get much worse for him, and probably pretty quickly. It'll get infected. Probably even gangrenous. He'll lose that foot if he doesn't take care. Around that time he might decide somebody needs to pay a price for that loss."

"I could find out where he is and how he's doing," Jeannie said.

"How could you do that?"

"I'd just have to ask the people I know in the warehouse. Everybody keeps track of Skate because nobody wants to run into him. I could find out. You said you'd take me to an in-person meeting if I wanted to go. We could go to a meeting in the evening near your work, and again in the morning, and in between I could talk to some people."

"No," Addie said. "I don't want you going in there. He could still be there. It's not safe."

"I don't have to go in. People come and go all night. I could catch somebody on the street. Talk to them right where you could see me from the office window."

"I guess," Addie said. "Yeah. I guess that would be okay."

It did sound like a relief to think of hearing news of where he was.

Maybe he had gone to an emergency room or a free clinic, gotten the foot looked at, and then gone far, far away. That would put her mind to rest.

Still, it might be throwing the girl close to danger. On the other hand, Jeannie had been in grave danger when Addie met her, and Addie had pulled her out of the vast majority of it.

"Okay," Addie said. "Next time I go to a meeting."

But eleven days would go by during which Addie still did not feel like going to any meetings.

Chapter Fourteen

Ding-Dong

The phone blasted Addie out of sleep. It was about eleven in the morning.

She tried to open her eyes, but ended up squinting and blinking and squeezing them closed. Because there was light pouring through the window. An unfamiliar and unexpected amount of light.

"Hello?" she mumbled into the phone.

"Oh, I woke you," Wendy's voice said.

Addie sat up and blinked some more without answering.

"I can never keep track of when you sleep," Wendy added.

"Days," Addie said. "Unless it's one of my two nights off. Why is it so bright out there?"

"Because it's day?"

"But it's been so dark and rainy. Is the rain over?"

"For maybe ten days it is."

"I know that can't be what you called to say."

Addie pulled the covers up closer to her, balling up the hems of the blankets in her fist and pressing them against her collarbone. It had seemed warm when she got home, so she hadn't put on any heat. It didn't seem warm now.

"No. I didn't call to talk about the weather. I called to ask where the hell you've been."

"Here. Or work."

"And not at any meetings."

"I was just taking a short break."

"Two weeks is not a short break."

"It hasn't been two weeks."

"Seems like it."

"It's been . . ." Addie counted up quickly in her head from the day she'd gone to see Tish. A hard date to forget. "Eleven days. I'm just trying to get my head together."

"Right. And guess where recovering alcoholics go to get their heads together?"

"Meetings," Addie said. "I know, I know. I just feel—"

"First let me tell you how *I* feel. I feel like you need to get your butt to a meeting. Okay. Go on now. How do *you* feel?"

Addie rubbed her eyes with the heel of one hand.

"Like I wanted to take a break from talking about myself."

"Which you did. For eleven days. See you tonight, then?"

"I guess."

"Let me phrase that more carefully. I. Will. See. You. Tonight. Correct?"

"Okay," Addie said.

She had planned to say more, but Wendy had already ended the call.

Addie rose, brushed her teeth, and dressed quickly, still not sure if she would go that night. She looked out over the backyard and saw Jeannie watering the as yet nonexistent vegetables.

No Jonathan.

She trotted downstairs and found him in the front yard, cutting back the forest of vines, especially where they crawled over the porch railing.

"Hey," she said, and sat down on the top step of the porch.

"Hey," he said back.

"Want coffee?"

"I'd love it. Jeannie would be happy with coffee too."

"Okay. I'll make some. And listen. If any of the neighbors strike up a conversation with you, you and Jeannie are my grandkids. Okay? You're having issues with your parents so you're living here for now. I'm not really sure what the legalities are around taking in minors who aren't yours."

Jonathan stopped cutting. He just stood for a moment, his eyes far away, the big manual clipper blades wide open.

"Sure," he said. "Okay. Actually, you mentioned that at the beginning."

She rose to go inside and make coffee. Or almost did. Before she could push to her feet, he stopped her with a whole new line of conversation.

"I need to tell you something," he said, "and it's none of my business, so you might get mad. But I'll just go ahead and say it anyway, and if you want me to shut up, I guess you'll say so."

"Okay . . ." Addie said, and settled on the step again.

"Jeannie looks to you to get a sense of what she's supposed to be doing. We both do. You're, like, the only adult we can sort of . . . watch. You know. To figure out how to live a normal life. She was kind of excited about going back to meetings, but you weren't going, so she couldn't get a ride with you. Now she's not even going to the online meetings, because she figures they're kind of . . . optional. I told her you've got eight years and she only has a couple of weeks, but she's still watching you and figuring it's okay not to go."

Addie closed her eyes against the bright late morning and sighed. She could hear his clipping resume. The thwack of the blades as they closed, shearing by each other.

"I'm going to one tonight," she said.

"Oh, good. That's great. She was also looking forward to finding out that thing you wanted to know. About you-know-who. She figured it would be like helping you. You know? And she was excited about that because there aren't too many ways we can help you." He paused again, blades still in the air. "We both thought you'd be more curious about that. Finding out about that. Like we figured you'd want her to ask."

"But then I'm afraid I'll find out," Addie said. "And once I know it, I can never unknow it again. It's one of those things that only goes one way."

———

"You're being awful quiet," Jeannie said.

They were on their way to the community center and their respective meetings. It was dark, and Addie could see the moon and a few of the brightest stars—for a change. Until Jeannie spoke, she had been lost in thought, with part of her dwelling on how long the sky had been overcast while most of her brain was much further away.

"Am I?"

"You didn't notice?"

"Do you see me as someone who spends a lot of time chattering?" Addie asked, trying to cap a mild irritation.

"I guess not."

They drove in silence for a time.

Then Jeannie asked, "Are you mad at me?"

"Why would you even ask that?"

"You seem mad."

"I might be a little mad at the world in general. I'm not sure why you'd think it has anything to do with you."

"Usually when people are mad or in a bad mood it's because of me."

"You might not be as powerful as you think you are."

Jeannie didn't answer for long enough that Addie thought maybe she never would.

Then the girl said, "I don't know what that means."

"It means we tend to think we're the center of the universe and everybody around us is responding to us in everything they do. But actually they're off in their own little universe and not thinking about us as much as we figure they are."

"What little universe of your own are you in?"

"Well, it's mine," Addie said. "Let's just leave it at that."

She slowed when she saw her freeway exit coming up and pulled onto the steeply curved ramp.

"Are you worried about the thing with Skate?"

"Maybe," Addie said, making a right turn onto the boulevard. She could already see the community center in the distance.

"We'll protect you," Jeannie said. "Jonathan and me, and I'll talk to all the guys who live at the warehouse, and we'll all protect you by coming up with the same story of who it was and who we saw do it, and it won't be you. We'll cover for you."

Addie sighed, and pulled into the parking lot.

She found a space fairly far from the door, but she could see Wendy standing outside with a few other familiar figures, vaping clouds into the cool evening air.

They sat a moment without exiting the SUV. Addie was wondering if she really needed to spell out the obvious.

"I already told my old lieutenant the whole story," she said quietly.

"Oh," Jeannie said. "Right. I still have no idea why you did that."

"Because I'm honest. Because I'm recovering, and the program is all about being honest, so you might want to think about that for yourself."

"I didn't shoot anybody."

"In general," Addie said, "you need to be prepared to tell people—at least the people you're recovering with—the truth about yourself. And you need to be honest with yourself first and foremost."

"What if I don't *know* the truth about myself?"

"You'll start to know it."

"I don't know if I can be that honest," Jeannie said, betraying nervousness and doubt for the first time since they'd set out together.

"Get ready to find out," Addie said.

———

As soon as Wendy was done sharing she called on Addie to talk. Which came as no surprise.

"I'm Addie," Addie said. "And I'm an alcoholic."

"Hi Addie," the group said back.

"I guess I took too long a break from meetings. At least my sponsor figured it was too long, but you know how sponsors are." A light rumbling of quiet laughter. "I'm working on an inventory, and I suppose I've got some things catching up with me. Some feelings and problems. I don't mean it like an excuse, and besides, I know this is where I'm supposed to bring them—the feelings and problems, I mean. I've just been feeling . . . it's hard to get my head around how I've been feeling, and it's hard to get it into words. But the way it feels . . . this might sound strange. It feels like just this complete . . . *calm*. I guess we pretty much normally associate good things with that word, but I don't think this is good at all. It feels like this perfectly glassy ocean. Like being out on the ocean but no surf and no swells and no wind. Just all this silence. All this lack of movement. Nothing moves at all. The world is just still. Which almost sounds nice, except it doesn't feel nice. There's some kind of heaviness to it. It feels dark and thick. And it gets even less nice when all of a sudden you realize you're a sailboat. And you're just going nowhere. I guess that's a weird thing to say, and I'm probably not explaining it right at all. I'm sorry if I didn't make any sense.

"Anyway, break's over. I'll come back to meetings regularly now. Like it or not. My sponsor'll see to that. Which I suppose is why we have them.

"That's all I've got to say. Thanks."

———

Wendy stepped up beside her right after the Serenity Prayer. As soon as people unclasped hands and took to milling about.

Before Wendy could open her mouth to speak, a woman named Fran came by, touched Addie on the arm, and said, "Awesome share."

"It was?" Addie asked, genuinely surprised.

But Fran was already gone.

Addie turned to her sponsor.

"Was she being sarcastic?"

"Of course not. She liked what you said. A lot of people did. I saw them nodding while you were talking. You couldn't have been serious when you said you were sorry if your share made no sense."

"I was being perfectly serious."

"You honestly don't know what you just described?"

"Not really."

"That was just about the best description of depression I think I've ever heard," Wendy said.

———

Addie met up with Jeannie just on the parking-lot side of the door, and they walked together to the battered SUV.

"How was your meeting?" she asked the girl.

"Kind of okay. Some people are boring and talk too long but other people I really get what they're saying and they could talk all night and I'd listen. Because it's like they know how I feel, and I didn't think anybody did."

"Humanity is more common than you give it credit for."

"No idea what that means," Jeannie said.

Addie unlocked the passenger door and then walked around to the driver's side, and they both climbed in. She twisted the key to start up the old engine. Just for a split second it turned without catching, and she felt it as a jolt in her stomach. But a couple of seconds later it roared to life.

"One of these days," Addie muttered under her breath.

"What'd you say?"

"Nothing."

But not today, she thought. *Fortunately not today.* She kept that one to herself.

They drove off toward Addie's work.

"How come you stopped going to meetings for so long?" Jeannie asked as they pulled out of the parking lot and onto the street.

"It was only eleven days."

"But don't you usually go to one every day?"

"I usually go to five a week."

"Then why did you stop for so long?"

Addie sighed deeply and audibly and drove for a few blocks without answering. Truthfully, she was deciding whether she needed to, and whether she should. On the one hand, it was a little like prying, and none of the girl's business, and it irked Addie slightly to be put on the spot to say. Then she remembered what Jonathan had told her. How both the teens looked up to Addie, and watched her, and followed her lead as a guide to living a more normal life.

"I had some things I needed to work out," she said.

She knew as she said it that she should be so lucky as to be able to frame her troubles in the past tense. But that was how she softened the personal information before it arrived at anybody else's ears.

"Aren't you sort of supposed to go to meetings to work stuff out?"

"Yeah . . ." Addie began. And didn't finish the thought.

"So why did you stop?"

Again Addie came close to losing her temper. Again she reminded herself that the girl might be using Addie to find her own way.

"Because I'm not perfect," she said. "I know you think eight years is a ton of time, and when you've got a few days, I suppose it is, but it's not that much time in the grand scheme of things. My sponsor has thirty-five years. My old sponsor had forty-eight years when she died. And even *they* didn't always do the exact right thing in every situation, because that's not how people are. It's progress, not perfection."

"I heard somebody say that in my NA meeting tonight."

"And it won't be the last time you hear it," Addie said. "Believe me."

They rolled along in silence for a time.

About a block and a half from work and the warehouse, the girl shouted suddenly, startling Addie. The SUV swerved slightly with her reaction.

"Stop the car! Stop, Addie! I know those people. Let me get out and talk to them. They'll know."

"I have to get to work."

"You're early for work. You usually have dinner in between. Besides, *you* don't have to talk to them. Go on to work. I'll meet you there."

Addie pulled over to the curb in a loading zone and stopped the vehicle. Three dark figures hung out on the dark corner, sitting cross-legged on the sidewalk, but Addie couldn't see much more than that. Just long hair and raggedy clothes. How the girl even knew them in this light and at the distance, Addie had no idea. Maybe she recognized their raggedy clothes. Or maybe she had better vision than Addie. Maybe most people did.

"Don't go in the warehouse," she said. "He might still be there."

"Duh," Jeannie said. "That's the whole point. I want to talk to these guys because they're not in the warehouse. They're here. I can talk to them here."

"Be careful," Addie said. "Please."

Jeannie turned and looked at her for the first time that evening. Addie had only the glow of the dashboard lights to go by, but the girl's face looked hard to her. Almost defensive.

"I can take care of myself, you know. I was doing it a long time before I met you."

Addie opened her mouth to tell the girl to have it her own way, but Jeannie had already jumped out of the SUV, slamming the door too hard and running to join her friends.

Addie took a deep breath, sighed it out, and drove on to work.

——

Addie sat in front of the bank of monitors, stopping to glance at them more often than usual, working on her inventory.

"I didn't know what I was feeling was depression," she wrote. "Which feels like just the craziest thing. What's up with that, anyway? I knew it was something big, and that it felt awful, but I couldn't match it to that simple word. I thought it was like a lack of locomotion. How could I not know that? How could I not feel it?

"When I was drinking, I used to sit around for hours at a time, thinking all these deep thoughts. Thinking about myself, and my life, and the world. Society. All that introspection. I should know myself better than anybody by now, and I don't. I haven't even scratched the surface. I don't even know what I feel.

"What do I know?" she wrote, underlining the word "do." "What was I actually doing all that time?"

Then she wrote about her father, and the dog, and her conversation with her brother, Bill, for what felt like an hour or two.

When she looked up at the big clock over the door, it was after six a.m. She had written twenty-two pages, front and back, in a very small and compact hand.

She got up and walked to the door, opened it, and looked around. No Jeannie, though it was not surprising. Why would the girl be within sight of the door and not knock or come in?

Though she was wrong to leave her post and she knew it, she fetched her keys and jumped into the SUV, and cruised around a few corners to the spot where she had left the girl. Jeannie was not there, and neither were her friends. The neighborhood was empty.

Addie drove back quickly and stationed herself inside again, hoping the owner would not review the tapes and see that she had left. She could say she'd seen something suspicious and followed it. But it didn't really track as an excuse. Why deal with any situation after it left the property? Besides, it struck her suddenly, there was that honesty-of-the-program thing. She shouldn't be lying to her boss. She would have to hope those tapes were only reviewed in the event of an incident.

She thought briefly of going over to the warehouse to see if Jeannie was there. To make sure she was okay. But she'd have to bring her gun for her own protection.

No, she decided quickly. *Definitely not going to do that.*

She pictured herself going in to see Tish again and telling her that she had made a second trip to the warehouse with her gun and some other unfortunate and borderline legal moment had occurred.

"No."

She said it again, out loud this time.

She had told the girl not to go there. She could advise Jeannie, but she couldn't control her.

You can't protect somebody against their will, she thought. *You can only protect somebody if they want to be protected.*

Then she wrote more on her inventory, this time about how decisions like this one took her around in circles and turned her inside out.

———

Jeannie knocked on the door at a minute or two before seven. Whether that was coincidence or whether the girl or someone she'd been with had a wristwatch, Addie didn't know.

By the time she had crossed over to the door, Jeannie had backed up several yards into the dark parking lot.

Addie opened the door.

"What are you doing way over there?" she asked the girl.

"Nothing," Jeannie said.

"Where were you all night?"

"Nowhere."

"You went to the warehouse, didn't you?"

"I found out what you wanted to know," Jeannie said.

"You shouldn't have gone there. You could have been hurt."

"No, it was safe."

"He could come back. You don't know."

"But I do know."

It struck Addie as a bit insane that they were calling words to each other across such a wide distance, but she wasn't sure how to fix it. And she had bigger issues on her mind. Jeannie knew what had happened to Skate; she had just said so. And now Addie was about to find out. It jangled in her stomach like a ring of keys. She wanted to know and wanted not to know in almost exactly equal measure.

"Why won't you come over here?" she asked the girl. "Come inside and talk to me."

"I can't," Jeannie said.

Addie chewed that over for a minute, the truth of the situation dawning on her in stages.

"Oh, I get it," she said. "You were in the warehouse getting loaded with your friends all night."

"I'm sorry," Jeannie said.

"Don't be sorry to me. I'm not the one you're hurting."

"Tell Jonathan I said I'm sorry."

"I meant *you*. Actually. I meant you're hurting yourself. But yeah. He won't be too happy to hear it. You shouldn't have gone to the warehouse. Even if Skate's gone. Even if he moved to the next state, he could still come back."

"No," Jeannie said. "Where he is . . . you can't come back from that." Then, surprisingly, she moved in about a dozen steps. Not close enough to literally be at Addie's office door, but close enough to speak in a more hushed tone. "You might not think it's good news, but I think it is."

"How about you stop prefacing and just tell me?"

"What's prefacing?"

"It's what you're doing right now. Just say it."

"He's dead. Skate is dead."

Addie felt the words like needles piercing her gut. No, more than needles. Ice picks. Cold ice picks that just would not stop.

Then I actually killed him, she thought. *Damn. Damn, damn, damn.*

It was the only possible outcome she had failed to consider. Or maybe she just hadn't allowed herself to go there.

"So he got an infection in that foot and died," she said. "So I killed him."

Her voice sounded too far away, and also it sounded like somebody else's voice.

It seemed too soon for that medical scenario to play out, and yet the girl had just said it. Skate was dead.

Jeannie stepped in another couple of yards.

"No, it wasn't you. It wasn't the foot. Well, it was and it wasn't. I do think it was infected, because they say he was sick and having trouble getting up and he was sleeping a lot. He was sleeping over in that abandoned storefront on Grant Street. He ran into some guy he molested when the kid was only about fourteen, and the guy strangled him in his sleep. I mean, I'm sure he woke up when he was being strangled, but he couldn't get up. He wasn't strong enough to do anything about it."

Then it really was me, Addie thought. *At least half of it was. I wanted him to be slower than his victims, but I never thought about him being slower than his attackers.*

But she didn't say anything of the sort to the girl. She needed to go home and sleep, and work it out in her own head before she said anything to anybody else.

"You can still come home with me," Addie said. "If you're looking to get clean again now."

But the girl only started walking backward.

"Tell Jonathan I'm sorry," she said again.

Addie opened her mouth to answer, but the girl had already turned and sprinted away.

Chapter Fifteen

I Ain't the Hugging Kind

Addie cruised by the early-morning meeting, even though she didn't plan to stay.

As soon as she pulled into the parking lot she saw Wendy vaping near the door.

She parked, jumped out, and approached her sponsor.

"Wow," Wendy said on a steamy exhale. "Two meetings in less than twelve hours. When you shift gears you really shift gears."

"I'm not staying," Addie said. "I promise I'll go to the one tonight. But I've had a hell of a shift and I need to go home and get some rest. I just wanted to tell you something."

"Okay," Wendy said. "Tell."

"The first night we talked, when we went out to that diner together, you asked me why I picked you as a sponsor. I didn't give you the full right answer. But it wasn't on purpose. I wasn't withholding. I told you what I knew at the time. But now I'm ready to tell you why. Why you. Yeah, we're very different people. I get that. But I'd been listening to you share for a lot of years, and you really do have an important thing that I want for myself. And I'll tell you what it is. You seem like you get along with the world."

Wendy let out a snort of a laugh.

"Not sure I'd say that. I have a low opinion of it most of the time."

"Maybe. But you take it as it is. You don't try to rearrange it to suit you."

Wendy took a deep drag on her e-cigarette and looked up at the cloudy morning sky before exhaling.

"You know why I don't try to rearrange the world to suit me?"

"Because it's impossible?"

"Bingo," Wendy said. "I believe that's what we call the serenity to accept the things we cannot change."

"I just feel like my life would be a lot more comfortable if I could do that."

"Oh, it would be," Wendy said. "Or maybe I should be more optimistic and say it will be. Now go home and get some sleep. You look like something the cat drug in."

"I'll come to the one tonight."

"You'd better."

Addie walked back to her SUV and drove home.

———

When she pulled into her own driveway, Jonathan was out front using an edger on the line where the lawn met the sidewalk. He had mowed her giant lawn to an even-looking inch or so, and weeded it from the look of things, and now he was edging it. It looked better than it had in years.

She parked in the driveway and got out, and he stopped working when she approached him.

"It looks amazing," she said. "You're doing a really nice job. My neighbors must be over the moon."

"Must be," Jonathan said, "because they keep waving at me and giving me thumbs-up. Where's Jeannie?"

Addie's face must have darkened when he asked it, because she could see him mirror the change back to her. She decided to go ahead and tell him, even though it was possible he already knew everything he needed to know.

"Jeannie's gone again."

"Oh," he said, his face falling further. "That's too bad."

"Come sit a minute," Addie said.

They sat down on the porch steps together, Addie looking out over her neatly tended world.

"She said to tell you she's sorry. She met up with some friends, and she wanted to talk to them and find out about Skate. Maybe I should have sat right there while she talked to them. I don't know. She just told me to go on to work and she'd meet me there, and I never thought twice about it. But I guess they were partying all night and she jumped in and joined them. And now I think I should have thought of that, and I feel bad. Here she's only got a couple of weeks clean and I leave her alone with old friends who use. I didn't think about them as maybe having drugs at the time. But still I feel like I made a big mistake. Should I have thought of that?"

"I wouldn't have thought of it," Jonathan said. "Most of those people who sleep at the warehouse, they don't have drugs because they can't afford them. And if they do manage to get their hands on some, they're not big on sharing. I wouldn't put it on yourself. Jeannie's gonna do what Jeannie's gonna do."

"But she was doing me a favor. Finding out about Skate."

"You didn't ask her to do it, though. She wanted to do that for you."

"I guess."

"But you'll feel bad anyway," he said. "Won't you?"

"Absolutely I will."

Addie's across-the-street neighbor, Ed Hoddington, pulled out of his driveway. Before he drove away he rolled down his car window and gave them a thumbs-up.

"Told you," Jonathan said. "Did you tell her she couldn't come back because she used?"

"No. Just the opposite. I told her she should come home with me if she was ready to start over again right now. But she just ran away."

"That answers that question," he said.

They sat without talking for a minute or two, looking out over the carefully manicured world that was her new front yard.

Then Jonathan said, "I should finish edging the lawn."

"Wait," she said. "I want to talk to you about something."

He was halfway to his feet by the time she said it, but he sank back down again, his face a mask of apprehension.

"It's nothing bad," she said.

"Oh. Good."

"I want you to move into the house."

That just sat on the porch for a minute. They were both looking down, which gave Addie the odd impression that they were both examining the statement where it lay, though of course that was not literally possible.

"*Your* house?"

"Of course my house. What other house could I invite you to move into?"

"You sure?"

"Positive. I have four bedrooms and three bathrooms, so it's pretty ridiculous to keep all that to myself and make you stay in an old garden shed."

"But you had just taken me off the street and you didn't know me. And you didn't know if you should trust me in your house."

"But now I do. I would've asked sooner, but I didn't feel quite the same about Jeannie. I'm sorry to say it, because I know she's your friend and all."

"It's okay. I know what you mean. She's in a bad place. She'd never hurt anybody, I don't think, but I wouldn't bet my life that your TV couldn't have come up missing if she really got it in her head she needed to use. I mean, I like her. I care about her. But I don't think you're wrong to feel the way you feel."

"I care about her too," Addie said.

"I like that about you," Jonathan said. "I'll gather up my things from the shed."

But for a moment they only sat.

In time Addie looked up into his face and caught him staring at her with a look she could only characterize as affection.

"Sometimes it's all I can do to keep from giving you a great big bear hug," he said. "But then I decide you're probably not the hugging type."

"Good decision," Addie said.

———

"This is probably the nicest room I've got that's not mine," she said.

She flipped on the light and was embarrassed by the thick layer of dust on every surface. But the bed was a queen, and there was a nice antique dresser and bedside table set, and a Persian rug.

"It's beautiful," he said, his voice thick with awe.

"Needs tending."

"That's not hard."

"There are others you could choose from, but this one has something the others don't. It has its own bathroom."

After a pause, Jonathan said, "I'm getting that feeling again."

"What feeling? The one where you want to hug me?"

"Yeah, that one."

"Just stay right where you are till it passes. I'll get you some sheets and blankets."

She rummaged around in the hall closet and found what she needed.

When she got back to his room, he said, "Did you feel like you wanted not to be alone? Is that why?"

"Might've been a small part of it. The bigger part is, you're too good for all this. You're too good to sleep in an old abandoned warehouse or a little tiny bare garden shed. I can't for the life of me figure how anybody could put a boy like you out on the street. I just can't get my head around it. I'm not trying to suggest that all the other kids out on the street deserve it. Nobody does. But you just *so* don't deserve it. It makes my head hurt to think about it. And don't think I don't see that look on your face. You were right when you said I'm not a hugger, so your feet can just stay right where they are. I'll go get you some dustrags and such."

She turned to leave the room without looking at his face to gauge his reaction.

Just as she reached the open doorway he said, "Wait. You never told me about Skate. Did she find out where he was?"

Addie stopped and turned, but she did not look at him when she spoke. She found herself suddenly fascinated with the Persian rug. She couldn't take her eyes off it.

"He's dead."

"Whoa," Jonathan said.

She glanced up at him quickly, then looked away. Turned out they were both fascinated by the rug.

"Of . . . ?" he began.

"Strangulation. Somebody he molested some years back took him out."

"Oh, so it had nothing to do with you."

"I wouldn't go that far. The foot was infected and he was sick. Why do you suppose somebody decided to go after him now but not before?"

"Got it," Jonathan said.

He might have had more he wanted to say, but Addie hurried away to gather him some cleaning supplies before anything like that could happen.

———

"Can I watch TV?" Jonathan asked her over dinner.

His voice sounded heady and awed, like a child talking about what toys Santa might bring for Christmas.

They were sitting at the kitchen table eating the leftovers of his very good navy bean soup, along with a baguette she'd had in the freezer.

"Of course you can watch TV. Anytime you want."

"I haven't watched TV for so long. I'm not even sure I know what's on anymore."

"There's a *TV Guide* on the coffee table."

They ate in silence for a minute or two.

Then he said, "Is it okay that I'm not sorry?"

"About which situation?"

"About what happened to Skate."

"Listen. Jonathan. Whatever you feel is what you feel. About any situation, but especially this one. The guy beat you up and tried to rape you. I don't expect you to hold a requiem for him. I'm not going to sit here and act like the world is a poorer place for the loss of him myself. I guess I just feel like he was probably really abused and messed up as a kid, and even though it's not like me to be a cockeyed optimist, I think there's at least a small chance that anybody can step up and redeem themselves at some point in their life. And that door just slammed shut on him."

"But you didn't shut it."

"But if I hadn't come along into his life that morning, then the whole thing would have played out differently."

"Right. I knew you felt that way. Are you going to be able to deal with that?"

"I suppose we're about to find out," Addie said.

———

Addie was fast asleep, having slept much longer than usual. When a soft knock came at her bedroom door, she resisted coming up out of sleep to deal with it. She could feel the resistance, even without being fully awake. It was something like an intruder she felt the need to defensively battle.

On the third round of knocks she shouted at the door.

"*What?*"

"It's me, Addie. Jonathan."

"I'm sleeping."

"You okay?"

"Of course I'm okay. People sleep, you know."

"But it's almost time for you to leave for work."

Addie sat up in bed and looked at the clock, a sick dread crystallizing in her gut.

"I might not go," she said.

A long, welcome silence fell. Addie wondered if that might be it. If he'd just go away now and leave the whole thing alone.

"Are you sick?" he asked after a time.

"No. I don't know. Maybe."

"Can I come in? Are you decent?"

"Yeah, all right."

He opened the door slowly. Almost hesitantly. He stuck his head into her room and looked around. Looked at her.

Then he stepped inside. He was fully dressed in jeans and a sweater. Not in pajamas like Addie. Then again, it was evening. Most people were dressed.

He walked over to her bed and perched on the very edge of the mattress.

"Is this okay?" he asked, his voice small.

"I suppose so."

"What's wrong?"

Addie rubbed her eyes. And rubbed them, and rubbed them, and rubbed them. A little voice in the back of her head asked her how long she was going to do that before answering. Or not answering.

She dropped her hands into her blanket-covered lap.

"I think I need to quit that job," she said.

"Why?"

"It might be hard to explain."

"Can you afford to quit?"

"No."

They sat quietly for a time.

Then Jonathan said, "I've only had one job so far in my life. I worked at an ice cream stand one summer when I was sixteen. Not too long before I left my dad's house. One thing I remember real clearly, though. Remember being told, I mean. They really drilled it into us that if you're going to quit you have to give your two-week notice. Otherwise a thing like that can go on their records and it can make it really hard to get hired anyplace else."

Addie almost rubbed her eyes again, but she caught herself and decided it was silly to keep going there.

"I hear you. It's probably good advice. It just feels really hard to go in to work right now."

They sat quietly for a minute or two, both staring down at Addie's quilt.

"Do you want me to go with you?"

"Why would I want that?"

"You know. For, like . . . moral support."

Addie opened her mouth to say *Of course not. Don't be silly.*

Instead she heard herself say, "That would be very nice. Thank you."

Chapter Sixteen

Defending the World, Until You Can't Anymore

It was about an hour after arriving at work when Addie's cell phone rang. Jonathan was sleeping soundlessly in the corner, looking—as he so often did—like a rough, realistic, and well-worn human version of an angel.

She slipped the phone out of her pocket and checked the caller ID. It was Wendy.

"Hey," she said, clicking onto the call.

"You at work?"

"Yeah, I am. And look. I'm sorry. I know I said I'd go to that meeting tonight, but then I overslept."

"Are you doing that thing again?"

"What thing?"

"The one where you say a thing that's true, but it's not the whole truth?"

Addie sighed, and paused a few beats before answering. If she was deciding what to say, it was happening at a level above or below her awareness. Because it only felt like a blank space to her, no matter how much she felt around in it.

"Yeah," she said. "I suppose I am."

"Do better," Wendy said.

"I think I need to quit this job."

"You told me you needed that job to get by."

"Yes I did."

"Has that changed?"

"No."

"Are you okay?"

"No, I don't think I am."

"I'll be right there," Wendy said.

———

"You've never been to my work before," Addie said, though it was obvious to both of them. She even added, "Have you?"

"Oh, we're stalling, are we?" Wendy asked.

Wendy was sitting in a vinyl chair on the other side of the very small office, watching Jonathan sleep in the corner.

"Sorry," Addie said.

"I'm thinking this is Jonathan."

"Yeah, that's Jonathan."

"He looks like a nice kid."

"He's an angel. He thinks *I am*, but I know it's the other way around. And I have no idea how he does it. He's been through all manner of trauma and he's still so sweet and calm. How does that even happen?"

"Undoubtedly saving it for later," Wendy said. "Like you used to do. Now talk to me about this crazy thing with quitting your job."

"It's not crazy. It's something I just have to do."

In her peripheral vision, Addie saw a movement of several figures across one of her monitors. But they were not on the property. She could just see them between two of the rows, moving across the vacant lot toward the warehouse. She thought she recognized Jeannie's hoodie, but it was hard to tell without light, and at the distance. And everything showed up on the monitor in night vision, devoid of color, with light colors coming off as a blazing, almost glowing white, as if lit brightly from within.

"What if I thought Jeannie was over there?" she asked Wendy. "Should I try to go get her?"

"Get her?" Wendy asked, her voice dripping with skepticism and maybe even something more. "As in, kidnap her?"

"Well, no. Of course I didn't mean *that*."

"Then what did you mean?"

"I don't know. Help her?"

"Help her how? How do you help somebody who doesn't want your help?"

"Invite her back, I guess."

"Didn't you already do that?"

Addie closed her eyes for a moment and allowed some uncomfortable feelings to move through.

"Right," she said.

"Is this a thing that you can change, Addie, or is this a thing you need to accept?"

"That second thing," Addie said. "And actually . . . I knew that. I just lost hold of it for a minute there."

"Why do you have to quit your job? And what will you do without it?"

"The second question . . . well, the answer to that one is, I have no idea. The first one I know, but it might be hard to explain."

"It's late," Wendy said. "And it was a long drive. Try."

Addie sighed deeply.

She ran her thumbnail along a groove in the wood countertop and avoided looking up.

"I just can't keep doing this, Wendy. I hit a wall with all this, and I hit it hard. I've been doing it all my life and I can't do it anymore."

"You've only been doing the job for a handful of weeks," Wendy said. "As a result, I'm going to assume that the 'this' you keep referring to is something else."

"Defending."

"Defending what exactly?"

"Everything. The whole world. When I was in the service I was defending the country. Then on the force it was the city. But I'm still doing it. I'm a civilian now but I'm still walking around carrying a gun to make sure that none of the bad people can get to any of the good people to hurt them. And I've been prepared to back it up with force, and I just did, and now a boy is dead. And now I'm starting to wonder if I even have the right to make that determination. You know. That a person is bad. I just don't know anymore."

"Good," Wendy said.

"It is?"

"Yeah. You're right. You don't know anything."

"Thanks a lot."

"I didn't mean you specifically. I don't know anything either. I don't know how things are supposed to be. I don't know what's supposed to happen, or what's best for the greater good in the long run. That's why I turn everything over."

"Oh," Addie said. "Right. I'm supposed to turn it over. Why do I keep forgetting that?"

"I don't know," Wendy said, "but it's a common problem. Do this for me. I'm going to go home and get some sleep. I came over because I thought you might really be losing it, but you seem okay for now. Am I right? Are you okay for now?"

"I can get through my shift and go home," Addie said.

"Good. Do that. Promise me you'll sleep on the decision one more day. Then, if it's really what you have to do, do it. You'll figure out something else to pay the bills."

Wendy rose and moved to the office door, shrugging into her coat. She looked back over her shoulder at the sleeping Jonathan.

"Why does he come to work with you?"

"He doesn't. Normally. He offered tonight and I took him up on it."

"Ah," Wendy said. "He's your security blanket."

"I shouldn't do that, I know."

"Who says you shouldn't?"

"Well. It's like a crutch."

"A crutch is a useful tool. Just don't forget to put it down when your leg is healed. But as far as not being alone when you're upset, or when you're going through something . . . I'm actually a fan of that."

Before Addie could even answer she slipped out the door, closed it behind her, and walked to her car.

Jonathan made a sudden snorting noise and rolled over.

Then everything was perfectly silent again. And everything stayed that way. All night long.

———

They drove home in silence for the first several minutes. Jonathan seemed deep in thought, and maybe somewhat downcast.

When he finally spoke, his voice sounded small. Maybe even a bit shy. As if speaking were something he might have no earthly right to do.

"I had a dream," he said.

"Oh? About what?"

"I dreamed you were talking to somebody and saying you'd hit a wall with having to defend what you thought was right. You know, like really defend it. With a gun and all. And that maybe you didn't even know what was right anymore."

Addie realized she was choking the steering wheel too tightly, and she made an effort to loosen her grip again. A big full moon, or a nearly full one in any case, hung over the windshield in the early dawn light.

"I don't think that was a dream," she said.

"Well, if it wasn't a dream, then what was it?"

"My sponsor came by my work and we were talking. You must've only been half asleep. You must've heard it but been close enough to asleep to think it was a dream."

"Oh," he said. "So you really do feel that way."

"Yeah."

"So you're not okay."

"I am and I'm not. It's been true for a long time, but I wasn't looking it right in the eye. When you first take a thing like that head-on it feels pretty bad. But I'm not sure it's really any worse than holding it in and trying to ignore it and live around it. If you know what I mean."

"I'm trying not to know what you mean," he said. "Because I'm not ready to try it."

After a silent mile or two he said, "I'm sorry."

"For what?"

"I'm the one you were defending."

"It's something I was doing before you were born," she said, "so I wouldn't take it personally."

They drove the rest of the way in silence.

Just as she was pulling into her own driveway, just as the sun rose over her back fence, Jonathan said, "I could get a job."

She turned off the engine but made no move to get out. And so neither did he.

"I'm not sure you can," she said.

"Why can't I?"

"If you're not eighteen you need working papers, and I think your parent or a legal guardian has to sign off on that."

"I *am* eighteen," he said.

"You told me you were seventeen."

"Yeah, I told you I was seventeen, and when I told you that, I was seventeen. But now I'm eighteen."

"You should've told me you were having a birthday. We could have done something to celebrate."

"You're doing so much already, though. I didn't think you should have to do anything more."

"It would be hard for you to get to a job. I have you pretty isolated out here."

"Can't you walk to a bus stop from here?"

"Yeah. I suppose. It would be more than a mile each way."

"That doesn't sound so bad. Did you give notice at your job?"

"No," Addie said. "I promised my sponsor I'd sleep on it one more day, and I'm going to do that, because I promised. But then I'm still going to quit. Because it's just something I have to do. I just don't feel like I have any other choice. I just can't keep doing this."

"That's what you said in the dream," Jonathan said.

And they walked into the house together without discussing it further.

———

Addie slept all day. When she woke up, her mouth was dry, she was hungry and thirsty, and a glance at the clock told her she'd been asleep for almost ten hours.

She picked up her phone from the bedside table and called her boss, the owner of the storage place.

"Blanche," she said when the woman picked up.

"Yeah, who's this?"

"Addie Finch."

"Oh right. Addie Finch. What's up, Addie Finch?"

"I need to give you my two-week notice."

Addie walked over to the window as she spoke and looked out over the backyard. Jonathan was doing something with the little sprouts in his vegetable garden, but it was unclear exactly what. It looked almost as though he was caressing them gently. Encouraging them, maybe. He might have been talking to them, but of course she was too far away to know.

This kept her busy in the seconds while she winced and waited, knowing she was about to find out if Blanche was mad.

"Oh," Blanche said. "Good."

"Good? What exactly do you mean by that? Were you unhappy with my work? Because if you were, you never said."

"No, you were fine, honey. It's just . . . I got a nephew who's been bugging me for a job is all. And how many jobs you think I got? I only own the one business. He'll be happy, and I'll be happy because he'll stop driving me crazy about it. Anyway, no notice required. I'll still say you're eligible for rehire if anybody calls. I know he'll start tonight if I ask him, so go on and go."

Addie said nothing for a time. She was half thinking how glorious it felt not to have to go in to that place, ever again. The other half of her brain was trying to add up how much she had in the bank and how long it would last. How fast she'd have to turn up another job without that two weeks of pay she'd been counting on.

"You okay, honey?" Blanche asked on the other end of the phone.

"Yeah, I'm fine," Addie said.

And as she said it, one of the two emotional directions snapped into place. The winner was . . . relief. She would find a way to deal with the bills somehow. But in the meantime, she didn't have to go in again. And that felt like the weight of the world had lifted off her. Like there had been an elephant parked on her chest for most of her life, and he'd finally gotten up and wandered away. And that she had taken her first real deep breath in as long as she could remember.

———

When Jonathan came back into the kitchen, he took one look at her and said, "You quit your job, didn't you?"

She said, "Yeah, I did."

"You look super worried."

"Well, she threw me a curveball. The boss. I gave her my two-week notice, but she let me off the hook for working those last two weeks. She's got a relative who wants to start right away."

"Oh," he said, and sank down into a chair next to hers at the table. "Is that good?"

"It is and it isn't. Just that I was kind of counting on those last two paydays. But don't worry. I'll get something new. Give me a couple of days, I'll get something. I always do."

Six

Jonathan

Chapter Seventeen

Disintegrating Boats

It was a long walk to his job interview.

He didn't know where Addie was. She hadn't been home when he'd left. He didn't know where she'd been going for the last couple of weeks. To job interviews, it seemed, but it was hardly reasonable to think there would be so many interviews without her coming home with good employment news by now.

As he walked, Jonathan couldn't stop picturing the paper boat he'd made when he was ten.

He could see that little paper boat in his head.

He had made it from newsprint. Not by folding one big piece of newsprint, because he hadn't known how to do that. He had heard of such a thing, but he had no idea how it was done. It would have been better for the project if he had known, because then he wouldn't have needed to use glue. Hindsight being twenty-twenty and all, a thing his mother used to say.

He did know that newsprint would get soaked and that it would sink, or disintegrate, or both, so he waxed the paper carefully, rubbing it with a bar of wax that his missing father had used on his hiking pants and cotton jacket for rainy days. Carefully, so as not to tear the paper. Starting all over if he made that mistake.

Then he put it together using, with the benefit of hindsight, the wrong kind of glue.

He'd taken it to the little man-made lake in the park ten blocks from home. Nobody asked him where he was going. Nobody ever did. Nobody seemed even to notice he was gone when he was gone.

He'd taken off his sneakers and socks, carefully rolled up the socks and stuffed them in the shoes, and waded out into the lake to just above his knees. Any farther and he would have gotten his shorts wet.

He set the boat down, and it just sort of . . . dissolved.

The wax on the paper seemed to hold. It wasn't as though the paper was getting soaked and dissolving. The glue just did not continue to exist. The water made it disappear, and he'd stood helplessly and watched as its pieces drifted apart, half sinking into the clear and shallow water.

He'd been thinking about that boat a lot lately.

Every time he looked at Addie for the past few weeks, in his mind he saw that little paper boat drifting apart from itself.

In a remote spot above and beyond that thought, it struck Jonathan as hard to believe that the memory was only eight years old. That eight years ago he had been ten. It seemed like half a century ago.

It felt like some kind of previous incarnation.

———

When he arrived at the Dairy Dream, there were eight people waiting out back, milling around with no place to sit, waiting for their interview for what he assumed was only one job opening.

One of them was Addie.

She was the only female in the group, and appeared to be the only one over twenty. And, being quite a bit over twenty, like three times the age of the others, she stood out from the crowd. Jonathan didn't know if she knew how much she stood out, but she looked deeply uneasy, so he figured she did.

"Hey," he said, and stood beside her.

"Jonathan, what are you doing here?"

"Applying for a job, just like you. But if you want this one, I can apply someplace else. I'll go home and you can have this one."

"No, stay," she said. "I don't know that I'll get it."

"But you have so much more life experience than all the rest of us."

As soon as he said it, he glanced around and noticed that some of the rest of the applicants were glaring at him unpleasantly. He looked back to Addie.

She snorted a harsh laugh, the way she did when she was dismissing something.

"Tell that to the last two dozen interviewers," she said. "You call it life experience. They call it old."

A woman of about forty with wildly curly dark hair stepped out the back door with a clipboard.

"Addie Finch," she said.

"I'll stay after I'm done," Addie said quietly to Jonathan. "Give you a ride home."

"That would be very nice," he said. "Thank you."

He was still having trouble breaking in his new sneakers, and he had blisters on his feet from the long walk down.

———

It was five or ten minutes later when Addie came out again, closely followed by Clipboard Lady. Addie had her eyes cast down toward the tarmac of the parking lot. Then she looked up very briefly and shook her head at him. A subtle gesture. One he was not sure anyone else even noticed. *Could* even notice.

"I don't think I got it," she said in a near whisper.

"Jared Jeter," Clipboard Lady barked out.

But a guy who was presumably Jared elbowed him in the ribs, jostling him into taking a step to rebalance himself.

"If she's your ride," Probably Jared said, "you can go next."

"That's really nice," Jonathan said. "Thank you." Then, to Clipboard Lady: "He says I can go in his spot."

"And you are?"

"Jonathan Westerbrook."

"Okay. Whatever. Follow me."

He walked behind her into the back of the Dairy Dream.

The floors were covered with thick, patterned rubber mats. Heavy-looking, and made of sections that locked together. The place smelled like fryer grease and burned sugar, and there was a lot of yelling. Not upset yelling. But everybody yelled everything. The people up front barked food orders to the people in the kitchen. The people in the kitchen barked the names of the same foods to announce that those orders were up.

The kitchen people wore silly orange uniform shirts and hairnets.

It was all more than a little bit intimidating.

She led him into a tiny, windowless office with a cluttered desk and no room for much more, including him.

There was one hard metal chair facing the desk, a space having been more or less carved for it from the stacks of boxes and files.

He sat, crossing one ankle over his knee and running his carefully scrubbed fingernails over the seam of his jeans where it trailed down his calf.

He only did that when he was deeply nervous.

"Jonathan," the woman said, and it made him jump a little.

"Yes?"

"Why do you want to work at the Dairy Dream?"

"I guess . . . to help out my grandmother. She's between jobs and I know she's worried about money. And I don't want her to worry. I want to be some help."

"You're not going to college this year?"

"I'm probably not going at all."

"Okay. Tell me about yourself."

At first, Jonathan said nothing. For a length of time that felt embarrassing, in fact, he said nothing. Embarrassing to him, at least. She might not even have noticed.

His face felt cold and possibly bloodless. He wondered if he looked too white. If he looked like a ghost to her.

Situations like this—that is to say, any situation in which he had to talk to another person, especially a grown-up stranger—made him feel exaggeratedly humble. Almost painfully so.

The only grown-up who didn't make him feel that way was Addie. When he was with Addie he felt like himself. No less and no more.

He decided to tell the truth. To be real. But it wasn't even a decision, exactly. It was just something that was about to happen, and he could feel it coming. He simply noted that life was going to play out that way.

"I got sent to live with my dad when I was sixteen," he said. "But I couldn't stay with him because of the way he was when he'd been drinking. And then I was homeless for a while. But now I've got a nice stable place to live, and I've got my life all cleaned up, and I'm ready to move on and live like an adult."

She said nothing for a beat or two, and Jonathan was filled with a deep sense of dread, assuming he had made a bad call. Guessing, after the fact, that he should not have been honest.

He watched her eyebrows knit down.

"But you have a grandmother," she said.

"Yes ma'am."

"Do you live with your grandmother?"

"Yes ma'am."

"I guess I'm just wondering why you were homeless when you had a relative who would take you in."

"Oh," he said. "Right." Then he struggled again, briefly, with the urge to tell the truth. And also with his innate fear of doing so. "I hadn't met her yet. I know that sounds strange, but . . . you see, she's not my grandmother by blood. She's more of an adopted grandmother. We adopted each other."

"She took you in off the street?"

"Yes ma'am. She did."

"She must have seen something good in you."

He sat up a little straighter when she said that, and realized it was true. Realized it had always been true, and he had always known it, at some level. He just hadn't framed it in those words.

"I hope you're right, ma'am," he said.

But mostly he only said it that way to sound properly humble. He knew she was right. That was one of the truly wonderful things about Addie. She saw something good in him.

"She sounds like a nice person. I'd like to meet someone like that."

"But you just *did* meet her," Jonathan said. "She was your last interview."

"Oh," the woman said. She flipped over a page on her clipboard. "Right. Addie Finch. That's your adopted grandma. I liked her. A lot. I don't think this is the right job for her, but I liked her. Now I like her even more."

Then they talked about the hours he'd be expected to work, and possible overtime, and she showed him the fryer, and the griddles and heat lamps for the burgers, and the big industrial fridges, and the soft-serve machines.

And after describing his duties, she told him she had to interview everybody who was waiting, but that so far she thought his chances were very good.

————

They drove toward home for a few blocks in silence.

Now and then he glanced over at the side of Addie's face and tried not to see that mental image of the boat, fading into its separate parts and sinking down into the clear, shallow water.

"Why do you think you didn't get it?" he asked after a time.

She frowned, but the look in her eyes didn't change. They continued to focus on something that was miles away, if indeed it was on this plane of existence at all.

"I could tell she wasn't all that impressed with me for the job," she said.

He thought about telling her what the interviewer had said, but no decision was final as far as he knew. He hated to bring her down without really knowing.

"Is it because you're overqualified?"

She let out one of her signature Addie Finch snorts.

"I have no qualifications," she said.

"How can you say that? What about the army and the LAPD?"

"Those are good qualifications for a security-guard job. What qualifications do I have to work at the Dairy Dream? You get to be my age, people expect you to have more going for you. They have to wonder why you don't. Besides, this is a young person's job. Supposed to be for high school kids. They don't like to hire people my age because they figure I'm going to be retiring soon enough anyway."

Her voice sounded alarmingly discouraged, as though the volume control was worn down by sheer exhaustion, and she simply didn't have the energy to project.

I have to help her, he thought. For maybe the hundredth time. *She helped me when I was at my bottom so I have to help her now.*

"How d'you figure *you* did?" she asked, knocking him out of those thoughts.

"She said I had a good chance."

"Good, good," she said. But with no improvement in energy or volume. "If you get it, you can take that bike that's in the garage. You can have it. I don't ride that bike anymore and I never will now. It'll need some work. The tires are flat, and the chain and gears probably need a good lube. Not sure how the brakes are. You'll have to put some elbow grease into it. There's a helmet hanging on the wall. I'd want you to wear the helmet, always."

"That's okay. I can do all that. It would be great to have a bike. It wouldn't be that far at all, for a bike ride."

"Well, I hope you get it," she said.

"Thanks. You'll get something."

"Will I?"

"Sure you will. Why wouldn't you?"

"This was my third interview," she said.

"In two weeks?" he asked, wondering where that meant she had been the rest of the time.

"Today," she said.

"Oh."

He should have known, he realized. She'd made a reference to two dozen interviewers. It struck him as an awful lot of times to feel rejected.

They didn't talk any more for the rest of the drive home.

———

About an hour after dinner, which Jonathan had made and brought to Addie in bed, the landline rang.

"Should I get that?" he called in to her.

"I guess," she called back. "Why not?"

He answered the phone with "Finch residence."

It was the woman from the Dairy Dream, telling him he could start at eleven o'clock the following morning, and that she would provide him with two aprons and two uniform shirts but that he would be responsible for keeping them laundered. And that he would be given a time card. And she said to come at least twenty minutes early, because there would be paperwork to fill out.

She asked if he had any questions, but he was having trouble thinking, and told her he didn't figure he did, though he allowed that in the morning he might.

He thanked her, and that was pretty much all there was to the call.

He walked to Addie's bedroom doorway, which was open.

She was lying on her back on top of the covers, fully clothed. Staring out the window the way she'd stared through the windshield on the drive home. As if gazing at something in a different dimension or universe.

He rapped lightly on the doorframe, and she grunted an acknowledgment of him.

"I got that job," he said.

"Good."

"Is this something you can talk to me about?" he asked, and it felt brave to say that out loud.

"Is what something I can talk to you about?"

"Whatever I'm watching you go through right now."

For a brief moment she turned her gaze to him. Drilled it right into his eyes and beyond. It was mildly alarming, and he vaguely wished she would stare out the window again. Which, a few seconds later, she did.

"I don't want to put all that on you," she said.

"I honestly wish you felt like you could."

She sighed deeply.

"I just couldn't live the way I was living, hon. Trying to protect everybody from everything."

"Right," he said. "I think I knew that."

"But then there's the other side of the thing. On the other hand it's who I was. It's who I've been my whole damn life." She waited, as if he might get there on his own. But he wasn't quite sure where she was heading. "So who am I now?"

It made his heart feel like it was falling. Getting heavier. Sinking too low into his gut. Because he wanted it to be something he could help with. Not that he was sure what kind of thing that would have been. Maybe if she'd said she was lonely. Or needed more encouragement.

Now he felt he should have known it would be something harder than that.

"I don't know," he said. "But I bet you'll find out."

"I sure hope so."

He waited to see if she would say more. She never did.

He stood a moment longer, thinking about the pieces of that waxed-paper boat. Seeing them behind his eyes, lying in the silt at the bottom of the lake.

And for about the hundred-and-first time, approximately speaking, he knew he had to put her back together. He owed her that much and more.

What he didn't know was how.

Chapter Eighteen

How It Feels to Be a Good Idea

It was after his ninth day of work when Jonathan parked the bike in the garage, hung up the helmet, and walked through the mudroom into the kitchen to see Addie talking to someone on the landline.

"I suppose you're right," he heard her say. "I guess it's just hard to find the energy to do all that."

He walked to the fridge and poured himself a glass of milk.

The plan was to take it into the living room, rather than sitting at the kitchen table to drink it. To give her privacy for her phone call.

But before he could even put the carton away in the fridge he heard her say, "Thanks for calling, hon, but I gotta go. Jonathan is home from work."

She hung up the receiver and looked into his face, and he sank down into one of the kitchen chairs and set his milk glass on the table.

"My brother, Bill," she said.

"Oh. I didn't know you had a brother. Any other brothers or sisters?"

"Nope. Just Bill. You?"

"No, I was an only child."

"That was probably why you liked having Jeannie around. She was like the sister you never had."

"Think so? Well, yeah. I guess. That makes sense. Weird that we don't know stuff like that about each other."

"Why is it weird?"

"I don't know. Just . . . people talk to each other about stuff like that. Don't they? I guess I wonder sometimes why we don't. But anyway. Even if I didn't know there was a Bill. At least Bill knew there was a me."

A pause fell, and Jonathan was hoping she would come back with some kind of reasonably detailed analysis of where they had gone wrong, with maybe a plan to do better.

Instead she only said, "I'll be up in my room."

He waited several minutes after she had gone. Until a minute or two after he heard her bedroom door close upstairs.

He was nursing a wild idea of something he might do, but it felt radical and strange, and he wasn't sure if he had the nerve to follow through. He wasn't even sure if following through was the right thing to consider.

And, oddly, he never exactly decided, either. The whole thing made his head feel a little swimmy, and he simply felt himself moving across the kitchen the way it all might feel in a dream.

He picked up the phone to see if it had a "*69" feature.

He hit the buttons, and immediately heard it ringing.

He felt it as a jolt to his belly, and his brain tingled and went numb. He almost hung up the phone. But before he could even send a proper signal to his hand, a man answered the phone.

"Addie?" it said.

He must have had caller ID.

"No."

That just sat for a moment.

"It's Jonathan," he added. "And I have no idea if it's okay to call, and maybe it's not and if it's not I'm sorry. I'm just worried about Addie, and I don't know who to talk to about it. I didn't know she had a brother until just now. She has a sponsor but I don't know her number or anything."

Another long pause.

Jonathan looked out the window as he waited. He could see little blossoms on his green bean vines, and it was the first time he had seen them. They must have burst out while he was serving fast food all day.

"Tell me why you're worried about her," Bill said, knocking his brain back into the moment. Into the problem.

"You're not?"

"Well, I don't know, son. I'm not sure what to say about that. She's been struggling for a long time. Maybe always."

"She didn't sound really down to you just now?"

"I guess . . ." Then Bill stalled, as if to think it all out before going on record. "I guess I mostly chalked it up to her being tired. I think it's hard on her, working the night shift. I kind of thought her system would have adjusted to the hours by now, but who am I to say how long that would take? I think maybe it's harder when we get older."

Jonathan stood staring at the garden through the window for what might have been a full minute, feeling an odd tingling around the tops of his ears. *See, this is why you shouldn't have called,* his brain said to him. *Now you have to decide if you're going to tell him something she obviously didn't want him to know.*

"You're not saying anything," Bill said.

Jonathan realized he had to decide. He had to do this or not do it, and the time was pretty much now. He asked himself a simple question in the silence of his head.

Do you think she's really in trouble, like the kind of trouble a person needs help to get through?

"I guess she didn't tell you she quit that job," he heard himself say.

"Wait. Her security-guard job? At the self-storage place? She quit that? No, she didn't tell me. How long ago?"

"Almost a month."

"How are you guys eating?"

"I got a job at the Dairy Dream. It's not much, but I think I can pay the water and electric and put food on the table. Better than we could without it, anyway. She says when the property taxes come due that's going to be a whole other ball game, but I think that's not for a while. I wonder why she didn't tell you."

"She doesn't like to worry me. And I think she still tries to put her best foot forward with me, even though I really wish she wouldn't. Do you know why she quit?"

"There was an incident," Jonathan said. "I don't want to say much more than that about it, because it should be hers to tell, not mine. But it just made her reexamine everything. Her whole life up until now. Something about not being able to defend everybody from everything all the time anymore."

The pause that followed felt dark and heavy to Jonathan, but he could not have explained why or how.

"Which is my fault," Bill said, after that weighty pause.

"How is it your fault?"

"Never mind. Just please tell me how worried I should be."

"That's a hard question. I'm pretty worried. I feel like she's having some kind of breakdown. But then I think, 'What if I'm wrong?' I ask myself that a lot. Like calling you just now. Was I wrong to call you?"

"I think I'm glad you did," Bill said. "I have to think what I want to do. I have to think about this. Do you have your own phone so I can call you back and tell you what I decide?"

"No, I don't have a phone. There's just this landline. But she's a lot more likely to hear it ring than I am, and even if I was here to get it, she'd probably be standing right next to me."

"Got it. Then I can't keep you posted. But anyway, thanks for calling. It's nice to know somebody out there is looking after my baby sister for a change."

After he hung up the phone, the gravity of what he had done hit him. She might be angry. She might even put him out again.

It was awful to think about, but not nearly as awful as the possibility that something bad could happen to Addie and he would always know that he could have done something, but that out of fear and indecision he'd let the chance go by.

———

It was only two days after that when he came home from work and found Addie sitting at the kitchen table with a man he'd never seen before. They were both drinking tea, their heads leaned fairly close together.

Oddly, Jonathan didn't make the connection, though in retrospect it was right there to be seen.

The man was about Addie's age, or maybe a little older. He had a shock of wild white hair and a full white beard. Like Santa Claus, except he was tall and solidly built but fairly trim.

They both looked up at him as he came through the back door.

"Jonathan," Addie said. "This is my brother, Bill."

Jonathan walked quickly to the table with his right hand outstretched, and Bill shook it. Meanwhile he kept an eye on Addie in his peripheral vision, and she did not look mad. Maybe calling Bill had been an okay thing to do. Something she could understand and appreciate. Or maybe he hadn't told her.

"You came for a visit," he said. "That's so nice."

"I wanted to check on my baby sister," the older man said. "I was worried about her."

"Oh. Okay. Is there a reason you were worried about her?" he asked, desperately feeling around for what she knew. "Don't get me wrong. I've been a little worried about her too. I just wondered if there was any specific thing that made you come all this way."

Bill leveled a very direct gaze at him, and held Jonathan's eyes as he spoke.

"When you know someone the way I know my baby sister," he said, "you can just tell. You can hear a lot in her voice. Or even in the silence in between sentences."

Jonathan wanted to say thank you a hundred times over, but that would have defeated the purpose of the moment. Instead he just said it as best he could with his eyes.

"I'll make us some dinner," he said.

"But haven't you been working all day?" Bill asked. "Why don't you let me go get some takeout instead?"

"I really don't mind. You two should just go on talking. Pretend I'm not even here. I like cooking. It relaxes me at the end of the day."

"If you'd ever tasted Jonathan's cooking," Addie said, "you wouldn't argue with the boy."

———

Jonathan was sitting out on the back steps—the concrete steps from the mudroom down to the back garden—between sunset and dark.

A moon just a few days before or after full was rising in the east, and such a small sliver of it was visible over the ivy-covered board fence that it took him a minute to realize it was the moon.

He was staring at his vegetable garden in the fading light of dusk and willing it to grow faster. Pressing it with his mind. Picturing himself picking corn and tomatoes and bringing them in for dinner. He did that a lot. He didn't believe it would make any difference in their growth. He wasn't deluded. It was just a thing he liked to do.

He heard and felt someone step out behind him. He figured it was Addie. But as the figure settled onto the step beside him, he realized it was Addie's brother, Bill.

"Hey," Bill said.

It was a soft acknowledgment, a greeting of the sort you offer someone familiar. Jonathan liked that, having so few people who took him into their circles.

"Hey," he said back, in the same tone.

They sat in silence, watching the moon rise for a time.

Then Jonathan said, "Is she okay, do you think?"

Bill sighed.

"I think she's going through what we used to call a 'dark night of the soul.'"

"Is that pretty much like being depressed?"

"Well," Bill said, "there's an overlap. If nothing more. I think her past is catching up with her and I think this time she has to meet it head-on and make some sense out of it, and I expect then she'll be okay. Might not be a speedy process, though."

Jonathan wanted to ask what would happen if she *didn't* meet it head-on and make some sense out of it. He also wanted to ask if she had told him about Skate.

He asked nothing at all. Just watched the moon clear the fence and gradually slip behind a few stray branches of the peach tree.

"This place looks amazing," Bill said. "I've never seen it look this good."

"How long have you known the place?"

"I was born here. I grew up in this house."

"Oh," Jonathan said. "Right. Duh." Then, when Bill did not immediately respond, Jonathan asked, "Is it weird to come back to a place that has so much history for you?"

"You have no idea."

"Is this really better than it *ever* looked? What about when your family lived here? What about when Addie had a gardener?"

"Our dad worked two jobs and our mom wanted no part of the upkeep of such a big property. She was against buying it. And Addie only ever paid a gardener for four or five hours a week. That's not really that much."

"I probably work four times that."

"It shows."

They fell into another long silence.

Then Bill said, "I'm going to do something potentially weird, and it might be a bad idea. But you had the guts to try something radical, so I'm going to go off your lead. I'm going to call Spencer, and I'd like to put you on the phone and have you talk to him. Tell him what you told me."

He slipped his cell phone out of his pocket and opened the phone app, then contacts. Meanwhile Jonathan wondered if he should ask the obvious question.

He decided, since he was about to be put on the phone with the person in question, he'd better ask.

"Who's Spencer?"

That seemed to surprise Bill, who let the phone in his hands sag down closer to the steps.

"Spencer," he said again. "Her son."

"Oh. I knew she had a son but I didn't know his name."

"Wow," Bill said. "She really has been compartmentalizing information, hasn't she?"

"I guess. Then she was married once?"

"No. She was never married. It was something that happened in the army. A guy who was a long way above her in rank, so it never should have happened. It's not like they were ever really together."

Jonathan felt a tingling at the back of his neck. It was the way he felt when he woke up and it took him a minute to remember that Skate could not possibly be skulking around.

"But it was, like . . . consensual, right?"

"Consensual has layers to it. Especially when the power dynamics are way out of balance. I know she regretted it, and that she was uneasy about it. She told me once that it never would have happened that way if the guy hadn't been who he was."

"Got it," he said.

Actually there was more he wanted to know, but it might not have been any of his business, and he should definitely hear it from Addie if he was going to hear it at all.

"Why is it weird to call Spencer?" he asked instead.

"It's not. Really. I call him fairly often. It's weird to call him about his mom. They haven't spoken in a really long time. He's the one who forced an estrangement. Not Addie. I know Addie would love to talk to him if she thought he'd have any part of it. But he's been stubborn on the subject for a couple of decades now."

And I'm the one who's supposed to talk him out of that stubbornness, Jonathan thought. *When his own mother couldn't.*

Meanwhile Bill was making the call. Jonathan could hear it ringing.

"Spence," Bill said, his voice booming and jovial. "How are you, buddy?"

A brief silence.

Then Bill said, "Good, good. Listen. I know this is not your favorite subject, but I want to talk to you a little bit about your mom. She's going through a rough patch."

Another brief pause. Jonathan strained to hear anything from the other end of the conversation, but it was just too distant and faint.

"I know, I know, buddy. But it just feels different this time. And she's not drinking. It's not about that at all. It's almost the opposite, if that makes any sense. It's more like she's really pitching into this recovery thing, and it's bringing up changes. And some really basic things about her seem to be breaking apart on their own. I don't know if they're the same things you couldn't handle about her, but it's sure a possibility. Anyway, I wanted to put you on the line with Jonathan, that young man I was telling you about, because he's been here with her during all this, and—"

And with that, Bill seemed to lose control of the conversation.

Jonathan could hear the faint buzz of the voice that had cut him off midsentence, but he couldn't make out words, much as he truly longed to hear them.

Bill held up one finger to ask Jonathan to wait.

Then he stood up and took the call into the house.

Jonathan sat in the moonlight and listened to something that might have been crickets and watched the stars come out. Just a few. The brightest of them, the ones that could stand up to the nearly daytime brightness of the moon.

When Bill returned, he was no longer on the phone. He didn't even seem to have the phone in his hand anymore. He sank down onto the step beside Jonathan with a deep sigh.

"I was being overly optimistic," he said. "I'm not sure why I thought I could get him to talk to you."

"You think he'll talk to Addie?"

"Probably not."

They sat for several minutes more in a comfortable silence. Well . . . uncomfortable in that something had happened to make them both uncomfortable. But comfortable in the fact that neither seemed to view the silence as a problem that needed fixing.

What might have been five minutes later Bill sighed again, and rose to his feet.

"I'm going to go have another talk with my baby sister, and then I think I'll call it a night."

"Good night," Jonathan said.

"Night, buddy."

He disappeared into the house, leaving Jonathan to nurse a warm spot in his gut. A spot that enjoyed the rare feeling of being someone's buddy.

A minute later Bill stuck his head back outside.

"I'm not sure if this is something I should tell you or not," he said.

Jonathan wasn't sure how to respond to that. He didn't know what the thing was, and couldn't imagine that he would know better than Bill regarding what should and should not be said.

"I guess . . . ," he began, feeling and sounding tentative, "try it?"

"Okay. Okay, then. Here goes. When Addie first told me she had taken you in off the street, I didn't think that was a very good idea. I thought she was showing poor judgment, in fact. I didn't say it, but I thought it, and I worried about it. But now that I've met you I can see that she was right and I was wrong. You were a good idea."

Jonathan felt that spot in his gut grow warm again. This time it buzzed with all that warmth.

"That's a good thing to say. Why wouldn't it be?"

"I don't know. I guess it felt a little like telling someone they look good now. You know. After making some big change. Kind of sounds like you're saying they looked bad before, if you know what I mean. Like a backhanded compliment."

"But you didn't know me before. The bad-idea thing was just a guess."

"Exactly," Bill said. "Glad you get it, buddy."

He patted Jonathan once on the shoulder and disappeared back into the house, leaving Jonathan alone yet buzzing and warm.

Seven

Addie

Chapter Nineteen

The Next Indicated Thing

Addie sat back against the pillows on her big bed and looked into her brother's face. She had been doing so at intervals, mostly when he was looking away.

Bill had planted himself on a chair near her bed, and they both mostly stared out the window at the brilliant moon. It propelled a shaft of brightness into the room and made it easy to see the details of her brother's expression, even though she had turned on no lights as daytime faded.

"From what you just told me," Bill said, "it sounds like that big, mean boy deserved all of what he got and then some."

"Maybe. But I'm not sure anybody deserves to die young."

"You didn't kill him, though."

"It was a whole chain of events," she said. "Like those dominoes we used to stack up when we were kids."

They watched the moon for a time in silence.

Then Bill said, "Is that what's behind this . . . I don't even know how to say what 'this' is. This breakdown of some sort, I suppose, if it's okay to call it that. This dark night of the soul you're going through. Is this about the boy who died?"

"It is and it isn't," she said. "That threw me. I won't lie. But it's more about my whole life. Like my life up till now was a keg of dynamite and that boy was the fuse. Or maybe the match that lit the fuse. Anyway, I can't go on being the person I've been, so I'm not sure where that leaves me. I mean . . . if I'm not me, who am I?"

"I think you're still you," he said. "In fact, I'm sure of it. You're who you always were, Addie, because what choice have you even got? You couldn't change that if you tried. I think what you're losing is the person you mistakenly thought you were."

"That still leaves me to wonder who I am now."

"You'll figure it out. You're a good person. You've always been a good person."

"I know some who'd disagree."

"They haven't known you as long as I have."

Addie sat a minute and absorbed that. And tried to let it be enough. But it wasn't enough. It felt good to hear, but it wasn't enough.

"One thing keeps bothering me, though, Bill. I mean *really* bothering me. I can hardly get any sleep and get by and live any kind of decent life. All my life I've lived like we shouldn't be hurting each other. Like I had to stop people from hurting other people. And then I went and hurt that boy. And now I wonder . . . and I want you to tell me the truth about this. You're my brother and I trust you, and no matter how much I'll hate it I just have to know the truth. Did I turn out to be just like him?"

"Him?"

"You know."

"That boy?"

"No. You know if you think about it."

"*Dad?* Addie, no. No way. Not for a minute. Not a chance in hell. How can you even ask me that?"

"I went over there and shot that boy."

"You went over there to try to stop him from hurting people. Dad hurt people because he was mean. Because it eased something in him that was eating him alive. He hurt me because he wanted to. You know that. His own pain was all he cared about. He didn't care how much pain he caused for anybody else. I don't know details about the inside of him and I don't want to know, but he obviously liked the way it made him feel. You don't have a mean bone in your body. The very fact that you asked the question is enough to give you your answer right there. You think Dad would ever ask anybody if he was right or wrong to do what he did?"

"You sure?"

"I've never been more sure of anything in my life, Addie. You're like the polar opposite of him."

"Good," Addie said. And pulled a big, deep breath. Let it out again slowly. "Good, because that's the one thing I won't brook. I can't live with that, Bill. Never. I'd rather leave this earth right now than find myself in his shoes. But if I know it's not that, I'm gonna figure I can get through the rest of this, even though it really, really doesn't feel that way now."

———

When he had left to make himself comfortable in his old room for the night, Addie called Wendy, who picked up on the second ring.

"You okay?" Wendy asked in place of hello.

"Depends on your definition of the word. Too late for a visit?"

"You mean an in-person visit?"

"That's what I was thinking," Addie said. "Yeah."

"As long as you're willing to get yourself over *here*. I won't be doing any house calls tonight."

"Oh." Addie nursed a sense of disappointment for a few seconds before saying more. She had really hoped not to have to get herself together to go out. "You don't like to drive at night?"

"I'm fine driving at night. My vision is great."

"Too much gas money?"

"I do okay with my retirement funds."

"Oh."

That left Addie wondering if she should ask more questions. Before she could, Wendy settled things for her.

"Look. Addie. If you were sick, I'd be there in a heartbeat. If you were injured, same deal. If the thing that makes you not want to drive over here was physical, I'd make the drive. You know I would. But you've just got yourself in a rut now, where it feels like too much to leave the house. Where it just feels like more than you can manage somehow. And when a person gets into a thing like that, it tends to spiral. The more you don't want to go out, the more you don't want to go out. I'm happy to do a little sponsor time with you, but you have to get up and get your butt over here. If you feel like you just can't, then we can talk on the phone. But if you want to see me in person, get up, put on some clothes and shoes, and grab your car keys. And look. Honey. I'm not judging you. I've been there, and I know it's a very real thing. I also know the only way to get out of it is to get out of it. You can waste your whole damn life sitting in your room waiting to feel like you can do better. But the actions change the feelings, not the other way around. You get my drift?"

"Yeah. I do."

"I understand the problem, but I don't plan to make a contribution to it. That's where I'm coming from."

Addie sighed, but as silently as possible.

"Yeah," she said. "I get it. Give me half an hour."

———

Addie sat on the couch, a few feet away from her sponsor, wondering where to begin. Wondering if there was even a door into all of this, or a way to wrap words around it.

Before she could open her mouth to speak, Wendy's little dog stepped off her owner's lap, walked across the couch cushions, and approached Addie directly. He looked up into her face with big, dark eyes that seemed full of deep questions. Then he stepped up onto Addie's lap, circled three times, and settled in a little ball.

"Well, you should consider yourself complimented," Wendy said, "because he won't do that for just anybody. Maybe two or three in a hundred. He tends to be drawn to people he thinks are in pain, but he still has to trust you first."

Addie opened her mouth to speak, but the words didn't happen.

Instead she looked down at the dog and burst into tears.

As she sobbed, she tried to remember any other time in her adult life when she had burst into tears, but there was nothing to remember. She couldn't even remember crying much as a medium-size child. And she hated to cry in front of anybody, but that made no difference, because there was no stopping it. It was out, and there was no way she was stuffing it back in again. That much was evident.

In fact, she was suddenly perplexed as to how so much emotion had ever fit into the limited space that was her.

She ran her hand down the tiny dog's wirehaired back, and he peered up into her face with what looked like a sense of worry for her.

Wendy rose and left the room.

Addie spent a minute trying to make sense of her sponsor's disappearance. Should she read some kind of judgment into that? Was Wendy even coming back?

A minute later Wendy reappeared with a box of tissues, which she set close to Addie on the couch. She settled a little closer than she had been sitting before, with one carefully manicured hand on Addie's shoulder.

"Thank you," Addie said.

The two words could barely be understood due to the sobbing.

"When you get to where you can breathe again," Wendy said, "talk to me."

Wendy's big dog came close and sat at Addie's feet, his big drooly chin resting on her knee. And with that, Addie gave up on getting anything under control, and just let go and cried it out.

———

"What if I don't even know who I am after this?" she asked her sponsor some fifteen or twenty minutes later. "What if I don't even know myself?"

"You should be so lucky," Wendy said. "We should all be so lucky that we change so much and so fast that we turn into a stranger. Doesn't work like that, hon. We're always who we are, maybe even more so than we were hoping. Most of the things that bother us about ourselves don't really go away. They get a little better, a little bit at a time. Maybe we have the same voices in our heads but we just don't listen to them as much. Instead of doing what they say, we learn to tell them 'Thank you for sharing, now please shut up and go sit in the corner because I'm trying to have a life here.' Our first thought on everything pretty much stays the same, but our second thought gets better with time. And our first action gets better. We're made up of all the same problems, but we just don't act them out the same way we used to. We see them for what they are and stop putting so much faith in them."

"I literally don't know what to do next, Wendy. I don't know where to go from here and I don't know how to get there."

"Listen to me and listen good, Addie. If ever in your life you're going to take in what your sponsor says, let this be the time. What you need to do next is simple. I'm not saying it's going to feel easy, but it's just as simple as can be. Get up and walk forward into your life. Do the next indicated thing. Do you need to brush your teeth? Do that. When did you last shower? Take a shower. Hungry? Feed yourself. Short on money? Go out looking for a job."

"I've been doing nothing but looking for a job for weeks now," Addie said, one hand on each of the dogs, stroking.

"And have you got one yet?"

"No."

"Then you'll have to do it for a while longer, won't you? But look. I'm not done with the important thing I have to tell you, Addie. I've barely just started. Here goes. You're doing it backward, hon. You're doing everything ass-backward. Lying in bed trying to figure out what kind of life to have so you can get up and have it. It doesn't work that way. Never did, never will. You want to know what life has in store for you? Then get up and start living it and you'll find out. You can't figure it out in your head first. Put one foot in front of the other. Take a step with your left foot. Then one with your right foot. Repeat as necessary. More will be revealed. Nobody ever got anywhere lying in bed waiting to feel ready to start something hard, because you never will feel ready. The longer you put it off, the less you'll feel ready. Once you're out there doing it, the ready will kick in after the fact. You with me on that?"

Addie took a deep breath and sighed it out.

"I hear you," she said. "I just feel so tired."

"I know you do. And I'm not without empathy for your situation. It feels hard. I get that. I'm not telling you not to feel how you feel, and I'm not telling you to just get over all this. But it's still simple. One foot in front of the other. It's the only way. Like we say in the program, the only way out is through. Or like my old sponsor used to say to me, 'If you're going through hell, keep going.' She swears Winston Churchill said that, but I heard it wasn't really him, and anyway, I'll always think of it as her old saying. Funny how people will find themselves in the worst pit of their lives, the most miserable place they could possibly be, and what do they do? They stop. They just sit where they are, which is just where they don't want to be. Don't do that, honey. Keep moving till you're someplace better. It's like I was saying about getting up the nerve to leave the house. You don't think your way into right acting. You act your way into right thinking."

They sat in silence for a time.

"Much as I hate to admit it," Addie said, "it makes sense."

"Yeah, nobody likes it when their sponsor is right."

"I think I'm going to go home and get a good night's sleep."

"I think that's a good idea," Wendy said. "In fact, I'd almost go as far as to say that's the next indicated thing."

———

When Addie turned into her own driveway, her headlights swept across her front porch and she saw Jonathan sitting there on the steps. Was he waiting for her? It seemed like a reasonable assumption, since he was more likely to sit in the private, sheltered backyard if his goal was simply to be outside.

She parked in the driveway and stepped out.

"What're you doing out here?" she called to him as she picked her way across the lawn in the near-darkness, moving slowly to give her eyes time to adjust.

"I wanted to talk to you," he called back.

"Yeah," she said, close enough now not to have to raise her voice. "I guess I saw that coming. Is this something bad?"

Addie hated even to ask, because she felt like one more bad thing would be too much. It might be the breaking point. A figurative spine can only have just so much heaped onto it before something gives.

She flashed back to the night she'd met Jonathan. To the idea that Karma would reward her with some kind of nice something in return for her kindness to him. And yet things just kept getting worse.

"I don't know if you'll think it's good news or bad news," Jonathan said.

Addie sank down onto the porch step beside him, listening to the air flow out of her in a sigh.

"Go ahead and hit me with it," she said, "and then we'll see."

"While you were gone just now, Jeannie came back."

"Oh," Addie said.

She sat a minute, nursing the sense of dread lifting away. It might not have felt cleanly in the category of good news, but it hadn't hurt to hear it. It wasn't anything that matched her deep negative anticipation.

"Is that okay?" Jonathan asked.

"Yeah. I guess. I said she could come back here if she wanted to get clean again."

"That's what she told me, yeah."

"And is she clean?"

"She says she is. She seems to be."

"Where is she now?"

"In the garden shed. Is that okay that I let her settle in there?"

"Yeah. It's fine. I'll go talk to her in the morning. Right now I've just had it. She can come into the house to eat if I'm home, but when I'm gone I don't want her in the house. Not till I know better how this is going to go. You'll have to bring food out to her if I'm not home. She can go into the mudroom and that bathroom, of course."

"Thanks. I'm glad you're okay with it. I was nervous you might mind."

Addie wanted to answer that, but she just couldn't find the energy.

Instead she reached over and tousled the top of his wild hair. It was the first physical contact of any kind between them, and she hadn't known she was about to do it, and she didn't know what had changed. She just knew she was very tired.

As she got to her feet and let herself into the house, it occurred to Addie that the things a person does when they're worn down to a nub were probably nothing foreign to their nature. Likely just the opposite, in fact. They were probably more the real nature of the person than anything that had come before.

She walked up the stairs, changed into her pajamas, and put herself straight to bed. But tired as she was, her eyes remained wide open and she didn't feel the least bit sleepy.

She threw back the covers and rose, crossing to the window.

Jonathan was talking to Jeannie at the open door of the little shed. She could see him fairly well in the light from the bare electric bulb inside.

She sighed, pulled on her worn robe, and made her way downstairs.

When she stepped out into the backyard, the door to the shed was closed, and Jonathan seemed to have gone back inside.

Addie walked along the carefully manicured path and rapped on the door.

When Jeannie opened it, she seemed surprised. She must have assumed it was Jonathan coming back.

"Change your mind about letting me stay?" the girl asked.

She had the hood up on her sweatshirt, which was filthy, and one side of her face was scraped and bruised. Addie made a quick choice to leave that whole topic alone.

"No. I just had a couple of things I wanted to say."

"Okay," Jeannie said, seeming wary and yet resigned at the same time. "Go ahead and say them."

"Some people believe in reincarnation. I'm not sure if I do. I guess mostly I don't, but I'll allow for the fact that I don't know everything. Simple truth is, until we die, it seems kind of arrogant to think we know. Obviously we don't know."

"I don't see what—" the girl began.

Addie did not let her finish.

"Give me a minute to make my point. Let's just say, for the sake of this conversation, this is your one life. The only life you'll ever have. Because it very well could be. One precious life, and every night you spend out on the street, hanging out with strangers because they have drugs, could be the end of that life. Because of the strangers or because of the drugs, but it can't come as news to you that this is not a safe activity. And look, I'm purposely not going to let you get a word in edgewise here, because I know what you're going to say. You're going to tell me your life is not precious at all, and you don't even know if it's worth keeping, and you don't care. But that's only how you feel now.

Twenty, thirty, forty years down the road your life might mean a lot to you. There might be a lot you'll want to do with it. But even one wrong decision now and you'll never get there. You'll never get to find out how it feels to have a life and want to keep it. What a waste that would be."

Jeannie shifted uncomfortably from one foot to the other.

"Well, I'm here," she said. "Right? But anyway, I'd be dead, so I'd never know what it was I wasted, and I wouldn't be able to care."

"But it's not only about you," Addie said. "Every time you go back out there you break hearts."

Jeannie snorted a sarcastic-sounding laugh.

"Nobody's heart is breaking over me."

"That's what *you* think, girl."

For a couple of beats, Jeannie said nothing at all. Addie couldn't read her face, because the only light on the scene was coming from behind the girl's head.

"Does Jonathan really care that much?" Jeannie asked after a time.

"I was referring to both of us," Addie said.

In the longish silence that followed, it was hard for Addie to know which of them was more surprised.

"I'll try harder," Jeannie said. "I'll go to more meetings. I'll get a sponsor."

"Good," Addie said.

Then she turned around, walked back into the house, and put herself to bed.

Maybe because she'd said what she needed to say, this time she slept.

Chapter Twenty

Karma, the Everyday Version

When Addie woke in the morning, Jonathan seemed to have left early. His bike and helmet were gone from the little covered porch outside the mudroom door.

Bill was apparently still asleep.

As she was crossing to the fridge, Addie spotted the note in the middle of her kitchen table. It froze her blood to see it. Somehow it had the ring of something bad to it, like a phone call in the middle of the night, but she could not have said why. Maybe she was simply not in a place in her life to anticipate anything but more problems.

It was written on the back of a flyer for somebody who cleaned storm gutters, and it had a business card paper-clipped to one of its upper corners.

"Addie," it said. "Would you be into a security-guard job if it was in a nice office building during the day and you didn't have to carry a gun or anything? If so, call this lady and see if you can get an appointment for an interview."

The note was not signed.

It didn't look like Bill's handwriting, but then she hadn't seen him write anything down for decades, and penmanship can change as people get older. And she had never seen Jonathan's handwriting.

And why would either one of them know of an opening in an office-building security team anyway?

Maybe somebody had left it stuck in the door, and Jonathan or her brother had brought it in? But who would that have been? Who else even knew what she was looking for?

She carried the business card over to her landline phone and dialed the number.

"Marty Greene," an efficient-sounding middle-aged woman's voice said.

And that was the name on the card, though she hadn't assumed it would be a woman.

"My name is Addie Finch," Addie said, noticing that her voice was shaking. Hoping Marty Greene did not notice. "I'm calling about that opening for a security guard."

"Can you come in this morning? I have meetings all afternoon, and it's Friday."

Addie glanced at the address on the card. Downtown. About a twenty-five-minute drive if traffic wasn't too horrible. Then again, when wasn't traffic horrible?

"It'll take me an hour to get dressed and make the drive, but yeah. Anytime after that."

"Okay. See you in an hour, Addie Finch. If it's more like an hour and a half, that's okay too."

Addie left a note for Bill, explaining that an opportunity had presented itself that might be too good to miss.

Then she jumped into the shower.

————

Marty Greene was a few years younger than Addie, but not young enough to be intimidating. She was a big, tall woman with a stocky build and short jet-black hair. She simply dripped professionalism.

Addie had no sooner sat down in front of this woman's desk than she was overcome with the idea that the job was too good. Too good for Addie, too good to be true. She found herself seized with a sense that she simply was not good enough or classy enough to rise to this occasion.

Marty spent a minute or two reading over Addie's application, her half glasses resting low on the prominent bridge of her nose.

Addie looked past her and out the window, and was bowled away by the skyline of downtown LA. It all looked so bright and clean compared to the darkness and squalor she had learned to accept.

"It's a good résumé," Marty said after a time.

"Thank you," Addie said.

"Why did you leave your last job?"

And here's where it all falls down, Addie thought.

She couldn't tell her about Skate. Or about how she'd plucked two homeless kids off the street, and how their treatment in the warehouse had started to feel personal. And it wouldn't do to complain about jobs that required Addie to carry a gun, since that one technically hadn't.

The truth was that she'd left as a result of some sort of personal mental breakdown, but that obviously was not the right answer.

"Owing to my military background," she said, "and my time on the force, I tend to be pretty good at accepting risk, but that gig was over the line even for me. Graveyard shift, not another soul around, and my job was to guard the place against an old abandoned warehouse full of homeless people. Not that I have anything against homeless people, and I don't just assume they mean trouble. But there was a lot of drug activity over there. A lot of assaults. I'm not too old to be a good worker, but I'm too old to think I'm immortal like we do when we're young."

Marty smiled with one corner of her mouth, and seemed pretty satisfied with the answer.

"This job would be nothing like that," she said. "There's a button to push if you need to call armed building security, but let me tell you, those guys have the easiest job in the world, because they almost never get called. Mostly you'd be running a sign-in sheet. Making sure that everyone who comes into the building has a work badge or an appointment. If they have an appointment you'd need to issue a visitor's pass and get it back when they leave. I'm afraid it might be too far to the other extreme for you. You might find it all quite boring."

That was the moment Addie consciously knew how badly she wanted this job, and it was a deeply uncomfortable feeling, because she didn't expect she would get it.

"I would love nothing more than a boring job," Addie said. "What I used to call boring, now I think of it as comfortable and serene. It's like a dream of mine to be bored. I haven't had enough of that in my life."

Marty Greene smiled that crooked smile again.

"I hear you," she said. "Tell me why you left the LAPD a few years before your pension would have kicked in."

Addie briefly scanned her options. Likely they would check references before hiring, so her only viable option seemed like the truth.

"Okay," she said. "I'm just going to be really honest here. I was having trouble with alcohol. With my drinking. But I'm not anymore. At all. And you can count on that. I haven't had even so much as a sip of alcohol in more than eight years."

Marty Greene's eyes came up to meet hers and held them for a few beats. She seemed more interested in Addie suddenly, as if she'd just been jolted awake.

"Are you a friend of Bill W.'s?" she asked.

It was a little bit of code. Bill W. was Bill Wilson, the cofounder of AA, and the question was traditionally phrased the way it was to protect the anonymity of potential program members. Thing was, Addie would have been surprised if anybody but a program member knew that coded question.

"I absolutely am," she said.

"As am I," Marty Greene said. She pointed to her own chest and added, "Seventeen years here."

It was as though someone had suddenly turned on more light in the room. Or, in any case, Addie felt it that way.

"That's great!" she said, which actually understated how great she thought it was.

"Great that I have seventeen years sober, or great that an honest answer worked in your favor in this case?"

"Yes," Addie said. "Both of the above."

Marty Greene smiled in a way that made her seem comfortable with the direction of things.

"Tell me your greatest strengths," she said.

"Okay. I take responsibility very seriously. Probably too seriously for my own good, but that works out great for my employer. I manage my own time well, so I'll never be late. I don't have issues with authority, and if something goes wrong I'll be honest. I won't cover my tracks and try to put it off on somebody else."

"Sounds good. Now tell me your greatest weaknesses."

"Oh. Okay. Well. Let's see. I guess there are a few. I fall into thinking I have to protect everybody and everything that's good, and that's more than one person can do. I think that's the thing I wrestle with most, but I also think it's fair to say I'm just starting to turn the corner on that. I'm not a big people person. I'm a loner and super introverted, so I don't let people get in too close. But I don't see that hurting my employer any. I know how to be polite to people and treat them right, I just don't want them sitting on my couch every night or knowing my innermost thoughts. Most of them, anyway," she added, thinking suddenly of Jonathan. "And I worry too much. Which is bad for my nerves, but I can't imagine you'd prefer it if I worried too little. Oh, and I can get pretty vocal with other drivers in traffic, but there's no driving required for this job, right?"

"Wow. You really *are* honest."

"I try to be, ma'am, yes."

"If I choose you for the job, when could you start?"

"When you tell me to show up, I will."

"You haven't asked what it pays yet."

"Oh," Addie said. "I guess that's true."

"Not as much as you're probably hoping, but it's nonnegotiable for the first six months, I'm afraid. Twenty-two fifty an hour."

Addie had been working at the self-storage place for fifteen dollars an hour.

"I can deal with that," she said.

"Then you can start Monday?"

"Yeah. I could start Monday. But you just mean hypothetically, right? Just if you happened to choose me."

"Not hypothetical at all," Marty said. "I'm asking you to start Monday. It's nine to five, but you'll need to get here at eight on your first day. You'll be probationary for the first six weeks, and after that your benefits will kick in."

She stood up and reached her hand across the desk, and Addie shook it.

"I don't think I've ever been hired on the spot," Addie said, her head still reeling from a success that had not yet sunk in.

"I liked your honesty. I especially liked the way you told me your actual weaknesses. Nobody ever does that. It's gotten to be almost funny. I say 'What's your biggest weakness?' and they give me a thinly disguised strength. They don't seem to know how much that's gotten to be a cliché. 'I care *too* much.' 'I'm *too* much of a team player.' They refuse to say they have a flaw. But everybody has flaws, so I don't think they're flawless, I just think they're liars."

"It's different inside the rooms," Addie said, using a euphemism for the meeting rooms of AA. "We're more used to being honest with ourselves and each other."

"Amen to that," Marty said. "And welcome aboard."

———

"I got a job!" Addie squealed.

She was in the car on the drive home, talking to Wendy on speaker.

"Excellent," Wendy said.

"A *good* job!"

"Even better."

"And it pays seven fifty an hour—"

Before she could complete the sentence a guy in a big jacked-up pickup cut her off. Badly. She had to slam on her brakes to keep from plowing into his tailgate. She almost honked or flipped him off, but decided she was too happy to let him ruin the mood.

"Isn't that less than minimum wage?" she heard Wendy ask.

"No, that wasn't the whole sentence. Some jerk cut me off and I didn't get a chance to finish. It pays seven-fifty an hour *more*. More than the awful job I just quit."

"Well, I like *that*," Wendy said. "You know what else I like? You didn't honk at the guy who cut you off, or yell cuss words at him."

"I decided I was too happy to bother."

"Where did you hear about this job?"

"That's the weird thing, Wendy. I don't know."

"How can you not know where you heard about it?"

"I know part of it. There was a note about it on my kitchen table. But I don't know who left it."

"Had to be Jonathan. Right?"

"Why does it have to be him?"

"Because . . . there's no one else there?"

"Actually, my brother, Bill, is here for a quick visit. And Jeannie is back, but she's out in the garden shed with no access to the kitchen."

"I guess you got a visit from the Employment Fairy," Wendy said.

"That's a joke, right?"

"Yes. That's a joke. But you wouldn't be the first recovering person to get a really unexpected bit of luck that could almost be classified as a miracle. If you're into such things."

"You think maybe that Karma thing finally kicked in?"

"You're asking the wrong person," Wendy said. "I still don't think I believe in it, and even if I do I figure it catches up with you in your next life."

"You don't believe that if you do good things you get more good things in your life?"

"Well, yeah. I believe *that*."

"How is that different?"

Addie thought she heard her sponsor sigh on the other end of the call.

"Talk to Jonathan. See if he left it. But don't fall into looking a gift horse in the mouth. You got a good job. Be happy and don't ask too many questions."

———

"You seem a lot happier," Bill said.

They were sitting in the backyard, drinking iced tea and waiting for Jonathan to get home from work.

"Well, it's a big relief, getting a good job."

"I'm glad, because I was dreading telling you I have to go home tomorrow."

"It's okay. Really. I'll be okay. I can't tell you how much I appreciate you being here at all. Coming all this way."

They sat quietly for a minute or two. Addie was wondering if Jeannie was in the garden shed. The curtains were drawn, so it was hard to know.

"This can't solve everything you were going through, though," Bill said. "I mean . . . can it?"

"No, of course not. I still have to sort out all this stuff in my inventory. But it definitely turns things in the right direction. Like I was sinking into a pit and now I'm up a little higher and I know the bottom is behind me. Doesn't mean I'm out of the pit, but it's better than what I had a minute ago."

"We should go out to dinner to celebrate," Bill said. "Someplace nice. On me."

"Is that offer just for me?"

"No, Jonathan can come. I like Jonathan. I had my doubts at first, but you did a good job picking him if you were going to take in a stray. Sorry if that came out sounding bad, but I hope you know what I mean."

"It's a little more complicated than that, though. Jeannie's back in the garden shed, and it seems mean for the three of us to go out and celebrate without her."

"Bring her along, then."

Before Addie could answer, she heard the click of the gate latch. She looked up to see Jonathan walk his bike into the yard, still wearing his orange Dairy Dream uniform shirt.

"Hey," Addie said.

Jonathan pulled off his helmet.

"Hey, Addie. Hey, Bill."

"Talk to me about the note on the kitchen table. Was that you?"

"I didn't write the note, but it was me that left it there. Is that okay? Are you mad? I knew you might not want that kind of job again but I figured I should at least tell you about it. You can always not go in for an interview."

"Except I already did go in for an interview. And it's a great job. And it pays half again what I was making at the self-storage. And I got it."

"You got the job?"

"I got the job."

"That's great!" He paused, and scrunched his forehead. "That's great, right?"

"I'm pretty happy about it, yeah. Now come sit down and tell me . . . if you didn't write the note, who did?"

Jonathan leaned the bike on its kickstand and hung the helmet over one of the handlebars. He perched on the very edge of the Adirondack chair closest to Addie.

"Jerri wrote the note and asked me to give it to you."

"Jerry? Who's he?"

"She. Jerri is my supervisor at the Dairy Dream."

"Wait. This is not making sense so far. Why would your supervisor at the Dairy Dream recommend a job for me? And how would she even know what kind of job I was looking for?"

"She likes you."

"She never met me."

"Sure she did. She interviewed you that day, remember? Right before she interviewed me."

"Oh. Right. That lady who was doing the interviews. She liked me?"

"A lot. She really went out of her way to say so. She didn't think you were right for *that* job, but she liked you. And then she hired me, and she likes me, and she knew you did something nice for me, so then she liked you even more and she wanted to do something nice for you. Her brother-in-law owns the building."

"Whoa," Addie said. "I have to think about all this for a minute."

But she didn't think, exactly. She just sat there and tried to let the whole thing sink in.

"It's almost like . . ." she began. But she had no clear direction for the sentence to go.

"Karma?"

"Yeah, almost. I guess. I kept complaining that it never kicked in, which is funny because I'm still not positive I believe in it."

"Maybe it's not something you have to believe in or not believe in," Jonathan said, his gaze—and the look in his eyes—far away. "Maybe it's just more simple than all that. She saw you do something nice for me so she wanted to do something nice for you. That's sort of like Karma, but it's not exactly mystical, if you know what I mean. It's just kind of an everyday thing."

"Which is weirdly similar to a conversation I just had with my sponsor."

She mulled things over a bit more, then added, "Bill offered to take us out to a nice dinner to celebrate. All four of us."

The news did not get the reaction Addie had expected. His face seemed to tense up and fall at the same time, as if she'd just suggested a nice IRS audit for everybody.

"Jeannie won't want that," he said.

"Why won't she?"

"She has nothing to wear. She doesn't even have clothes she'd feel okay wearing to a fast-food place. I don't have much myself."

"Oh. I'm sorry. I never thought of that."

"I'll just go get takeout," Bill said, "and we'll eat here." He rose and checked his pockets, presumably to be sure he had his wallet with him. "Requests?"

"Surprise us," Addie said.

He walked to the gate, then stopped and turned back.

"By the way," he said, "the reason I didn't tell you I was coming is because I thought you might tell me not to. I know you're not big on unannounced visits, but I thought if I offered to come out you'd say I shouldn't go to the trouble and that you were fine."

"It's not a problem," Addie said. "But just for the record, I wouldn't have said I was okay, and I wouldn't have discouraged you from coming."

Bill stood a moment, his hand on the gate latch.

Then he said, "Wow, you really *were* in trouble."

He let himself out, the gate clicking closed behind him.

Eight

Jonathan

Chapter Twenty-One

Walking with Space Heaters

They ate out in the back garden, just because it was a nice evening.

Bill had brought Chinese food—a lot of it.

As they ate, Jonathan kept glancing over at Jeannie, trying to get a better sense of what was wrong. But it didn't answer any questions. Each time he looked directly at her face she looked relaxed to him. She was watching the person who was talking, and occasionally smiling at just the right moments.

She never spoke, though. She remained perfectly silent throughout dinner.

Then where was Jonathan getting the idea that something was off with her? He asked himself that question several times, but never got a satisfying answer. It was just something he could feel.

She didn't eat all that much, either.

She ate a few mouthfuls of broccoli beef and some white rice, then pushed her plate away.

"I'm going to go inside and lie down," she said. "I'm just tired."

She disappeared into the garden shed, and Jonathan watched Addie turn her attention onto him.

"She okay?"

"I don't know," he said.

"Did she tell you what happened to her face?"

"No, and I didn't ask. I figured if she wanted me to know she'd tell me."

They ate in silence for a minute or two more. Then Jonathan felt his own appetite slipping away.

"I'm going to go check on her," he said.

He rose, and walked to the door of the garden shed, rapping lightly with his knuckles.

"Who is it?" he heard her voice call out.

"It's me. Jonathan."

"Oh. That's okay, then. You can come in."

He opened the door.

Jeannie was lying on her back on the air mattress, her hands laced behind her head. She was staring at the ceiling with such intense concentration that one might have thought she was gazing on an endless universe of bright stars, or a sky full of clouds in fascinating shapes.

It even made him glance up briefly. But there was nothing up there except the shed ceiling, which he had practically memorized on sleepless nights.

He closed the door behind him and sat cross-legged on the rug Addie had given them to cover the concrete floor.

"You okay?" he asked.

She didn't turn her head to look at him.

"Yeah. Why wouldn't I be?"

"I don't know. I just know you. And it felt like something was wrong."

"No. Nothing's wrong. I'm fine."

Jonathan sat a moment longer, wondering whether he should take her at her word and go.

Just as he began pushing to his feet, she spoke again.

"It's just that . . ."

He sank back down to the rug and waited, but she said nothing more.

"It's just that what?"

"It doesn't fit."

"What doesn't fit?"

"Me."

"Why are you calling yourself an 'it'?"

"I'm not, really. I meant more like . . . *the situation* with me. I'm eating with those people, but I'm not like them and I never will be. I'm pretending to be alive like they're alive, but I know it's not true."

"You're definitely alive," he said.

"That's not what I meant. I meant I'm not alive *in the same way*. I have to pretend to be something I'm not to be around those people, and I don't like it, and it's too heavy. And I don't want to do it. They want me to be like them, but I'm not."

"I think you're wrong, Jeannie. I'm not even sure how you can say that. Addie is a recovering alcoholic and she and Bill grew up with an abusive father and Addie's just barely trying to get back up again after a really serious depression."

"Still not the same," Jeannie said. "I can't explain it. It's just something you can feel. They're one thing and I'm something else, and I don't want to be around people, anyway. I just want to be left alone."

"Even me?"

"Yeah," she said, still looking straight up at the ceiling, "even you."

Jonathan sat for a beat or two, nursing the sting of that brief statement.

"Anything I can do for you before I go? You want a plate of food for later?"

"No, I'm fine. But if you really want to do something for me you can ask Addie if I can borrow her iPad. I want to go to one of those Zoom meetings."

"Yeah," he said. "Sure. That's a good idea. You can talk to them about how you're feeling."

She offered no response to that.

Jonathan let himself back out into the yard, where Addie and Bill were still eating and talking.

Addie looked up when she saw him.

"She okay?"

"I don't know. I hope so. She's in a weird space. She wants to know if she can borrow your iPad to go to a Zoom meeting."

"Of course she can," Addie said. "And the fact that she asked makes me think she'll be okay. It's a good instinct to want to go to a meeting when you're feeling off."

"I thought so too," Jonathan said.

———

In the morning, at a little after seven, Jonathan made Jeannie a breakfast of coffee, orange juice, and cereal with the milk on the side. That way it wouldn't get soggy if she didn't start in on it right away.

He carried it out to the garden shed and knocked on the door.

No answer. No movement inside. Nothing.

"Jeannie?" he said, and knocked again.

Still nothing.

"I'm going to open the door," he said. "If you're, like, dressed and everything. If not, say so now."

Nothing.

He set the tray down on the concrete garden path and eased the door open.

The shed was empty.

No Jeannie. No Jeannie's backpack. The iPad was gone. And, though it took him a moment to notice, the space heater was missing as well.

He stood staring for a long time, not thinking much. Carefully postponing reactions that involved feeling.

Then he closed the door, picked up the tray of food, and carried it back into the kitchen.

Addie was standing at the counter pouring herself a cup of coffee.

"Bill still asleep?" he asked her.

"Yeah. He's been taking care of his grandkids, so he's relishing a chance to sleep in."

"I have to tell you something," Jonathan said.

Her eyes came up to his face for the first time that morning.

"Something bad from the sound of things," she said. "And from that look on your face."

He sat at the kitchen table, setting the tray in front of him. He would eat it himself. He had made Jeannie something to eat before eating his own breakfast, so this could be his. The only problem was the fact that his appetite had completely abandoned him.

"Jeannie's gone again."

"Already?"

"Looks that way."

"How do you know?"

"Well . . . she's not there."

"Maybe she just went out for a walk or something."

"But she took your iPad. And the space heater. I never heard of anybody going for a walk with a space heater."

Addie plopped down beside him at the table with her coffee.

"Yeah," she said. "That does sound pretty gone."

For a minute they only sipped at their coffees.

Then Addie said, "You think she really wanted to go to a Zoom meeting last night? Or you think she just wanted my iPad?"

"I don't know," Jonathan said. "I've been trying not to wonder that myself."

———

When he arrived home from work, Addie was sitting on the living room couch, staring at the TV. Or at least in the direction of the TV. But the TV was not turned on.

He sat beside her, and she grunted a wordless greeting.

"Where's Bill?" he asked her.

"He had to go home today. He didn't want to leave his wife to take care of the grandkids all by herself for too long."

"Oh. Are you okay with that?"

"Yeah," she said. And she sounded like she meant it. She turned her face to him for the first time since he'd arrived home, and offered him a small and vaguely sad-looking smile. "It was just so nice that he came all this way. How long he could stay feels less important."

"Okay, good," he said, and leaned back against the couch cushions. "Then you're okay."

He was not at all sure that *he* was okay, but he felt unclear on how to broach that subject.

"I will be," she said. "Given some time. I think starting work on Monday will help. At least I'll feel like I'm moving forward in my life instead of standing still. Why? Do I not seem okay to you?"

"I don't know," he said. "Maybe. You were sitting here like you're watching TV, but the TV's not turned on."

"I was just thinking," she said.

For a few moments he wrestled with whether he had any right to ask her what she was thinking. Before he could resolve the issue in his head she saved him the trouble.

"Just worrying about Jeannie a little bit," she said. "Wondering if she's okay. If there's any way she can keep being okay. You know. Out there."

"Oh, I know," he said.

For what felt like quite a long time they didn't speak. Jonathan was hungry, but not quite ready to disconnect from her company to do anything about it.

"If she came back," he said, "I'm guessing you wouldn't take her in. Right?"

He heard Addie pull in a huge breath of air and sigh it out again.

"If that girl comes back," she said, "and asks me for some kind of help, I'll help her if I can. I'll help match her up with a sponsor, or some kind of shelter or recovery house, so she can live long enough to maybe get clean. But I'm not taking her in again. Not onto my property. Because she stole from me."

"I get it," he said.

"It's not even the things, so much. The iPad was not cheap, but now that I've got a decent job I can get another one. It's the breach of trust. She hurt me in ways that go much deeper than the things, because I gave her what I could and she broke my trust."

"I guess I always had it in my head that she would make it," he said. "You know. With the staying clean and all. And now I'm not sure why I thought that. Because I guess a lot of people don't."

"You can say that again," Addie said.

"But I still want to know why she couldn't just stay with the meetings and do it."

"Because she's an addict, honey. I know that's not a very satisfying answer, but it's an honest one. When an alcoholic or an addict goes back to drinking and using, they can't even tell you why themselves. There's no thought process behind it. It just happens, and they can't even track why. But most people don't make it. It's pretty rare for someone to stay."

"Do you know how common it is?"

"How common what is, exactly? Staying with recovery?"

"Yeah. That. Like, when people come into meetings, do you know how many actually stay and how many drop away?"

"It's a little hard to get statistics on a thing like that. But if you're talking about actually staying sober till the day you die, some think it's as low as three percent."

"Oh, that's not bad."

"It's not?"

"Only three percent dropping out? That's good."

"No. Other way around, buddy. Three percent actually stay clean and sober their whole lives."

They sat quietly for a bit longer.

Then Jonathan got up, walked upstairs to his room, and got the big square candle that had been sitting by his bed as long as that room had been his. He carried it downstairs and set it on the coffee table in front of the couch and stood over it, and her, for a moment.

"You might think this is really silly," he said.

"Try me."

"I thought we could light a candle for Jeannie. I don't really know how to pray, or even if I believe in anything to pray to, but it would be like putting it out into the universe that two people are wishing for her to be okay. It's probably silly."

"I don't think it's silly."

"Probably won't do any good."

"Won't do any harm."

"Yeah," he said. "That's true."

He got a book of matches out of a drawer in the kitchen next to the stove. He knew where to find them because the stove wouldn't light without one.

He carried the matches back out to the living room, settled on the couch, and lit the candle.

They stared at the bright, flickering point of its light for a long time. Long enough that the daylight coming through the windows began to fade into dusk.

Once he glanced over and saw the candle flame reflected once in each of Addie's eyes.

He had no idea what she was thinking. He was not thinking, exactly, but more wrestling with a feeling that he was not going to see Jeannie again—pushing it away every time it came up, then feeling it drift back in again. There was no reason to think he could know such a thing. Still, the feeling was there, and it seemed to do no good to deny it.

Not everybody makes it out.

———

He rode his bike into the driveway after work on Monday, dismounting as he slowed. He walked the bike a few steps, mostly focused on the fact that Addie's SUV was not in the driveway. Not that he had expected it to be. He knew this was her first day of work, and he knew she would work until five to his three, and that she would have a much longer trip home.

No, he stared at the empty spot where she normally parked because it was so wonderful to see it empty for a change. She had been home when he got back from work for as long as he'd had a job. Other than a bit of job searching in the morning, which had tailed off as of late, she had been home.

It felt good to see that she was out in the world. Moving forward with her life. It felt like a relief. Like something he'd been silently pushing into being with his mind. Something that finally took off just as he was accepting his powerlessness over it.

He stared at the empty, slightly oil-stained spot as he walked the bike up the driveway.

It wasn't until a movement caught his eye that he realized there was a man sitting on the front porch.

He looked to be about forty, compact and small, with dark hair thinning at the temples and a touch of gray in his short sideburns and his neatly trimmed beard. He wore wire-rimmed glasses and the kind of clothes that never entirely went into or out of style—tan chinos and a pastel polo shirt.

Jonathan set the bike on its kickstand and walked over to the porch, unclipping and pulling off his helmet as he did.

"You must be Jonathan," the man said.

He was not a total stranger, then. Maybe to Jonathan he was, but he must have known Addie, or how would he have known the name of the person who lived here with her?

"Yeah, I'm Jonathan," he said.

He wanted to ask *And who are you?* But it seemed rude. This man was his elder. He had not been raised to speak thoughtlessly to his elders.

"You're here to see Addie?" he asked instead.

"Seems that way. Unlikely as I would have said such a thing was, right up until the time I left the house."

"She's not home."

"I thought she was always home. I got the impression that she more or less wasn't getting out of bed these days."

"She just started a new job today."

"Oh. Well. That's good." He looked Jonathan up and down. A sort of appraisal, from the feel of it. As though Jonathan were goods he might consider buying, but he was skeptical about the purchase so far. "I'm sorry I wouldn't talk to you on the phone," the man said. "Nothing personal. I'm just not good on the phone with people I don't know."

Jonathan said nothing, because he had no idea what to say. The man seemed to think Jonathan knew who he was. But Jonathan had no idea.

"You look confused," the man said.

"Because I *am* confused."

"I'm Spencer."

"Spencer," he repeated, still not quite getting the connection.

He knew he had heard the name recently, but he couldn't produce the context in which he'd heard it. Not so immediately. Not on such short notice.

"Addie's son."

"Oh," Jonathan said. "Well, you should come in, then. I'll make us some coffee or something."

"But she's not here."

"No."

"Any idea when she'll get back?"

"I know she works till five. But leaving downtown at five o'clock . . . that's kind of brutal, traffic-wise. I'd say it's anybody's guess."

Spencer glanced at his watch. Actually, more than glanced at it. Stared at it, as though trying to figure out something complicated.

While he waited, Jonathan felt the pressure of not wanting the man to go away again. It would be devastating to have to tell Addie that her son had come to see her after all these years and she'd missed it.

"It's a two-hour drive home for me," Spencer said. "And I'd be turning around to come back here more or less right after rush hour. I guess I could come back on a different day. Although it sounds like she's not in as much trouble as Uncle Bill thought."

"No, please don't leave," Jonathan said. He could hear the panic and need in his own voice. And Spencer couldn't have helped but hear it as well. It was too much, but it was also too late to stop it. "Please stay. I know she'll want to see you. She'll just kick herself if she misses your visit."

A long few seconds ticked by in silence. Jonathan wasn't sure if he was breathing.

"I guess I'll take you up on that coffee, then," Spencer said.

———

"Actually, do you have tea?" Spencer asked. "I really like tea better."

He was sitting at the kitchen table, watching Jonathan take mugs down from the cupboard.

"I think she has tea." Jonathan opened a drawer near the sink and saw two boxes. "Mint and English breakfast."

"English breakfast is fine."

Jonathan set about filling a kettle and putting it on to boil, because Addie did not have a microwave. She didn't believe in them.

As he lit the burner with a match, he asked, "How long has it been since you've seen her?"

"Eleven years since we had any real talks," Spencer said, without hesitation. He did not seem to need to figure the time in his head first. He knew.

"You know she's been sober for most of that time, though."

"I know. I heard."

"I guess I just thought . . ."

But Jonathan never finished the sentence, because it might have been inappropriate to say what he thought. Probably it was none of his business.

"You thought when I heard she'd stopped drinking I'd welcome her back. Or at least give her another chance. But the drinking wasn't the problem. I mean . . . it was *a* problem. But it wasn't the heart of the thing."

Jonathan set the burner to a fairly high flame and sat down at the kitchen table across from Spencer.

"I'm surprised to hear that."

"I'm not sure why."

"Because Addie is so wonderful."

Spencer snorted. It was a big sound, and it startled Jonathan. It took him a few seconds to realize it had been a disdainful laugh.

"I guess you can't understand unless you grew up with a mother like that."

Jonathan took a big, deep breath. He thought he was deciding whether or not to go forward with what he had on his mind to say. But it turned out there was nothing to decide. Before he could consider his options, he was already speaking.

"I grew up with a mother who sent me away because her new boyfriend didn't want a teenager around. She sent me to live with my father, even though she knew what he was like when he'd been drinking. Some nights when I was little she had to take me and go to some kind of women's shelter because of how he was. So she knew. And when I had to leave there I called her and told her I was about to be out on the streets, and she never called me back. So I think I know what it's like to grow up with a tough break in the mom department. But if I thought she wanted to talk to me, and I had any reason to believe she was sorry, or had changed her ways, or even was just *trying* to change her ways, I'd let her talk. I'm not saying I'd forgive her, and I'm not saying it would fix everything. I'm just saying I'd hear her out. At least give her that chance to tell me her side of the thing. Because she's my mother."

Then he stopped and just waited, wondering if he'd stepped over a line.

Spencer seemed lost in thought, and said nothing.

The kettle began to whistle, but Jonathan only sat frozen, waiting to hear the reaction to his words.

The sound intensified.

"You should get that," Spencer said.

Jonathan rose and poured the hot water for tea for both of them.

He set the mug next to Spencer with a spoon and ramekin, so he could remove the tea bag when it had steeped enough.

"Sugar?" he asked. "Honey? Milk?"

"No, just the way it is will be fine."

Jonathan sat at the table again with his own mug of tea, feeling the steam rise into his face and still having no answer as to whether he had overstepped, or how his words had been received.

"I'm here now," Spencer said.

"Yeah, you are. That's good."

"I'm late. I know it."

"But you're here now," Jonathan said.

———

They were sitting on the couch together, and had been for some time. For the majority of that time Spencer had been doing something on his phone.

In other words, they had long ago run out of things to talk about.

Spencer looked up suddenly from his phone, his gaze drilling so directly into Jonathan's face that it felt a bit startling.

"Can I be honest with you about something?"

"Um," Jonathan said, wondering if he had the option to say no. "I guess. Yeah."

"It kind of pissed me off that she took you in the way she did. Nothing about you. Please don't take it personally. It just felt like she kind of . . . went out and got another son."

"More like a grandson, really."

"I think you know what I mean, though."

Jonathan sat a moment, painfully aware of his own breathing. As if it no longer worked automatically.

"Can *I* be honest with *you*?" he asked after a time.

"Sure," Spencer said. "Why not? I started it."

"I don't think that's fair. She didn't leave your life. It was the other way around. It was your decision. She's not married. She has no other kids. Her brother lives all the way in Texas. Don't you think it's normal that she might get a little lonely and want more people around her? It's not like she wouldn't have wanted it to be you."

For a moment Spencer just stared at him, but not right into his face. More like a spot near his ear.

Then he said, "That's a fair point, I guess."

"It's human to feel the way you do, though. Even if what I just said was true. I mean . . . you have a right to feel the way you feel."

"If just once in my life she had said that to me," Spencer said, "we wouldn't ever have found ourselves in this situation."

Then he went back to whatever he'd been doing on his phone.

Nine

Addie

Chapter Twenty-Two

More Important than a Parking Space, Scarier than an IED

Marty Greene came by the front desk to see Addie at the end of her working day. It hit Addie like a fastball to the gut, because she figured that's what bosses do when there's a problem and they're about to let you know in no uncertain terms what it is.

Addie hurried awkwardly to her feet, as if the queen or a president had just entered the room.

"Sit," Marty said. "Relax. Just checking in to see what you thought of your first day. Bored to tears?"

Addie sat, and breathed deeply a couple of times, trying to be quiet and not too obvious about it.

"If you mean was I able to be pretty relaxed all day, and the sky didn't fall in, and I had nothing to get upset about, then yeah. Bored to tears. It was great."

"Then it went well."

"I hope so," Addie said. "I feel like it did."

"Well, the good news is, so did everybody else. I got nothing but good feedback."

Addie glanced around as if expecting to see an unnoticed crowd over her shoulder. She had been working the desk alone all day, which was one of the things she liked best about the experience.

"From . . . ?"

"The people who work in the building are always quick to weigh in on the security staff. They didn't like the last day person. They felt like he was throwing his weight around for no good reason. You they liked. Everybody said you were very polite and professional."

Addie breathed in the feeling for a moment. The relief of the thing.

She was about to answer when Marty said, "Now go home and get ready to do it all again tomorrow."

———

She called Wendy at a long stoplight and put her on speaker.

"Hey," Wendy said. "How was your first day?"

"It was so good, Wendy. I just can't tell you how good it was. I feel so lucky. Everything there is bright and clean and everybody seems professional and nothing feels dangerous and I don't feel like I'm carrying the weight of the whole world on my shoulders. I'm just so relieved to get this job."

"I think the word you're searching for, hon, is 'grateful.'"

"Right. Grateful."

"How's that inventory coming along?"

"It's almost done," Addie said. "I was working on it a lot during that time I was home. I'm going to be ready to read you my fifth step soon."

"Ready when you are," Wendy said.

"Can I ask you a question?" Addie asked, just as the light finally turned green and she was able to touch the accelerator and crawl forward again.

"I think that's what sponsors are for."

"Does everybody fall apart like that before they come back together?"

"No. Not everybody. Some people don't really change from the inside out. Some just drink tons of coffee and smoke too much and gamble or get addicted to shopping—what we call retail therapy—or whatever they're going to do. And they just kind of hold on like that. They don't really move forward, but they don't back up either. But most of us can't stay unless we grow. Whatever we were holding down with all that alcohol, it's going to want to come up. After a while there's just no more room under the rug to sweep anything. And then there's no rug anymore. There's just us and whatever brought us here. That's what happened to you, I think. You got to that part of the process we call 'grow or go.'"

"I'm glad I grew."

"That makes two of us, hon," Wendy said.

———

When Addie had finally made it home through all that traffic, there was a car parked right in front of her house. Addie hated it when somebody took the space right in front of her house. She'd always figured there was a sort of unwritten pact for neighbors, in this case stating that people should always have first crack at the curb in front of their own homes.

She parked in the driveway, trying to unhook from the irritation in her own gut. Trying to decide whether she would say anything to the driver of that car if she saw him, and whether she would waste any of her evening glancing out the window at intervals to see him.

She decided it would be best to let it go.

She let herself in through the front door with her key.

Sitting on the couch next to Jonathan was her son.

He looked up from his phone, right into her eyes, and she held his gaze. For a second or two, she didn't breathe. She almost thought her heart had stopped, but a split second later she felt a big, panicky beat.

Meanwhile neither of them was saying a word.

"Look, Addie," Jonathan said, possibly overwhelmed by all that silence. "It's Spencer."

"Yeah, I see that," Addie said.

Then another deadly silence fell.

This time Addie felt it was her job, her responsibility, to break it.

"You grew a beard," she said to her son.

"And you hate it," Spencer said.

"No, I don't hate it."

She actually did hate it. But that wasn't important in light of the fact that he was here.

Jonathan said, "I'm going to leave you two alone to talk. I know you must have a lot to say to each other after all these years."

And with that he hurried out of the living room.

I sure hope so, Addie thought.

She walked over and sat on the couch next to her son.

She was so nervous she felt as though she couldn't breathe. If she hadn't sat down, she knew she might have passed out, or something close to it.

It flitted through her head that she had once watched the armored vehicle right in front of hers get blown up by an improvised explosive device on a road near an Iraqi airport, and she hadn't been this scared. She'd had a perp try to wrestle her gun away from her, firing off a wild shot in the process. She hadn't been this scared.

"This is a really nice surprise," she said, and the words sounded nearly unintelligible because she couldn't catch her breath. "To what do I owe it?"

"What's wrong with you?" he asked.

For one awful moment she thought it was a general comment about her life. About her. Then she realized he was probably wondering why she sounded like she couldn't breathe.

"Just a little overwhelmed is all. But as I was asking . . ."

"Uncle Bill said you were in trouble, because Jonathan called him and told him you were. Uncle Bill said if I was ever going to think of paying you a visit, it should probably be now. He thinks you've really changed."

"I haven't had a drink in over eight years."

"That's not what I meant."

"What did you mean, then, Spencer? What's the one big thing I did wrong? I know I was anything but a perfect mom, so I'm not saying you're not supposed to have any criticisms, but I honestly don't know what I did that hurt you so much."

"I'm not sure I could get you to understand," he said.

"You could try."

"Tell me how you've changed," he said.

"Yeah. I could do that. You want a cup of tea?"

"Actually Jonathan made me one. But . . . yeah. I'll have another. And I'll at least hear you out. Speaking of Jonathan, that part was mostly him. The part about hearing you out. He told me what his own mother did to him, but he said he'd hear her out anyway if he thought she had changed, or even if he thought she wanted to change. That he would listen to her side of the thing. You can thank him for that."

Addie made a mental note to thank Jonathan for saying that to Spencer. Also to bring up the fact that he had called Bill and told him she was not okay. Though as to that second thing, she wasn't sure if she felt inclined to thank him or not.

———

Nearly forty-five minutes later she stopped talking, drew a deep breath, and risked a look over at Spencer to see how the story was being received.

They were sitting together at the kitchen table, in the dimming light of evening. Their tea mugs had long since been emptied, and she had been doing her best to avoid eye contact with her son.

"You keep referring to this 'incident,'" Spencer said. "Is there a reason why you're not telling me what kind of incident it was?"

The heart-hammering came back, but Addie breathed as best she could and talked through it.

"I discharged my weapon to defend myself from an aggressive person who was approaching me."

"Fatal shot?"

"No. Just wounded him enough to stop the advance."

"Didn't you pretty much do that your whole career?"

"My whole career it was my responsibility to do that. I was authorized to do it when necessary, and it was my job."

"Isn't any citizen authorized to defend herself?"

"I suppose so, yes. But I took it hard anyway."

"Good," Spencer said. "I'm glad that's not something you could do lightly."

"I think it was because of all this stuff that's been coming up. Or maybe all this stuff came up because of that. It's really hard to get it all sorted out in my head."

Spencer sat back. Addie could hear the light sound of his back bumping against the wooden back of the kitchen chair.

"You still carry the gun?"

"I don't carry it, no. I have it, but I don't walk through the world with it every day. It's in the drawer of my nightstand, on the off chance that somebody should ever break in."

"Let me mirror back to you what I'm hearing," Spencer said. "It sounds like you're saying that the whole tough-guy bit just completely fell apart and left you high and dry, and now you have no choice but to admit that you were never as tough as you wanted everybody to think you were."

"That's about the size of it," Addie said. "Yeah."

"Well then, that does put us on much better footing than we were before."

Addie could not have been more surprised to hear it. She couldn't help feeling that he could have knocked her over with the proverbial feather.

"It does?"

"Absolutely. That was the problem. You really didn't know that?"

"The problem was that I was tough?"

"The problem was that you tried to make me tough. Every time I had any kind of feelings about anything, every time something hit my sensitive side, you told me to man up and tough it out."

"I'm pretty sure I never said 'man up' to a toddler."

"I don't remember exactly what you said, but that was the message I took. I was a sensitive boy. I grew up into a sensitive man, in spite of you. Do you have any idea how hard it is to be a sensitive boy, even if your mother wants you to be? Even if you're getting support for it at home? I could have taken all the crap at school, because my peer group meant almost nothing to me. But you were my mother, and you were my only parent, and you were telling me all the same crap. And don't tell me I should just have ignored you, or not believed you, because when you're three years old, or five years old, you don't question your parents. It doesn't occur to you that they could be wrong. I figured you must know everything, and you were telling me that everything that was true about me was wrong. You wanted me to be something I wasn't. Like an iron-man kind of kid. The kind where everything just bounces off of me. And I couldn't do that for you. I just figured I was unlovable and bad."

For a moment he did not go on, and she was not quite ready to begin. They just sat and breathed. It was so quiet in the house that Addie could hear their breath.

"I am so, so sorry," she said after a time, "for making you feel like you weren't right just the way you were. For acting like you didn't have a right to be who you were and feel what you felt. I didn't mean it that way at all, but I take full responsibility for the fact that it came out that way. And for the fact that I hurt you."

"Tell me how you *did* mean it," he said. "I think I know, but tell me anyway, so I can see if I was right."

"I just wanted to protect you," Addie said. "It's such a vicious world. I wanted to throw myself over you like a suit of armor and be your protection, which is the main reason I wanted to be tough myself. But I knew I couldn't go everywhere with you, and I wouldn't always be there to take care of you. So I guess I tried to get you to put on your own armor. And I'm sorry. I just loved you so much, and I was so afraid the world would hurt you."

"Yeah," Spencer said. "That's what I figured. I kind of knew that. As an adult, I mean. But knowing it really doesn't make it any easier to have grown up that way."

"Granted," Addie said.

They sat without talking for a while longer.

The daylight outside had completely faded, leaving them illuminated only by the light over the stove. It was enough, though. In fact, she thought, it was probably better that way.

"That was the big thing?" she asked him. "Not the drinking?"

"The drinking sure didn't help. But that was the main thing, yeah. That and the fact that you wouldn't tell me anything about my father."

"Same answer as last time," Addie said, wishing they could talk about something else. Anything else.

"I have no idea what that means."

"It means it was another attempt to protect you. Probably another misguided one."

"In what way would it hurt me to know anything about my father?"

"Because he was not a good man," Addie said.

She expected some kind of immediate parry from him. Something about how his rights remained the same. Instead he seemed surprised by the answer, and willing to let it be for a moment.

"I never meant to be with him," she said. "Sexually, I mean. I never wanted to. He was my commanding officer, and he coerced me, which good men don't do. I'm not saying he forcibly raped me, but he pressured and manipulated me, and it was a bad thing for me, and I didn't report it because I was afraid of him. And when I got pregnant he acted like it could have been anybody, but he was the only one. It's hard to tell your son about his father when you have nothing good to say. Not one good thing."

She waited, but he said nothing for a long time. Over and beyond his head she could see a few bright stars out the kitchen window. While she waited, she wondered if she had been wrong to tell him even now.

"I'm sorry you had to go through that," he said after a while.

"Thank you."

"And I'm sorry I treated you like you were being mean and bad for not being all the things I wanted you to be. Now that I know what I know, it seems like a pretty selfish interpretation of the whole mess."

"It means a lot that you would say that to me. Anything else while we're putting it all out onto the table?"

"I was mad that you wouldn't get me a dog. Wouldn't even think about it or talk it out with me. Or tell me why not. Is there a story I never knew behind that too?"

"As a matter of fact," Addie said, "there is. But I have to work in the morning, and you have a long drive home. Maybe I could tell you that on your second visit. I realize I'm being presumptuous, thinking there'll be a second visit. Well, more than presumptuous, actually. More like completely lost in wishful thinking. But if you're willing to come back again, or let me come to you, I promise you I'll tell you anything you want to know."

"That's fair enough," Spencer said. "This went a lot better than I thought it would, so I guess I'm willing to try it again."

———

After he'd left, she walked upstairs and rapped on Jonathan's door.

"Come in," he called.

He was mostly propped up in bed in a T-shirt, with the blankets pulled up to his chest.

"Were you sleeping?" she asked him.

"No."

"What were you doing?"

"I don't know. Just thinking, I guess."

"Thank you for what you said to Spencer."

His eyebrows knitted together and down, as if to accommodate deep thoughts.

"What did I say to him?"

"That even after everything that happened with your mom you'd still hear her out."

"Oh. Right. I'm glad if it helped."

She opened her mouth to say more, but he beat her to it.

"I have to tell you something," he said. "I'm sorry I didn't tell you sooner, but I was scared you might be mad. I called your brother and told him I was worried about you. I know it probably wasn't my business to do that, but . . . well, I was worried about you." He stopped talking for a few seconds, picking at a thread on the silk border of the blanket. Looking where he was fidgeting. Then he looked up into her face. "Are you mad?"

Addie had thought she was. At least a little. But that was when she thought he'd done it without telling her, rather than doing it and telling her later than he should have. His confession took every bit of the wind out of her sails.

"It was a bold move," she said. "Could've gone either way in terms of how I'd feel about it."

"Right. And I knew that. And that just goes to show how worried I was. Are you mad?" he asked again.

"I suppose not," she said. "It needed to be done and I wasn't brave enough to do it myself, so it fell to you. And I'm sorry about that. It's hard for me to ask for help. Next time I'll step up and do it myself and save you the worry."

He smiled in a way she'd never seen him smile before. Something that went deep, and let her see all the way in, though she couldn't have described it better than that.

"We both need some sleep," she said.

She moved to let herself out, then turned back again.

"Oh," she said. "Jonathan. Tell your supervisor at the Dairy Dream thank you from me, okay? Jerri? Was that her name?"

"Yeah. Jerri."

"Tell her I said thank you. That job is really a blessing. Here I don't even know her and she sends this amazing thing into my life."

"Or maybe Karma sent it."

"Maybe. But I don't know how to thank Karma, and I do know how to thank your supervisor."

"I'll give her the message," he said. "She'll like that."

Chapter Twenty-Three

Searching and Fearless

Addie was at her sponsor's house, doing her fifth step—which was to say, reading her fourth step to Wendy for the purpose of admitting the exact nature of her wrongs to at least one other human being.

She had started out nervous, but now it was almost three hours in, she had essentially covered everything she had written, and the feeling had worn itself down.

The little dog was sleeping curled up in her lap. She had one hand on the animal's warm back. The big dog was asleep on the floor with his head on Addie's shoe.

"That was a pretty complete fourth step," Wendy said.

"Pretty complete? What did I miss?"

"Nothing as far as I know, but just now you missed the compliment looking for the insult. Emphasis on 'complete' and not 'pretty.' Take the praise."

"Right," Addie said. "Got it. Sorry."

"We should talk about amends."

"But that's skipping six and seven. What about being ready to have my defects removed? What about asking my higher power to remove them? Aren't we supposed to do all this in order?"

"We're not going to skip them," Wendy said. "We're just going to make a plan for your amends. For when your sixth and seventh steps are finished."

"Okay."

"Now, I wasn't your sponsor when you did your first fourth step. But you made amends for everything that came up in that one, right?"

"Oh yeah. Joan saw to it."

"Then this will just be for what happened since that first time through the steps," Wendy said, "plus anything you hadn't seen yet when you did your first inventory."

"Okay."

"Kind of seems like the person you most need to make amends to is yourself."

"Myself?"

It was a concept Addie had not even considered. Her whole life felt as though it had been geared toward what she did or did not owe everybody else.

"Well," Wendy began, "who's left? You said you made an amends to your son."

"I wrote him a letter, yeah. The first time with Joan. And just recently I did it in person. And probably over and over until the day I die. And I made amends to my brother, too."

"I don't see that you owed an amends to your brother."

"That's what he said."

"An amends for doing what?"

"Nothing," Addie said. "For doing nothing. For watching my father beat him to a pulp and doing nothing."

"What could you have done, though?" Wendy asked, pulling her vape pen out of her cardigan sweater's pocket and removing the cap.

"That's what my brother said. But I still felt like I needed to do it."

"Well, there's nothing wrong with saying it. Just so long as you're not getting in the habit of taking responsibility for things that are outside your control."

"Too late," Addie said.

Wendy laughed, inhaled, and spewed out a cloud of vapor.

"I sensed that," she said.

"How do I make amends to *me*? That seems weird."

"I'm not suggesting you look in the mirror and say you're sorry to your own face. It's more of a living amends I had in mind. You make amends to yourself for treating yourself badly by treating yourself better."

Addie said nothing for an awkward length of time. Just stroked the sleeping dog's warm back and tried to get the concept to click into place inside her. It never really clicked.

"I never even considered a thing like that," she finally said.

"It shows. Don't you think it's time to consider it?"

"I was picturing more like being dutifully sent off to apologize to people I'd hurt. Somehow I can get my head around that better."

"Who's left, though?" Wendy asked, the breath behind the words spewing out another stream of vapor.

Addie said nothing for a time, trying to decide whether or not to say it. Then she decided that the whole point of the exercise was to be searching and fearless. It was right there in the description of the step. To withhold anything would turn the whole exercise into a "half measure."

"There is *one* thing," Addie said. "But actually making the amends would be pretty much impossible."

"I'm listening," Wendy said.

"The stuff I told you about Spencer's father . . . and of course I'm using the word 'father' in only the very loosest sense of the word . . ."

She watched Wendy's face as she spoke. Watched her eyebrows lift slightly.

"You're not going to tell me you owe an amends to *him*."

"Oh hell no. Over my dead body."

"Well, tell me what you meant, then."

Addie pulled in a deep breath, closed her eyes, and jumped.

"I feel like I owe an amends to the women who had to deal with him after me. The ones who were unlucky enough to come in contact with him later. I don't know for a fact that there were more, but you just kind of know there were. I mean, obviously it's not that I was so devastatingly attractive that he couldn't resist me. It was just who he was. It was his pattern."

"Okay. And . . . ?"

"And I didn't report it."

Wendy vaped for a minute or two in silence, her gaze far away.

"If you'd reported it, would that have stopped it from happening again?"

"I doubt it. Which was one of the reasons I didn't. I was scared. That was part of it. I thought things would only get worse for me if I told, and I was probably right about that. But also I knew it wouldn't do any good. It wasn't straight-out force. I didn't scream and try to get away. It was more like intimidation and manipulation. And he would have said it wasn't, and it's not a thing you can really prove, and the whole thing would have gone nowhere."

"Then why make yourself responsible?"

"Because that way at least I would have tried. Maybe if I'd made a big deal about it, maybe more of the female troops would have known. Maybe they would have found ways not to be alone with him. Seen him coming and gotten out of the way. I don't know. But at least I'd feel like I'd done something for them. But I was scared and I curled up in a little ball and did nothing. But I have no idea who these women are who he might have gotten to after me. And I can't make amends to somebody I can't even identify."

"Back to the living amends," Wendy said.

"How would that go in this situation?"

"Be the person who speaks up. Do things even though they scare you. Be a different person than the one you were when that happened. But at the same time, let yourself off the hook for the past, too. You know the old saying 'If they knew better, they'd do better'?"

"I've heard that, yeah."

"If you'd had better tools at the time—better options—you could have done better. You were young. You were pregnant. You were scared. You had no support. Don't judge yourself."

"Not my specialty," Addie said.

"So I've noticed. Go home. Get some sleep. You did good work. We'll talk more about the sixth and seventh steps on another night. But the amends you have left to make seem to be the ones you need to make to yourself."

Addie looked down at the sleeping dog in her lap.

"I hate to move him," she said.

"He'll live."

Wendy held the vape pen tightly in her lips and used both hands to lift the little dog off Addie and onto the couch. He woke up looking seriously aggrieved.

"You think it was a good inventory?" Addie asked, pushing to her feet.

"Fishing for compliments, are we?"

"Sorry."

"Mostly kidding. Yeah. It was a good inventory. It felt honest. It felt complete. Which is not to say that you won't immediately recognize something you missed. I find that happens a lot. But just be open to it. Don't push it. Enough work for now is enough. Just go home and rest. Don't you have work in the morning?"

"Yeah, I do. Fortunately."

"Get some sleep," Wendy said, and walked her to the door.

Still, all the way home Addie could not shake the feeling that she owed one more amends, and that it was not something she had any inclination to postpone.

But it would be nearly eleven by the time she got home, and she figured he would be asleep.

———

He was not asleep.

She came in through the kitchen door and found him sitting at the table, hunched over a mug of something hot.

"Jonathan," she said. "You're not sleeping."

"I'm working on it," he said.

She suspected he was worried about Jeannie, but he didn't say and she didn't ask.

"Don't you have work in the morning?" she asked him.

"No. I'm off tomorrow."

"Oh. Well, I'm not sure sitting here drinking coffee is the way to go."

"It's not coffee."

"Same for tea."

"It's hot milk," Jonathan said.

"Oh. Then you really are working on it."

She sat next to him, and they coexisted quietly for a moment.

Then Addie said, "I kind of wanted to talk to you anyway."

She watched his face register alarm. Would he ever outgrow waiting for that second shoe to drop? Probably not, she figured.

"Uh-oh."

"No, it's not an uh-oh," Addie said.

"Oh. Good."

"I wanted to make an amends to you for something."

His eyes came up to hers, and from the look on his face she felt as though she must have switched to a foreign language before beginning that last sentence.

"What could you possibly have to make amends to *me* for?"

Addie sighed, and rose from the table.

"I'll tell you," she said. "But *I do* have work in the morning, and it's late, and while I do I'm going to make some of that hot milk for myself."

She poured what she thought would be a mug's worth of it into a saucepan and set it to heat on the gas burner.

Then she sat down at the table with him again.

In her peripheral vision she could see the flames dancing in blue patterns under the pan.

"That first night I met you," she said, "you remember how you said you wanted to believe in Karma because you wanted the universe to give me some nice thing for being kind to you? I don't think I said much about it at the time, but I really latched on to that idea too. Because I needed some nice thing. I was feeling unhappy and lost, and like things just kept getting worse, and even though I wasn't sure I believed in that whole Karma thing, I wanted to, because I wanted the good thing. But things just kept going downhill. But then I got that really good job, and we started talking like maybe that was it. Maybe that was my Karma. My nice thing from the universe. And I only just realized tonight how much that was so unfair to you and so wrong."

He took a sip of his milk and then stared into the cup for a moment. He did not look up into her face.

"I don't get why that was wrong," he said.

"Because I had already gotten my nice thing from the universe, and I can't believe I was too dense to see it. Right away the universe gave me something good for my trouble. Right there in real time."

He brought his eyes up to her face for the first time.

"What did it give you?" he asked.

"You really don't know?"

"Not a clue."

"You can't even guess?"

He thought a minute, then shook his head.

"No guesses," he said. "I'm lost."

"*You,*" she said. "It gave me *you.*"

She watched him nearly collapse under the weight of the compliment. Watched it soften and change the look on his face. He looked as if he might cry at any moment.

Addie stood.

"Bring it in, buddy," she said.

She spread out her arms to receive him.

He looked up at her, frozen, his eyes wide.

"I just know that's got to be a joke," he said.

"I've never been more serious in my life."

For a moment he just sat there blinking too much.

Then he pushed himself up from the table and walked into her arms. She could feel him grasp two fistfuls of the back of her shirt, and she heard him begin to cry.

"Now that I've done my turn at falling apart," she said, "it can be your turn if you want it to be."

He stepped back from her, wiping his eyes on his shirtsleeve. He was obviously trying to hide the tears, or push them back away, or both.

"Why would I want to fall apart?"

"Well, nobody *wants* to fall apart," she said. "But you've been through a lot. And you're handling it so well I swear it's a cause for concern. If you want to let it out I'll support you, like you did with me. Or maybe you'll be more like your old adopted grandma and wait until you're sixty-two. But I honestly don't recommend it."

The milk boiled noisily, and Addie poured her mug of hot milk and carried it to the door of the kitchen.

"Okay, enough with the mushy stuff," she said. "I'm going to drink this in bed. Good night. Get some sleep."

She took two steps toward the stairs, then turned back and stuck her head into the kitchen again.

"We should get a dog," she said.

He looked over his shoulder at her, and he looked less certain than she had imagined.

"You don't like that idea?" she asked him. "I thought you would."

"I like dogs," he said. "But also when I was out on the street I met a couple of scary ones. What kind of dog were you thinking?"

"Maybe like a sheltie," she said. "Doesn't have to be a purebred or anything. Just something along those lines."

"Oh. That would be nice. I wouldn't be afraid of a sheltie. But we both work all day."

"I don't think it matters," she said. "We'll go to the shelter. The dogs in the shelter are going to die if no one takes them, and don't for a minute think they don't know it. Imagine if you were them and somebody came to you and said 'We'll give you lots of love and a nice house but you'll be alone in the yard all day, and we'll have to love on you double when we get home from work.' Wouldn't that sound like a pretty good deal to you?"

Jonathan wiped his eyes again and smiled, but a little sadly. Addie had begun to accept that he might have to do everything a little sadly for a long time to come. Happy simply was not a speedy proposition.

"Yeah," he said. "I definitely think we should get a dog."

Chapter Twenty-Four

Addie, a Year Later

They sat together in her SUV for the longest time, in a kind of stunned silence, watching the sky threaten rain and staring at the old abandoned warehouse. Now and then someone would come or go from that awful place in the morning twilight.

"You sure you want to do this?" she asked Jonathan.

"I'll be okay," he said.

"Please don't get the sudden idea that you should go in."

"I won't go in. I promise."

"The chances you'll find out anything useful are pretty slim, you know."

"You have to take the chance, though. Right, Addie? I mean, whatever you do, you can basically forgive yourself for. Sometime, anyway, even if it's years later. But I'm not sure we ever really get over that thing where we freeze up and don't take the chance."

Addie smiled a little, but it might only have been on the inside. Jonathan might not have seen. Besides, he was still staring at the old warehouse.

"There you go again," she said. "Talking like a wise fifty-year-old."

He reached for the door handle and popped the passenger door open, and Barney jumped up from the back seat, realizing there was something he'd almost missed during his nap. He began wildly licking Jonathan's ear.

"I'll be right back, buddy," Jonathan said, scratching under the dog's jaw. "Don't worry about a thing."

Then he jumped out of the SUV, slamming the door behind him.

Barney turned his gaze on Addie. As if he had questions.

"He'll be fine," she told the dog. "He'll be back."

Barney set his butt end down on the seat and watched Jonathan's retreating figure.

Barney was not a sheltie. Quite far from it, in fact. He was about the size of one, but all similarities ended there. He was a grayish color with long, wild hair and ears tipped over just above the base. He had deep brown eyes that could only be seen because Jonathan regularly trimmed his bangs.

He had been Jonathan's choice.

Addie had wandered up and down the shelter aisles that day, nearly a year earlier, and then finally realized she hadn't seen Jonathan in quite a long time. She'd found him standing in front of the cage of the future Barney Westerbrook-Finch, who was a seriously starved and bedraggled creature at the time.

"That one?" she'd asked him, sounding almost as unsure as she felt.

"That's what I'm hoping," he said.

"Jonathan. That's not even in the general neighborhood of a sheltie. That's about the opposite end of the planet from a sheltie."

He had turned his eyes to her, as deep and sad as the pathetic little dog's eyes.

"But Addie," he'd said. "It's his last day."

It had been a good decision, though.

Addie pulled her attention back to the moment and watched Jonathan talking to two young men outside the warehouse door.

"Don't go in," she said, out loud but quietly.

In time he moved around the corner of the warehouse to a spot where she couldn't see him, following an older woman as they conversed.

Both Addie and Barney sat up straighter in their nervousness. But as time ticked by, Addie allowed her attention to drift elsewhere. Barney never did. Barney was a laser, focusing on every aspect of his two humans. Barney did not drift.

Jonathan came back to the car a few minutes later, his head down, staring at the pavement in front of him. Just before reaching for the door handle he raised his gaze to Addie and shook his head ever so slightly. Almost imperceptibly.

He climbed in and they both just sat for a moment, with Barney licking Jonathan's neck.

"Nobody's seen her for probably a year," he said.

"She could be okay, though. She could just be somewhere else."

"I guess it's possible. The bad ideas I'm having are also a strong possibility. And I just hate that we'll never know."

"Story's not over yet," Addie said. "She knows where we live."

"She's had *a year* to come back, though."

"Takes most people longer than a year. Took me decades longer."

"I just thought she'd at least let us know she's okay. And now I don't know if she doesn't care enough about us to let us know she's okay, or if she thinks we don't care enough about her to *want* to know. Or if she's . . . you know. Not okay."

"Well. We knew that could happen."

"Didn't want it to, though."

"No."

Addie started up the SUV and drove off down the boulevard in the direction of home.

"Care to share your thoughts?" she asked him after a few silent blocks.

He pulled a deep breath and sighed it out before answering.

"I was just thinking . . . I guess in a lot of ways I didn't even know her all that well. Not really. But I knew her *enough*, so I care. And now I'm just sitting here thinking . . . all the people who are homeless or addicted or both—and that's a pretty big crowd—if I knew them, would I care about all of them? That would be hard. Jeannie is hard enough."

"Probably some more than others," Addie said. "But yeah."

"That would be hard," he said again.

He stroked the dog's ears as he spoke, his gaze and attention appearing far away.

"Which is why people limit their caring," Addie said. "Because it would be too much for them otherwise."

"Really? I thought when people didn't care it was because they just didn't care. You think they care too much?"

"A lot of people," she said.

They drove on in silence for a time. Until they passed that bank with the outdoor sign that read out the time, date, and temperature.

Then Jonathan spoke up suddenly.

"Addie," he said. "Look at that."

"Look at what?"

"The sign."

"Okay. It's fifty-nine degrees. Isn't it usually around this time of year?"

"No, not that," he said. "The date."

"What about it?"

"It's a year to the day since you first drove me home. Remember that day? We were expecting all that biblical flooding from those atmospheric rivers. And it was windy and these palm fronds were hitting the windshield and lying all over the street."

"You remember the date after all this time?"

"I memorized it," he said. "Because I thought maybe that would be the day my life turned around."

"I'm glad you were right."

"You and me both," Jonathan said.

———

They were just a few blocks from home when she asked him what she'd been wanting to ask him for a very long time.

"A question," she said.

"Okay," he said, still staring out the window and looking lost.

"Probably none of my business."

"It's okay, I guess. I mean, as much as I can tell without knowing what it is."

"You ever think about calling your mom?"

He looked over at her quickly, then out the window again.

"To do what?" he asked after a time.

"Maybe just to let her know you're okay?"

"I thought about it once," he said. "Right after I moved in. When I was still living out in the garden shed. I came to the back door to ask if I could use your phone."

"But you never asked."

"No."

He didn't say more—at least not right away. Addie decided not to push.

Just as she pulled into the driveway, he continued without any urging from her.

"I decided it wasn't my job to give her all this reassurance that I'm okay. I hope that doesn't sound terrible. I don't mean it to. But I called her five times and told her I was about to be homeless. Or that I already was. And I just kind of feel like . . . if she cared about me being okay, she should have let me come home. She could have done something about it. She could have *made* me okay. And now I'm just not sure what she's done to deserve the peace of mind of knowing I landed in a good place, no thanks to her."

Addie turned off the engine and they sat a moment, just listening to the silence. Neither moved to get out and go into the house.

"I guess I'm coming more from the point of view of the mother," Addie said.

"You never did anything like that to Spencer."

"No," she said. "But we make mistakes. Us mothers, we make mistakes. Some are bigger than others, I guess. But we mostly torture ourselves over them, wishing we had everything to do over. If you had any idea how much of a miracle it is that I've seen Spencer four times in this past year. I mean, if you had any idea."

"I have some idea," he said. "But I'm not sure my mother is torturing herself over the mistakes she made with me."

"No, you can't be sure," Addie said. "That's just the point. You haven't talked to her, so you just have to guess about everything. All the information you have to work with, to form an opinion about the situation, comes from your imagination. And I don't know about you, but my imagination is a dangerous place to linger. Maybe she's really sorry for what she did. I would think so. Maybe she's found some way not to be, I don't know. I guess I just figured you would want to know. Purely for yourself. Whether calling her helps her or not, and whether or not she even deserves to be helped, I just figured some part of you would want to know."

He stared out the window for quite a bit longer. Barney periodically wiggled his butt frantically in the back seat, probably wondering why the humans didn't seem to know they were home.

"I guess I could think about it," Jonathan said.

And with that, they climbed out of the car and went inside.

———

Nothing more was said about the situation for days, and Addie didn't push. She had said her piece, and the ball was in Jonathan's court now, and she knew it.

She was sure they both knew it.

———

"Are you positive you don't want to talk to her?" Addie asked a few days later.

"I've never been surer of anything in my life," he said.

"You just want me to tell you the gist of what she says?"

"I just want you to tell me the parts you figure I can live with."

He headed for the stairs, and Addie sat down on the couch and picked up her phone.

"I don't have to do this if you don't want me to," she said as she listened to his footsteps on the creaky old steps.

"No, it's okay. I want to know. I just . . . you know . . . don't want to know."

Then he hit the landing and headed, she assumed, for his room, Barney following closely at his heels.

Addie brought up, in her contacts, the number he had given her. She chose the FaceTime option. Jonathan hadn't been sure whether his mother had figured out FaceTime calling yet or not. But Addie really wanted to see her face during all of this, thinking it would help her gauge the woman's sincerity, or lack of same. Besides, what was there really to figure out? It rings and you press a button to answer it.

It rang about seven times, and Addie was just beginning to think the woman wasn't near her phone, or wouldn't answer. She felt it as a deep sense of disappointment all the way down into her gut. She hadn't known how much she needed answers from this woman until she felt that sense of loss.

Then a face appeared on the screen.

Addie didn't think the face looked enough like the woman in the photo, though it did look something like her. But this woman looked exhausted, disheveled, and caught off guard. But the uncertainty in her face did seem familiar.

"What *is* this?" the woman said. "I never got a call like this before."

"Mrs. Westerbrook?"

Addie watched the face on the screen change. Apparently the woman had been assuming this was some kind of wrong number, or unwanted junk call, right up until she heard that name. Now she just looked downright spooked.

"No," she said. "I *was*. That was my married name once upon a time, but I don't use it nowadays."

"But you're Jonathan Westerbrook's mother."

The face on the screen quickly fell apart. Her chin began to quiver, and she opened her mouth and said, "Oh no, oh no, oh no," over and over again until Addie cut her off.

"It's not bad news," she said.

Jonathan's mother fell silent for a few beats.

"It's not?"

"No. He's okay."

"Oh thank goodness. I thought you were some kind of official somebody who got given the job of calling me and telling me bad news. He's okay. Thank goodness he's okay."

No thanks whatsoever to you, Addie thought.

She did not say it out loud.

"He's been through some bad times," Addie said. "He was living in an old abandoned warehouse, and he didn't always eat, and he got beaten up and nearly raped out there. And he's still carrying a lot of scars from that, things he hasn't even begun to deal with yet. But he made it through."

"He's okay," the woman said again. "Thank goodness he's okay."

Conveniently dismissing all the other truths, Addie thought.

Before she could think how to answer, Jonathan's mother spoke again.

"How do you know Jonathan?"

"He lives here with me."

"Why?"

"What do you mean why?"

"I guess I mean how did you meet him?"

"I was a security guard at a business next door to the old abandoned warehouse where he was squatting. With a whole crowd of other people, including a lot you wouldn't want your son hanging around with. It was real clear to me real fast that he was this amazing kid. Somebody who deserved a lot better than what life had dished him out. Not like everybody doesn't, but he's just a really unusually good guy. At least that's my point of view."

"You're telling me you just took him in off the street? Just like that?"

"He needed a place to live, so he lives here with me. He should have had the option to live with you, but you took that away."

Addie had meant to withhold recriminations until much later in the conversation, to minimize the chances of the woman hanging up on her.

"Do you have any idea how hard it is to find a special someone in your life? And how hard it is to hold on to a special someone once you find him?"

And with that, Addie felt her temper slip away.

"You already *had* a special someone in your life! You had your son! He's just about as special as people get, and he's your child, and he was supposed to be your number one priority. When you bring a human being into the world they have to be your number one priority, and you can't just abdicate that responsibility because something that feels more important comes along."

As she railed and fumed, Addie watched the woman break down into tears.

"Can I talk to him?" she asked, between sobs, when she was sure Addie was done.

"I'm afraid not," Addie said. "He doesn't want to talk to you. He didn't even want to be here when I made this call."

"He's right there," the woman said, pointing into the screen of her phone. "He's sitting on the stairs behind you."

Addie whipped her head around.

Jonathan was indeed sitting on the stairs behind her, one arm around the dog. Jonathan, like his mother, was crying. Addie had turned just in time to see him wipe his eyes on his shirtsleeve.

"You want to talk to her?" Addie asked him.

He shook his head and scrambled up the stairs, Barney in close pursuit.

Addie turned back to the image of Jonathan's mother.

"Just tell me whatever it is you want him to know," she said. "I'll make sure he hears the message."

"Tell him I'm sorry," she said, still sobbing. "Tell him someday he'll understand. Someday when he's older he'll look back and understand."

"I don't know as that's true, to be perfectly frank. I'm sixty-three years old and I don't understand. But I'll tell him. I'm going to hang up the phone now before I say anything that would hurt you even more. I didn't call to hurt you, but I don't think you deserve to be coddled, either. I'm not saying you're a bad person at heart, but you did a really wrong thing and you need to look it in the eye. But it's not my job to make you face up to reality, so I'm just going to hang up the phone."

Addie pressed a button on the screen, which erased the woman's tear-streaked face and returned her to her home screen.

She set down the phone and sighed.

She held still for a couple of minutes, breathing deeply, trying to get the anger to move through her. But it would not happen on the spot. It would take days to process that woman.

She rose and walked upstairs, where she knocked on Jonathan's bedroom door.

"Don't come in, Addie," he called out to her.

It was obvious by his voice that he was still crying.

"You're not decent?"

"No, I am. I just don't want you to see me cry."

"Why not? Everybody cries. It's like not wanting me to know that you hiccup or sneeze. Who doesn't sometimes?"

A long silence fell. Addie only leaned on the doorframe and waited.

"Besides, I've already seen you cry," she added.

"When did you see me cry? I almost never cry."

"The first night I ever met you. The first time I ever shone a flashlight in your direction and laid eyes on you. When you were trying to sleep in that empty storage space. And I didn't blame you one bit, by the way, after the night you'd had."

"Oh," he said. "Right."

"And when I made those amends to you."

"Oh yeah."

Then, for a full minute or so, he said nothing more.

"I guess you can come in," he said at last, his voice small.

Addie opened the door and walked into his room.

He was sitting cross-legged on the bed, surrounded by used tissues. His shoulders were slumped forward as if he could fold himself in half to protect his soft underbelly.

Barney was on his belly on the bed in front of Jonathan, positioned like a sphynx, now and then stretching up to try to lick tears off Jonathan's face.

Addie perched on the edge of his bed, and they sat together without talking for a while.

"I guess I don't want anybody to know how bad she hurt me," he said after a time.

"I hear *that*."

His eyes came up to meet hers for the first time.

"You do?"

"This kind of life stuff is hard, kiddo. This is what my old sponsor used to call 'when life gets lifey.' Everybody hates it, but I especially hate it when somebody is watching me go through it."

"I thought that was just me," he said.

"Nothing is just you. Welcome to the human race."

They sat quietly for a minute or two.

Then Addie said, "How much of what she said did you hear?"

"All of it."

"Even after you ran up the stairs again?"

"Yeah. I was still listening. You think she's really sorry?"

"Yes. I think she's really sorry. I also think that's not nearly good enough. There are two parts to a genuine, useful sorry. One is that you regret what you did and the other is that you'll do better next time.

The first part is easy. Most people never get the second part right. Or even try to. I guess what I'm trying to say is . . . if you're asking if you should accept her apology, well . . . I'd say you should accept that she's sorry to whatever extent that helps you, but don't go running back and expecting better next time. Because I didn't hear anything that even felt like a move in that direction."

"Thank you for telling her off the way you did."

"Honestly, my pleasure."

"You pretty much said everything I wanted to say to her. Everything I've been saying to her in my head when I can't get to sleep at night. And that made me feel better, because when you hear somebody else talking like they see the situation just the way you do, then you feel like you were right. Like you're not so alone in what you were thinking."

They sat quietly for another minute.

Then Addie asked, "Are you sorry I called her? Would it have been better if I had just left well enough alone?"

"In this case 'well enough' wasn't very good," he said.

"True."

"I don't think I'm sorry, no. It was weird. But now it's a little better than it was before. At least, I think it is. I have to think about it for a while. But when I was listening to her, I felt like . . . I hate to say this, because it feels like a terrible thing to say about your own mother, but she seemed kind of . . . pathetic. Like she knew she wasn't doing very well but she couldn't seem to do better. And so now I feel like it wasn't about me."

"I wish you'd always known it wasn't."

"I did. Sort of. Well. I did and I didn't. I knew in my head it was about her, but when I was listening to her just now it's like all of me got it. Not just my head. If that makes sense."

"It does."

Addie waited to see if he had more to get off his chest.

Then she said, "If you want to let all this out now, you can. Even if it means falling apart, like I did last year. But if you're still not ready, you can do it down the road. Whatever works for you."

For the second time his eyes came up to hers, the way they tended to do when she said something welcome but unexpected.

"That's the nicest thing anybody's ever said to me."

"Really? How so, hon?"

"I don't know. Just . . . everybody always says 'This is the right thing to do, so do it.' Nobody ever says 'I think this is the way to go, but maybe you're not ready, so just in your own time.'"

"We should talk to each other that new way more often."

"Agreed."

"You hungry?"

"Very."

"I'll make dinner."

"I have beans and onions and winter squash in the garden. And probably the first of the red potatoes."

"You can make some really nice veggie sides and I'll rustle us up some kind of main dish."

She rose from the bed and moved off toward the door. But he had more to say.

"Addie? Thank you. For everything. I guess I'm trying to say something like I've been so much happier since I've been here, but I don't know if 'happy' is exactly the right word. But I've been feeling . . . I guess . . . secure. Safer, you know?"

She paused in the doorway and looked back at him.

"Well, that's a pretty low bar, though, hon. I mean, anyplace is safer and more secure than that old warehouse."

"No, that's not what I meant," he said. "I meant as opposed to living with my mom."

Addie took a moment to let that sink in. While she was waiting he said more.

"I was never really relaxed living with her. I always felt like she was about to come out from under me."

"And you were right," Addie said.

"Huh. This might sound weird, but I never really looked at it that way. I guess I always felt like if I was insecure that was on me. You know. That it must be my problem. It never really occurred to me that if I had my doubts about her it was for a good reason. That's weird, isn't it?"

"Not really," Addie said. "I think we all do that."

She moved to leave, then stopped and turned back just outside the doorway.

"I have to admit," she said, "even though it's not all that magnanimous of me . . . I'm really happy to hear you say what you said. That you're more secure here than living with your mom. Even if living with her were possible. I was a little scared calling her, because I thought she might not be with that guy anymore and she might want you home. And you might go."

"Oh, that was never going to happen. But it's nice you didn't want me to go."

She hung just outside the doorway a moment longer.

"We'll get through this, you know," she said. "Both of us will get through. Maybe not fast, but we will."

He nodded, sniffling slightly, and said, simply, "Yeah."

"Now go pick us some nice stuff for dinner from your garden."

Chapter Twenty-Five

Jonathan, a Year Later

Jonathan set down his handled wicker gardening basket and fell to his knees on the concrete pathway along the vegetable patch.

For a moment he only looked up at the sky, assessing the weather. The clouds were thick and heavy, threateningly dark, with the air beneath them electric and dense with moisture.

It rocketed him back to the previous year, when all this had been new to him—having this place to live—and when it had not been anything he'd expected to last.

At the time he'd had dreams of a vegetable garden. Now he looked down and the garden was real.

He tried to think of another time in his life when he'd watched a highly anticipated dream become real, but he came up short.

He reached over and dug up a red potato.

He brushed dirt off it, then just held it up in front of his eyes for a moment and said what he always said.

"You did it!"

He knew it was silly to congratulate his vegetables on growing, and as a result he never said such things when anyone was around to overhear. Really, though, when you thought about it, it *was* remarkable. It *was* a thing worth celebrating. In a spot where there had been only dirt and weeds there was now food.

If he'd been called upon to examine his reaction more deeply, he likely would have recognized and admitted that he was congratulating himself as well. He had created something. Made it exist where nothing useful had existed before.

Best of all, it was something he could share with Addie.

He pulled up three more red potatoes, then a small sweet potato, two young carrots, an onion, and a good-size beet.

He had decided that cubed root vegetables roasted on a sheet pan would be a good choice for dinner. Though, thinking it over, he wasn't sure it had even been a decision. It simply appealed to his senses. It was winter, albeit in Southern California, and root vegetables were winter vegetables, and it sounded right. And it felt right.

Ever since he'd begun gardening he'd been noticing how nature designed food to fit the seasons—simple carbs for summer, starchy complex carbs for the winter when more warmth was needed—and how most people seemed determined to ignore and defy that carefully planned system.

He carried the basket into the kitchen, where Addie had two fish fillets arranged on a sheet pan with lemon slices and sprigs of dill on top. She was sprinkling them with salt and pepper as he walked in.

Then she wiped her hands on a dish towel, picked up a pen from the countertop, and made some notes on a yellow legal pad. She didn't seem to notice he was there.

He paused in the doorway and watched until she looked up, giving him a crooked and slightly curious smile.

"What's on your mind?" she said.

"Nothing. What are you writing? If you don't mind my asking."

"A new inventory."

"Didn't you just do one?"

"That was a year ago now. Wendy likes the women she sponsors to do one every year."

"But you don't have to, right?"

"No. I don't have to. There's plenty of free will in the system. But she hasn't steered me wrong yet, so I'm inclined to follow her suggestions." She glanced over her shoulder at the temperature read-out on the stove, then set down her pen and picked up the pan of fish. "This is bass. You like bass."

"I like all the kinds of fish you make."

He stood a while longer as she loaded the fish into the oven. Then a little longer after that. In his peripheral vision he could see the swish of Barney's tail near his feet.

"Why are you just standing there staring at me?" she asked him.

"I was just thinking," he said. "I was just remembering when I first got here and I was telling you how nice it would be to have a vegetable garden. I said one day I'd be able to say 'Hey Addie, want some tomatoes? I just picked some,' and you said they should be for me if I grew them, but I said no. I said I would want to share them. And then you said if I shared my vegetables with you you'd share your eggs and bread and tuna fish and such with me, and we'd both eat well."

"Wow, you have a good memory."

"When something is important, I do. And it was important to me, because I thought a garden would be a really good thing."

"And you were right," Addie said. "You've been right a lot in your life."

———

Addie took a few bites of his roasted root vegetables and chewed almost thoughtfully, with her eyes closed.

"I love the way the onions and garlic kind of . . . caramelized," she said. "I honestly don't know how you take something as basic as carrots and beets and potatoes and get them to taste like heaven."

"The fact that I just picked them has a lot to do with it. That and the seasoning."

They ate in silence for no more than a few seconds before the rain let go, clattering on the roof. Ticking loudly against the windows. Flowing audibly along the downspouts.

They stopped eating and listened for a moment.

Jonathan said, "It's been such a quiet rainy season so far."

"Yeah, but we're in for the genuine storms now. They're just late."

"Is it going to be biblical like last year?"

"I don't think so," Addie said. "It's an El Niño year, so it'll be wet. But I haven't heard anything to suggest it's going to be a superflooder like last year. Or at least like last year would have been without a break in between systems."

He took a bite of fish. Savored it. It seemed almost to dissolve on his tongue.

"Good weather to live indoors," he said.

"And I'm grateful that we do."

"I wish everybody did," he said, without naming any particular member of "everybody" out loud.

"So do I," Addie said.

They took another bite, both seeming to think that over.

Then Jonathan added, "But I guess we don't control that."

"Exactly," Addie said. "All we can do is be grateful for a nice dry roof over our heads."

They ate the rest of their dinner without talking, or needing to. The only sound to accompany their feast was the pounding of rain on their sturdy roof.

ABOUT THE AUTHOR

Photo © 2019 Douglas Sonders

Catherine Ryan Hyde is *The New York Times, Wall Street Journal,* and #1 Amazon Charts bestselling author of fifty books and counting. An avid traveler, equestrian, and amateur photographer, she shares her astrophotography with readers on her website.

Her novel *Pay It Forward* was adapted into a major motion picture, chosen by the American Library Association (ALA) for its Best Books for Young Adults list and translated into more than twenty-three languages for distribution in over thirty countries. Both *Becoming Chloe* and *Jumpstart the World* were included on the ALA's Rainbow Book List, and *Jumpstart the World* was a finalist for two Lambda Literary Awards. *Where We Belong* won two Rainbow Awards in 2013, and *The Language of Hoofbeats* won a Rainbow Award in 2015.

More than fifty of her short stories have been published in the *Antioch Review, Michigan Quarterly Review, Virginia Quarterly Review, Ploughshares, Glimmer Train*, and many other journals; in the anthologies *Santa Barbara Stories* and *California Shorts*; and in the bestselling anthology *Dog Is My Co-Pilot*. Her stories have been honored by the Raymond Carver Short Story Contest and the Tobias Wolff Award and have been nominated for *The Best American Short Stories*, the O. Henry Award, and the Pushcart Prize. Three have been cited in the annual *Best American Short Stories* anthology.

As a professional public speaker, she has addressed the National Conference on Education, twice spoken at Cornell University, met with AmeriCorps members at the White House, and shared a dais with Bill Clinton.

For more information, please visit www.catherineryanhyde.com.